We almost had him, but we screwed up. So far, this psychopathic killer had kept one step ahead of us...

Sometime Tuesday morning, while at the FBI headquarters in San Francisco, I was informed by Special Agent in Charge Steward Harden that the *Examiner* had received another hand-written note from the Gaf Killer, mentioning, in so many words, he was onto the sting the FBI had set up.

My first reaction was, "What do you think this means, Hardin?"

"Drake, did either of your agents, on the stake-out, order food to be delivered? If they did, that was a big mistake."

"I don't know, but I'll find out."

I called Vack at the Hayes's house and found out he ordered the pizza. He told me, at the time, he didn't see the harm in it. If it had been anyone besides Vack, I would have come down hard on them.

"Okay, Vack, hand your cell over to Simmons. I've got something I need to tell her."

"Sure, boss, no problem."

"Carla, I'm shutting down the sting. Vack messed up by apparently placing a call on his cell to a pizza shop. Somehow, Miller found out about it, or else he probably would've shown up yesterday." I explained about the note sent to the *Examiner*. "I want both of you to head back here and meet up with me and Martinez at headquarters. We need to re-think what we're doing. So far, what we've done isn't working. Right now, it's the Gaf Killer, six—the FBI, zip. There's one attempted homicide, three murders, an FBI Agent who was held hostage, and a sting operation that went nowhere."

A serial killer, calling himself The Gaf, starts an interstate killing spree that quickly propels him to the top of the FBI's most wanted list. Special Agent David Drake and his hand-picked team of agents drop everything and form a taskforce with one purpose—to track down this psychopath and bring him to justice. Crisscrossing the country from one crime scene to the next, Drake and his team can only hope the killer gets careless and makes a mistake. But this killer is no novice. His father, serial killer The Zodiac from the late 1960s and early '70s, has taught him well and the taskforce has its hands full. How many more innocent victims must die before Drake and his team can track down this monster and stop the carnage?

KUDOS for *The Gaf Killer*

In *The Gaf Killer, Son of Zodiac* by Jerry Otis, FBI Special Agent David Drake is tasked by the director of the FBI to head up a task force to track down a serial killer calling himself Gaf. He and his team of three other special agents assemble the clues and chase the killer across the country, trying to track him down before he can kill again. Meanwhile, Gaf is traveling around the country killing people who disrespect him, or whom he feels disrespect him or insult him from a waitress who serves him a cold patty melt, to his ex-boss who fires him for cross dressing at the airline where he works as a flight attendant. As psychotic as he is, he still manages to keep one step ahead of the task force, much to their frustration. The story is fast-paced, hard-hitting, and things never seem to go as the task force or the reader expects—a page turner that will hold your interest from beginning to end.
~ *Taylor Jones, Reviewer*

The Gaf Killer, Son of Zodiac by Jerry Otis is the story of a psychopathic serial killer, who thinks of himself as a "friendly people person" and only kills people who insult, offend, or disrespect him. He leads the FBI task force assigned to track him down on a merry chase from California to Seattle to Utah and back to California as the body count piles up. The hero, FBI agent Drake, seems to be up to the task of catching the man, or is he? All his hard work and dedication can't seem to locate his man, and regardless of what he tries, the killer always seems to be way ahead of him. Like his father, the Zodiac Killer of the '60s and '70s, Gaf send notes to the local newspapers taunting the FBI agents chasing him—a fact that does not please the director of the FBI. Otis's characters are interesting, and I like the fact that he tells the story from both the hero's POV as well as the villain's. It's a fast-paced, edge-of-your-seat crime thriller that should keep you up at night for more than one reason. ~ *Regan Murphy, Reviewer*

The Gaf Killer gets your attention from the get go. I Love the fast pace, edge of your seat, drama and intrigue, as you wait to see what happens next. It's a mix of sex appeal, drama, and humor...Otis's crime thriller will be hard to put down. It's a true page turner. ~ *Susan Bunch*

ACKNOWLEDGEMENTS

I'd like to acknowledge Kimberly Lovoy, my proof reader, who's been with me now for nearly four years while I wrote two manuscripts, one of which is *THE GAF KILLER-SON OF ZODIAC*, the other was a YA novel I self-published. Trust me, without a second set of eyes looking at your manuscript, it's an even more daunting task.

I also would like to thank Faith, my editor at Black Opal Books for translating my finished manuscript into a polished, grammar-corrected, readable book. She did a great job.

tHe
GAF KILLER
Son of Zodiac

JERRY OTIS

A Black Opal Books Publication

GENRE: CRIME THRILLER/MYSTERY-DETECTIVE/ROMANTIC EL-EMENTS

This is a work of fiction. Names, places, characters and incidents are either the product of the author's imagination or are used fictitiously, and any resemblance to any actual persons, living or dead, businesses, organizations, events or locales is entirely coincidental. All trademarks, service marks, registered trademarks, and registered service marks are the property of their respective owners and are used herein for identification purposes only. The publisher does not have any control over or assume any responsibility for author or third-party websites or their contents.

Published by Black Opal Books **http://www.blackopalbooks.com**

DEDICATION

To all those former students out there who struggled in English classes, as I did in school. Even though grammar is important, it's the story that's actually more important. Without a good story, all you have is nothing but a bunch of rambling mumbo-jumbo. Grammar can be corrected, but good story telling can't be faked.

CHAPTER 1

The Call

I was sitting in my office in Phoenix when the phone rang. "Special Agent Drake here," I said.

"Agent Drake, this is Ms. Janson, from the director's office in Washington, DC. Hold please, I'm transferring you to Director Becker."

Director Becker and I went way back, once working as partners out of the Washington, DC office, tracking down and arresting several interstate and international murder suspects on the FBI's Most Wanted list. Director Becker was old-school FBI with several more years of experience than me, and for the last five years had been director of the FBI. He was gray-haired, slightly overweight, and never wore designer clothing. Becker bought his suits right off the rack at the local Walmart.

"Hello, David," he said when he got on the line. "I've got an assignment I want you to head up. I'll need you here at headquarters tomorrow morning, then I'll fill you in on the details. I can tell you this, it's a taskforce I want you to head up to track down and arrest a serial killer who's now on our Most Wanted list. This case is the number one priority of the FBI, so drop what you're working on at the Phoenix office, and catch the first flight out."

"No problem, Director Becker, I'll see you in the morning." I hung up the phone, and right away let my supervisor at the Phoenix office know that I'd been requested by Director Becker to meet with him and told him what I could, going on to add, "That's pretty much all I know right now."

With that, I headed back to my duplex on the outskirts of Phoenix, and gathered up a few things I'd need for the trip, fully knowing I might be gone for who knew how long. I knew I stood a good chance of never coming back here.

I caught a non-stop flight on FTTA-Air to DC at three p.m., landing at ten p.m. DC time. By the time I picked up a rental car and made it to my room at the Hilton, it was midnight. I set my iPhone alarm for five a.m. It was going to be a short night.

೧೩೧೩

I arrived at headquarters around seven-forty-five a.m. then went straight up to the director's office on the fifth floor, checking in at Ms. Janson's desk. Then she let the director know I was here. "Go right in, Special Agent Drake, the director is ready for you." As she opened the door to the director's office, I thanked Ms. Janson, walked toward Director Becker, shook his hand, and took a seat at one of the three, rather cushy-looking, cordovan brown leather chairs that were situated in a semi-circle in front of his huge desk. This office seemed as large as my thousand square foot duplex in Phoenix and was done in cherry wood paneling.

Both the director and I got right into it with Becker explaining to me that he wanted this sum-bitch tracked down and arrested ASAP.

"If need be, shoot and kill this lowlife scumbag no matter whether the killer's a man or woman," the director went on to explain. "Those are the perimeters. Are we clear, David? I want this motherfucker caught. It doesn't matter to me how you do it, but make sure you don't fuck up and kill some innocent person. If that happens, we here at headquarters, and that means me, we're gonna declare you're a rogue FBI agent out on some kind of vindictive payback." He paused and studied me, letting his words sink in. "Any questions, David? Are we clear? You're free to get up and leave this office with no hard feelings if you decide you don't wanna head up this case."

I had to admit, I thought about walking right out of the director's office and kissing this assignment off, but I knew I wasn't going to leave. After all, my job as an FBI special agent was to track down murdering lowlifes.

"No problem, Director. I'm on the case, but I do have one question and one request. First question is, do you have any leads on this case?"

"We don't have much to go on, except for one female by the name of Sandy Bandfield living in Norfolk, Virginia, who escaped after being confronted by a burglar in the middle of the night, while sleeping, three nights ago. We think that burglar is the serial killer, mainly by comparing MOs of other unsolved murders with the MO of this attempt.

"What makes this attempt different is what was said to Ms. Bandfield just before she jumped up and bolted out of her condo. From what I understand from reading the police report, the burglar nudged her while she was sound asleep, at approximately three a.m. in the morning, telling her 'I'm Gaf. Are you ready to die?' I want you to meet with her and do an in depth interview. Get all the particulars and make sure nothing was missed, no matter how insignificant it may seem. That's a start. And, by the way, what was your request?"

"My request is that I handpick my team of FBI agents for this taskforce. I figured this isn't gonna be a run of the mill track down, so I have several FBI agents in mind who are all highly experienced in their fields, whom I've worked with in the past and would feel comfortable working with again. I have a list I've put together, narrowing it down to these three FBI agents."

"Okay, who are they?"

I opened my briefcase and pulled out a list I had typed up on my laptop during the flight out, noting the fields these agents specialized in, and handed the list to the Director.

The director eyeballed the list. "It's a rather impressive list. I know we've both worked with these three agents in the past, and I have to say they definitely are the 'Cream of The Crop,' as far as FBI agents go. They're like bulldogs. They don't let up. And, I might add, Carla Simmons is easy on the eyes. By the way, David, that last remark I just made stays in this office. That's all I need— a sexual harassment lawsuit brought on by a female agent." The director then chuckled as he continued studying the list. "FBI Special Agent Carla Simmons. Fifteen years of experience specializing in criminal profiling and also as an FBI sketch artist. FBI Special Agent Joe Vack. Has nearly twenty years of experience with the Bureau. Vack Believes in old-school gumshoe investigations— making calls, following up on every lead, and taking lots of notes in his small spiral notepad, while leaning on informants for info. Special Agent Vack's an exact clone of TV's Detective Columbo. FBI Special Agent Juan Martinez. Ten years of experience doing dual duties as an expert at analyzing crime scenes, and as a crime scene photographer with the Bureau.

"Okay, David, I like the list. Now go down the hall to a spare office and start calling these agents. I want them all here in my office by eight a.m. tomorrow morning, then we'll start working on a plan. I want your taskforce to hit the streets running. I want this serial killer bad. Do you have any other questions, thoughts, or requests?"

"Tomorrow morning, we'll need a spare office and any additional background you may have."

"No problem, you'll have total access to all FBI resources. Anything you need that'll help in catching this sum-bitch, you got it. If you have any problems along the line in getting help from any of my divisions here—well, you know what to do. You have my cell number."

With that, we both shook hands, with me knowing as I walked out of Director Becker's office, that this would be a tough case to crack. But I was confident that I and my team of experienced FBI special agents would catch the serial killer the bureau had labeled the Gaf Killer.

I called all three agents and gave them the rundown on what little I knew. They all agreed to come on board and meet at headquarters tomorrow morning. I especially enjoyed talking to Special Agent Carla Simmons again. Unbeknownst to Director Becker, Carla and I did have a fling while working on a case in New Orleans a few years ago. It had just happened. It was a mutual attraction between the two of us at the time, with no commitments. It was just sex. Fuck Buddies would be a better name for it, I guessed.

Director Becker was right about one thing, she was easy on the eyes, but I'd put it in modern terms—Carla was a looker with a great personality, brains, and a smokin' bod to match.

I knew I'd have to keep my cool as much as possible. After all, our main focus was to track down the Gaf Killer.

CHAPTER 2

Brain Storming

I made it back to headquarters early, around seven a.m. and began setting up an office where my team and I could meet without being interrupted. I had let the agents know to check in with Director Becker's secretary, and she'd direct them to the office we'd be using as our home base while in DC.

Before I made it down the hall to the spare office, Director Becker pulled me aside and told me the Bureau thought the Gaf Killer had struck again, this time in Seattle, less than a week after making the failed attempt on Sandy Bandfield in Norfolk.

"Now it's really critical that we catch this scum," the director went on to add. "I want him caught and strung up."

Director Becker was old school. He often used those types of phrases when referring to criminals. He didn't care whether or not they'd gone to trial. To him, they must be guilty of some type of crime or else they wouldn't have been arrested in the first place. Like he'd told me before, "The FBI doesn't arrest innocent people." In his mind, anyone arrested by the FBI was guilty until proven innocent.

By seven-fifty a.m. I had everything setup in the office. Five minutes later, my new team came walking in and grabbed seats at the ten-foot conference table. I thanked them all for coming on such a short notice, letting them know they were selected because of their work ethics and knowledge in the field they specialized in. While I schmoozed my team with compliments, I couldn't help but notice how great Carla looked. I had to quickly forget about that and move on, or else I'd find myself spending the rest of the morning day dreaming about the night we spent cooped up in that New Orleans hotel, getting it on like a newly married couple on their honeymoon night.

Before we got started, Director Becker walked in and gave us what details the Bureau knew about the Seattle incident yesterday. "The FBI office in Seattle believes the murder was committed by the same killer, because of the MO used. He broke in late at night, killing the female victim in her bed as she slept. This sick bastard scumbag left the name 'Gaf' smeared in blood on the dresser mirror. Now, this killer is taunting us, getting cocky, thinking he'll never get caught. I want whoever this is caught soon, and when we do, I'm gonna take pleasure in seeing him fry."

Becker never minced words on the way he felt about criminals in general. I believed he'd always looked at anyone outside the law enforcement community in a different light, and looked at civilians as "us against them." Being as old school as he was, and I was pretty sure Director Becker would never change his way of thinking.

"We've made arrangements for the team to interview Ms. Bandfield at her residence tomorrow morning in

Norfolk, at ten a.m.," Becker informed us. "Check out every inch of that place, especially the bedroom. After interviewing Ms. Bandfield tomorrow in Norfolk, I want this team to head straight out to Seattle and when you get there also go over every inch of that crime scene thoroughly. Look for clues that'll help the Bureau catch whoever did this. By the way, Special Agent Drake, I had a meeting with President Anderson yesterday and he's authorized the use of a government owned Gulfstream G4500 jet, along with a couple of air force pilots who'll be on constant standby, to fly the team to wherever your next important lead comes from. I did this mainly so the team doesn't have to spend endless hours standing in some line at an airport, while waiting to board. Time is of the essence, so when we get a hot lead, we need to act on it without delay."

Director Becker did go on to warn me that having access to the government jet 24/7 wasn't going to be an excuse for us to hop-scotch around the country like we were on some kind of vacation. "I'll be closely watching the results of this taskforce. I'm sure we're all on the same page, so let's capture this sum-bitch. If there aren't any questions, that's all for now, except to say, 'Be safe out there.'"

Yeah, that old school saying, "Be Safe Out There," was a phrase most law-enforcement agencies these days no longer used.

We kept our meeting short and to the point. After Director Becker gave us his pep talk, it was already eight-thirty a.m., so I directed my team to go back to their hotel rooms, rest up a bit, and meet me at Andrews Air Force Base at three p.m. for the flight to Norfolk Naval Air Station, going on to add, "I'll notify the pilots and have them preflight the Gulfstream for takeoff at three-thirty p.m. We'll load up and be in Norfolk in less than an hour. After we break from this meeting, I'll also get a hold of the FBI travel department and have them reserve us hotel rooms in Norfolk. There's one other thing. I want you all to be thinking about the questions you'll have for Sandy Bandfield. Agent Simmons will start the interview process, with all of us chiming in when appropriate."

I turned to Special Agent Martinez. "Other than profiling the killer, I want you to also look for anything in the condo the police might have over looked. And I'll need a sketch of the suspect from her description." I glanced around the room. "Are there any questions? If not, I'll meet the team at Andrews at three p.m."

We got up, shook hands, and headed for our hotel rooms.

CHAPTER 3

Norfolk Virginia

The flight down to Norfolk was nice. It was on a rare occasion that I'd had the opportunity to fly on what was essentially a private jet. Not much time to enjoy the flight though. It lasted less than thirty minutes, landing at Norfolk Naval Air Station at three-fifty-five p.m.

Before walking down the stairs to the tarmac, I went up front to the jet's cockpit and let both air force pilots know how much we all appreciated the fact they would be flying the team around to these different crime scenes, until we've solved this case. I went on to tell both pilots that I also knew being on standby wasn't easy. "Plan on being back here at the base, and have the jet fueled up and ready for take-off no later than eight a.m., day after tomorrow. Please don't stray too far from the base, just in case plans change. You never know, the director may just want us to hot-foot it to a new crime scene location on a moment's notice."

With that I shook both their hands and told them to

rest up, because from now on I had a feeling the schedule was going to be grueling until the case was solved.

I picked up a rental car at the base airport. We all jumped in and headed to the Wayside Inn, a combination bed and breakfast motel constructed from an old farmhouse that only charged the FBI $120 a night per agent. I thought the government got a bargain on that deal. The Wayside Inn did have a lounge with a full bar, a small dance floor, and even enough stage space for a three piece combo to play music, mostly playing classic rock and doing requests, as long as it wasn't heavy metal.

Carla and I agreed to meet later on at the lounge after Vack and Martinez told me it had been a long two days and both planned on kicking back in their rooms and doing room service. I was kinda glad to hear that actually, knowing it would make Carla's and my little rendezvous more private. We wouldn't have to be on guard, watching every little thing we said to one another, hoping what we said to one another wasn't heard and then turned into a rumor mill.

Around seven p.m., we met and I bought Carla dinner, splitting a bottle of Robert Mondavi Chardonnay. In the back of my mind, I had wild thoughts about fucking her brains out later on, but that would have to wait for another time and place. I knew it wasn't a good idea to go sticking your pen in the company ink, but sometimes it was too hard to resist when in the company of a woman this good looking.

We sat there, mainly doing a lot of small talk, reminiscing about our fling in New Orleans, dancing around the thoughts of becoming fuck-buddies again, but we knew for right now it wasn't the right time. In my mind, I knew it wasn't, but who's to say it wouldn't happen again while we're working this FBI track down.

I enjoyed Carla's company, but we ended the night

early, both knowing we weren't here to party all night like we did in New Orleans. At least, not this time around. As we got up from the table, Carla leaned over and kissed me on the cheek, thanking me for including her in the taskforce, then we parted ways for our separate rooms, knowing tomorrow we needed to be clear headed and focused when we interviewed Sandy Bandfield at ten a.m.

The next morning, we all piled into the rental car, and headed for Sandy Bandfield's residence, with Carla giving her a call on her cell, informing Ms. Bandfield we were on the way.

Sandy Bandfield lived in an up-scale neighborhood. The condo complex she lived in was well kept, with the main three-story structure done in beige stucco, with white trim, and nicely landscaped. This building was dated, but not so much that it resembled some ghetto condo complex, with peeling paint, and bent window screens. Even though it was an older building, I was still impressed with the location. *Ms. Bandfield must be knocking down some decent coin to afford to live in an up-scale neighborhood like this one*, I thought.

As we walked up the sidewalk leading to the security door, I noticed there was a call box to notify the tenant you were out front. That was the first thing I made note of. "How would a criminal gain entrance, unless he or she was let in?" I muttered.

We all looked at each other, thinking the same thing. I saw that Special Agent Vack noticed it also, because he was scribbling away in his small spiral notebook. That's what I liked about this team I put together. All of us were on the same wave length.

"Ms. Bandfield, it's Special Agent Drake, with the FBI," I said. "Can you ring us in please?"

"Oh, sure, hold on, I'll let you in right now."

The buzzer went off, then we went through the front door. The second thing I made note of was that there was a laundromat on the left, half way down the lobby. That's when I knew this complex was really dated, because the newer condos that I'd been in, all had washer/dryer hook-ups in each unit. We took the elevator up to the third floor, and rang unit 310's door bell.

"Oh, come right in. Man, you're right on time, unlike the police when they interviewed me."

"Yes ma'am, we try to always be on time."

I noticed right off Ms. Bandfield looked like she was in strikingly good shape. Tall, blonde, with long legs and not an ounce of fat on that trim body of hers. At least from what I could tell, just from eyeballing those skin-hugging, low-cut, black spandex pants she was wearing, along with that hot pink halter top. For an instant, I almost forgot why I was there.

After introducing her to the rest of my team, I asked Ms. Bandfield if it would be okay if we all sat at her dining room table. "We have some questions we'd like to ask you first, starting with Special Agent Carla Simmons, who specializes as a criminal profiler, just so we can start getting a feel as to this person's psychological and behavioral characteristics. It's an investigative tool the FBI uses to help us accurately predict and profile the characteristics of unknown criminal subjects. Agent Simmons also does double duty as my team's sketch artist, so she will be drawing a sketch of the subject from your description."

"No problem, Agent Drake. I've watched a lot of cop shows on cable, and I have a pretty good idea of what you're talking about. Go ahead."

Carla pulled out a yellow legal tab from her small briefcase and began asking questions, questions she had put together yesterday. "Ms. Bandfield, two nights ago, before this incident happened, had you gone out that night?"

"Yeah, I was out till around twelve a.m. That's rare for me since most of my time is spent in training as a long distance runner."

"Oh. Well, that's interesting. Is it a hobby, Ms. Bandfield? Tell me more about it."

"No, far from it. Long distance running is pretty much my life. It's a full-time job. I was on last year's US Olympic Track Team, but had to drop out because of a torn ligament in my right knee just before we were scheduled to leave for the European track meet trials."

"How's your leg now?"

"It's fine, see?" Ms. Bandfield stood up from the table. "I can now raise my right leg up over the top of my head."

Vack, Martinez, and I paid special attention to this particular display of dexterity by Ms. Bandfield. Special Agent Vack actually laid down the spiral notepad, he had been taking copious notes in, just to gawk.

"That's why I was able to just jump up from my bed and bolt outta the condo."

"Can you tell us where you went earlier that night, and who you met, if anyone at all, while you were out?"

"Sure, I hung out at a local dive called, Flash in the Pan. Not a great looking place, but they have great food and drinks. Besides, I kinda like the bartender working there. His name is Mike."

Agent Vack was making notes, knowing we would be following up on Ms. Bandfield's statement and talking to that bartender before we left for Seattle tomorrow morning.

I chimed in to ask a personal question. "Ms. Bandfield, don't take offense to this, but while you were there, did any men hit on you? If so, what were their names?"

"Okay, yeah there was a guy there who bought me several drinks, but he seemed harmless. He didn't give me his number, and I didn't ask for his either. I do remember him telling me he worked for an airlines, and that's about all I remember him telling me."

I turned to Agent Vack, asking him to make note of what Ms. Bandfield just told us and do a follow up at the bar, when we're done here, to see what he could dig up on that guy. Also, to check out the bartender's whereabouts after he closed up the bar.

"Ms. Bandfield, now back to what happened in the bedroom," Carla said, continuing with her questioning. "Did you manage to get a good look at the person?"

"Yeah, as a matter of fact, I got a quick glance of him from over my shoulder as I made a bee-line out the bedroom and out my front door. This creep was wearing one of those black leather face masks. You know, like the ones people wear who are into S and M. It had slits for the eyes and mouth. I got a good look, and other than that, he wore all black." She described what she remembered of his facial features while Carla made notations, knowing before they left she'd put together a sketch of the suspect.

"How do you know it was a man?"

"That voice was the voice of a man. No doubt in my mind. Only other thing I noticed is that he was shorter than me. I'm five foot, ten. And I'd guess he was around five foot eight, with a slim build, and probably weighing around one hundred, fifty pounds."

"Okay then. Well, at least we now have a physical description. Repeat to me exactly what he said."

"After poking me with what looked like the handle grip of some type of hunting knife, you know, like *Rambo* used, then he said something like, 'I'm Gaf. Are you ready to die?' That's when I sprang up from bed and pretty much flew outta my condo and into the street where I flagged down a passing car and had the couple call 911, since I had left my cell on the nightstand."

"One other question, Ms. Bandfield. How do you think he gained entrance to your condo? Do you have any ideas?"

"Sorry, I have no clue. What really bothers me is how he got inside the building to start with. I never heard a thing, and I'm usually a lite sleeper. By the way, I've had the locks changed, and now plan on getting a dog, most likely a Pit Bull."

"Okay, thank you Ms. Bandfield." Then Carla turned to me. "Do you have any other questions for Ms. Bandfield?"

"No, but what we'd like to do now is check out your bedroom, and have you re-enact exactly what went down the other night. Special Agent Martinez is an expert in analyzing crime scenes, and he'll be taking photographs while asking you some questions, as he looks for anything the police may have missed."

Ms. Bandfield nodded. "Sounds like a plan, just follow me."

Then we all got up from the table and followed Ms. Bandfield down the hallway and into her bedroom. Special Agent Martinez walked in first, ahead of the other agents, and started photographing the bedroom from all angles.

"Ms. Bandfield," Martinez said. "If you don't mind, I want you to demonstrate how you were laying in the bed before being nudged."

She got into her bed and crawled under the covers. "I was laying with my backside to him, initially, that's when he poked, or nudged me with the knife."

"Do you remember what hand he was holding the knife in? Was it his left or right hand?"

"Hum...let me think...Oh, yeah, I remember. He held it in his left hand."

"Okay, thank you, Ms. Bandfield. I think we're done in the bedroom."

Back in the dining room area, I turned to Ms. Bandfield. "Can we sit back down at the dining room table?" She nodded. "I need you to describe to Agent Simmons, to the best of your recollection, the male patron who bought you drinks that night who, for now, we'll refer to as a person of interest," I continued. "She'll also do a sketch of the person who broke in then have you look at both for accuracy."

"Sure, no problem."

We spent another forty-five minutes in the condo while Carla held her sketch pad, and listened intently to Ms. Bandfield describe what she remembered about how both males looked. When she was done, Carla had Ms. Bandfield look at her handiwork for accuracy.

"That's right on the money. That's exactly what I recall both those characters looking like."

"Thank you for your time, Ms. Bandfield," I said. "If we come up with anything at all, or if the team has any other questions for you, we'll be in touch. The police will be surveilling this neighborhood for the next several weeks, looking for anything specious."

Before leaving, I had Martinez take several more shots of the interior, then we headed downstairs to take shots of the hallway, lobby, and the building's exterior, both front and back. After walking out front with the team, I turned to Vack. "We'll drop you off at Flash in the Pan to see what you can dig up on this guy who bought Ms. Bandfield the drinks. I also want you to question the bartender on his whereabouts after his shift was over. Then, when you're done, just catch a cab back to the Wayside Inn and fill me in on what you find out."

"Sure, boss. No problem."

To me, it looked like we had a serial killer on our hands, who was using the name Gaf. This had to be the same person who'd committed the murder out there in Seattle, a crime scene we'd be flying to in the morning.

On the ride back to the Wayside Inn, I told my team to meet me at the restaurant/lounge at five p.m., and I'd buy everyone a working dinner. We'd go over the Sandy Bandfield interview, including the feedback I'd be getting back from Vack as soon as he returned from the Flash in the Pan bar. I went on to inform the team that after getting all their feedback, I'd be contacting Director Becker and informing him on what we'd found out today.

"So keep your feedbacks short and to the point. And make them meaningful as possible." I then turned to Carla. "I'll need your profile and artist's sketch of this guy who calls himself Gaf. At least then we'll have something to go by, even if it's not gonna be one-hundred percent accurate. When I talk to Director Becker in a few hours, I'm gonna suggest we go nationwide with your profile and sketch, along with offering a decent reward to the public for leads, hoping we'll get at least one good one that'll help us find him sooner, rather than later, before he strikes again."

☙☜☙

Special Agent Vack got back to the Wayside Inn at five-thirty p.m. and did a quick run through with me on what he found out. "The guy that bought Bandfield drinks left the bar at around ten p.m. and didn't return." "The bartender, Mike, told me he paid in cash, using no credit cards at all, and as far as names go, he only mentioned once that his name was Jeffrey. The bartender also told me he didn't believe this Jeffrey was straight, mainly because the only men he'd ever met with that kind of name were all gay. I gathered, from what a few patrons told me about Mike, that he's sort of a redneck from Oklahoma, and didn't much like big city life at all. I think we should do a deep background check on this guy Mike," Vack suggested. "It's probably nothing, but my gut tells me we should."

"Okay, thanks for the feedback, Vack. Let's go with your gut instinct, and do it. That's why you're here. I don't have all the answers."

Special Agent Vack and I then proceeded to the lounge where we met up with the other agents for our planned working dinner to discuss the interview we did with Ms. Bandfield. Right after sitting down, Carla handed me her sketch of what she thought the Gaf Killer might look like, according to what little we had to go on. I thought the sketch looked eerie, to say the least. As I sat there, looking at the sketch, I felt like the killer was at the table, staring me down. It was a weird feeling.

Just then my cell rang, and it was Director Becker, wanting to know what I had. I told him I would get the profile and sketch to him within the next couple of hours, along with my suggestions on getting the public involved.

"The sum-bitch has killed again, less than seventy-two hours after the Seattle killing," Becker told me. "This time it was in San Francisco, and it was the same MO, but now the victim was a male who was viciously attacked and killed in bed late at night. The killer not only left his name, Gaf, smeared in blood on the dresser mirror, but also drew a smiley-face in blood just below Gaf."

The director was now steaming and getting louder as he talked to me. "I want this fucker caught! Get a hold of the air force pilots and have them gas up the jet and get it ready to take off, because you're heading to Seattle tonight. I want you on that crime scene early tomorrow morning and then jump right back on the jet and head to the Frisco crime scene, and analyze it while it's still fresh. Have Vack check with everyone living nearby. Maybe someone saw something. I need results ASAP. The president is all over me on this one. Do you get my drift? Remember, it all flows downhill."

We cut the dinner short, headed back to our rooms, packed up, and headed for Norfolk Naval Air Station, where the two air force pilots were standing by, ready. It was nine p.m. when we took off, with an ETA of approximately five hours, while cruising at 477 knots. We were scheduled to land at McChord Air Force base around midnight West Coast time, giving us a chance to get some sack time on the way out.

During the flight, I had Carla send her profile and sketch to the director, using a secure military scanning device aboard the Gulfstream. That multifunctional device would turn out to be a valuable tool we'd be using in the near future to help our team in tracking the movements of this serial killer around the country. I came to find out the Gulfstream had all kinds of secret electronic spying devices that I never even knew existed.

While in the air, I also had Vack use that device to run background checks on the bartender and the guy who bought Sandy Bandfield the drinks, claiming to be Jeffrey. I also had him check out the part about him telling Bandfield he worked for an airline. It wasn't much to go on, but for now, no one was going to be ruled out if they'd had any contact at all with Ms. Bandfield.

Before crashing for a few hours of needed sleep, I mentioned to Martinez, "I'll need your thoughts on what took place at Bandfield's, as far as how Gaf broke into the condo, and I'll need that analysis before we land. Director Becker wants answers, and the president wants answers from the director."

"I'm on it, boss. I'll have it typed up before we land in Seattle."

With that, I leaned back in my chair, and checked my eyelids for holes.

CHAPTER 4

San Francisco

I was just beginning to nod off in the cabin, when my cell went off. It was the director.

"Hello, Director."

"David, a few minutes ago, I called the pilots up front and had them divert to Frisco, because that's a fresher crime scene." He sounded anxious. "The pilots told me they were over North Dakota and would re-set the autopilot for NAS Alameda with an ETA approximately the same as if you were landing in Seattle."

"I want you, and the other FBI agents from the San Francisco office, to be all over that crime scene in the morning. By the way, I've informed that office you'll be the agent in charge, directing all other agents who'll be collecting evidence and analyzing that crime scene, so we don't have duplicate evidence gathering going on. Take charge, David, and get back with me. Let me know what's going on. The president wants to see me in his office at one p.m. for an update on what we've found so far. One other thing, the victim's residence is located out there in what's called the Castro District. I don't know much about that area of San Francisco, except for the fact that's where all the gays live."

Director Becker didn't hide his feelings toward a group of people he couldn't or didn't relate to. To me, that was a fault that I didn't particularly like. I often wondered why President Anderson appointed him director. I would have thought that particular personality trait of Becker's would've been a liability that one day could come back to haunt the president.

One of the air force pilots walked back to the cabin to let me know we'd be landing at NAS Alameda in about one hour, and if any of us wanted to freshen up a bit, we could do so by using the on board men's or women's showers located in the rear of the plane. Having those showers on board the Gulfstream was definitely a plus. With only two hours of sleep since taking off from Norfolk, taking a shower was something I needed to do just to wake up. I woke up Carla first, and let her know. *I'd love to be showering with her,* I thought. *Who knows, maybe we'll have some time to ourselves later today after analyzing the crime scene. I'll see. Whatever we do together, it'll have to be discreet. I can't have any of that getting back to the director, only because I know how Becker thinks. He would be wondering, Why him, and not me?* I knew if the director had a chance, he'd love to fuck Carla ASAP, and, as he would put it, since being a romantic was something he wasn't.

Carla told me in confidence the director had hit on her once during a phone conversation. She went on to tell me that he was *so* not the type of man she liked, that having sex with Becker would never have happened, because he made her skin crawl from just the thought of them two being in bed together. She went on to inform me she'd warned the director, telling him she didn't appreciate the nature of his call. I was sure Becker got the hint. I knew the one thing he feared almost more than anything else was having a female agent bringing him up on a sexual harassment complaint. If that happened, he knew President Anderson would replace him.

I didn't have that problem. Both Carla and I had feelings for one another, even if it was mainly being fuck buddies. Other than that, we did truly love working together on FBI investigations, but I thought I loved it more.

After landing, I had the motor pool drive the team over to one of the base hotels that civilians, or vendors, used while conducting business on the base.

After we threw our carryon bags into our rooms, I decided to head out to the crime scene now, rather than waiting till morning. I called the NCIS office to have one of their agents drive us out to the Castro District crime scene.

Now it was getting late, after midnight. As it turned out, several NCIS investigators were also headed out there.

This time The Gaf Killer victim happened to be a lieutenant in the navy, so the NCIS would also be investigating the crime scene.

They were the navy's version of the FBI, investigating crimes against military members.

I knew right then I'd have to pull rank, and I also knew NCIS probably wouldn't appreciate me heading up the investigation, even after explaining that we were all in this together, and that both agencies thought of the lieutenant was one of their own. I was confident because I and my team were seeking the same answers to the question, "Who did this, and why?"

エ⁊エ⁊

When I got out to the crime scene, I explained the situation to the NCIS agent in charge, Criminal Investigator, Jacob Barnes. He didn't give me any flack, which surprised me, because I did expect to get some push back since the victim was a military member, and we FBI agents were treading on his—for lack of a better word—turf.

Barnes and I entered the roped-off house, located on Martha Street, first, passing by the two cops guarding the entrance so no one could contaminate any evidence that might have been left by the killer. Even though it was dark out, there was just enough moonlight for me to notice, from the teeth marks on the handle, that the door knob on the entry door had been twisted back and forth with a pipe wrench of some type. I had Martinez get some close up photos of the knob then remove and bag it for the lab to check out. Later, I found out that one of Barnes's agent's had twisted the front door knob back and forth with a pipe wrench to open the door and gain entrance to do a home check when the lieutenant didn't report to the base that morning. The fact that the lieutenant's SUV was still parked in the driveway and that no one answered the door was a big red flag.

After Barnes and I entered the bedroom, where the body of the navy lieutenant was still laying nude in the bed, I noticed his hands and legs had been bound together, as if he had been hog-tied. And, from the looks of the body, he had apparently been stabbed a number of times. This was probably the one of the most gruesome crime scenes I'd had the unfortunate task of having to investigate in a long time.

One thing that stuck out in my mind that connected this killing to the one in Seattle and the foiled attempt on Sandy Bandfield were the letters G-A-F carved into the victim's back. To me the wound looked post mortem.

That made this crime even more gruesome, if that was possible.

It was then that I pulled Barnes aside to ask him for some personal information on the victim and to also ask how I'd go about obtaining a spare navy photo of the deceased lieutenant. One personal question I did ask Barnes, and felt odd doing it, was, "Not that it matters, but was the lieutenant gay? I'm thinking if he was, it might help in finding his killer if he had been to any of the gay bars in the area last night, picked up someone, and brought them back here."

"Agent Drake, the NCIS doesn't check the status of a military member's sexual orientation unless there's a strong indication it had something to do with a crime. Let's just assume he was gay. What's that got to do with anything?"

"Nothing to me, but if he brought someone home from a bar in the area, it is of importance."

I then turned to Vack and waved him over. I'd have him hit the streets early this morning, soon as the sun rose, and start checking all the gay bars in the area to see if maybe someone recognized the lieutenant from a photo NCIS had emailed to Vack's FBI cell.

"If anyone saw the lieutenant with someone, who he either met at a bar, or came back here with, we'll find out who they are and question them," I mentioned to Barnes. "If they have a good alibi, then they'll have nothing to worry about. If they don't, I'll escort them to the base and both you and I will interrogate whoever it is, until we either believe what they have to say, or they lawyer up. Who knows? More than one person could be involved here."

Even though I knew I was now really treading on NCIS's turf, the way I looked at it, I wasn't here to play favorites or worry about egos. Director Becker and the president weren't going to cut me any slack until the Gaf Killer was arrested.

Next, I had Martinez, Carla, and the other NCIS investigators turn this small house on Martha Street upside down, photographing and tagging anything that remotely looked like evidence. I got NCIS to dust any surfaces that could have been touched by the killer. Who knew? Maybe the killer or killers weren't smart enough to wear gloves. Nothing was going to be taken for granted.

The last thing we did before leaving was to spray all the rooms in the house with Luminal, looking for blood spatter patterns we couldn't see with the naked eye.

After spending over three hours on the crime scene, we gathered up all the evidence we'd collected, then the NCIS coroner bagged up the body and headed back to the base for an autopsy. Maybe, with any luck, they'd find the killer's DNA on the body. That was what Barnes and I were both hoping for.

When I got back to the base, at around four a.m., and after maybe getting three hours sleep, I called Vack and told him to meet me back at the base when he was done checking out the Castro District gay bars. "By the way, I'll need the results on those background checks you ran on the bartender and the guy who claimed to be Jeffrey, the one that bought Ms. Bandfield drinks at the Flash in the Pan."

"No problem, boss, you got it."

Later on that afternoon, I planned on having the team pool its ideas together, along with having Carla work on another profile of this killer since we'd now seen his handy work. I was really hoping Vack had dug up something concrete that we could use. I knew that if there were any good leads out in the streets, Vack would be the one to find them.

Right after I met with my team members, I'd get on

the horn to Director Becker with what we'd found out so far. What I was hoping was that NCIS had found some DNA other than that of the navy lieutenant's and put a rush on getting that profile run through the criminal data base. Maybe we'd get lucky and identify this psychopath.

After I got the feedback from my team, no matter what it was, I was going to recommend to the director that the FBI go on national TV to let the public know The Gaf Killer was now on the FBI's Most Wanted list. I'd suggest we broadcast what we had and tell the public what we thought the Gaf Killer's looked like, using Carla's profile sketch, along with what she thinks the killer's personality traits were, stating his known height, weight, and the name we thought he was going by. I'd also recommend that the reward offered should be huge, in the hopes of getting a hot lead, one that would put an end to the carnage and put this person on death row.

During our little pow-wow back at the base, Vack did come up with one good tidbit of info from the streets. He found the bar the lieutenant had spent some time in last night. It was called Last Chance, and the bartender there, just like Mike, the bartender in Norfolk, told Vack there was a guy who bought the lieutenant drinks, but never came on to him, and, in fact, left the bar early, around ten p.m. According to the bartender at Last Chance, he paid in cash and only once mentioned his name when ordering drinks, stating it was Jeff.

Now that was a hot lead! I was beginning to see a trend. I knew then this had to be the same Jeff or Jeffrey who had bought Sandy Bandfield drinks in Norfolk. But how did he move around the country like he did? He had to be working for an airline.

"As far as criminal background checks on both the bar patron at Flash in the Pan, who went by the name of Jeffrey, as well as the bartender Mike, Mike's came back showing no record. We couldn't really do one on the patron, Jeffrey, with only a first name. But we didn't find one on anyone with that first name in the area," Vack informed us.

Martinez chimed in with his analysis of what he thought took place at all three crimes scenes, even though one of the three, the one in Seattle, hadn't been checked out as of yet. "The killer most likely scopes out a likely victim in the bars he randomly picks, buys them drinks, then leaves the bar early. He then just sits outside in his car and waits for them to leave and follows them home. Later on that night, he breaks in their home and commits his dirty deed."

Just before I got Carla's input, I chimed in. "I'm thinking this could be a recent crime spree being committed by someone with no previous record. They have a hatred for both men and women, and it possibly started from some episode in his life that made him snap and set him off, then the killing began.

"Special Agent Drake, you must be reading my mind," Carla said. "I'm assuming its work- or relationship-related and that this killer could be a cross dresser. The way these most recent killings are taking place, I'm thinking The Gaf Killer might be working for an airline company. Maybe this person is a flight attendant, or they could even be a pilot."

With that, I completed our get together by asking Vack and Martinez to contact all the major airlines and see if they could come up with a lead. I knew it was a long shot, but maybe we'd get lucky.

Right after I was done with the meeting, I got on the phone to Director Becker and gave him what we had.

"Call the pilots and get the jet gassed up. I want you and Simmons here early in the morning, The FBI is going on all the national and cable news shows at twelve noon tomorrow with what we have, in the hopes of getting some good leads on this sum-bitch. All the cable network news reporters will be here, at headquarters in DC, so I want you two here to speak to the press and answer their questions. Even though I'm the director, I'll admit you two are much better at dealing with the press than I am, so you and Simmons will be doing the majority of the talking. I'll be there simply to introduce you two, and then you take it from there.

"By the way," he continued. "I've had the reward money okayed by President Anderson. It's one million dollars. The reason the reward is so high is because the killer snuffed out that naval officer, and no matter whether the lieutenant was gay or not, now it's personal, with both the NCIS, and the FBI. Don't mention any of those gruesome details on how the lieutenant died. It's an image thing. The navy wants to keep that info quiet. You get my drift?"

I was surprised to hear that coming from the director, knowing how homophobic he'd always been. "Yes, I do. No problem. We'll be heading out ASAP."

Right after the phone call, I let Carla and both pilots know we were heading out tonight. Carla gave me that crooked half-smile, knowing we'd be going alone to DC. I knew she was actually reading my mind now, acting as if that was the best news we'd both had since starting this track down.

I informed Vack and Martinez about the news conference, Carla and I would be attending in DC, and told them to cover for us until we returned in a couple of days.

I also directed both agents to keep me informed on any forensics NCIS came up with, especially if it was a DNA profile that told us who the killer was. "Even though the Seattle crime scene is stale now, be prepared to leave for Seattle on a moment's notice," I said. "I still wanna check that crime scene out, in case anything was missed by police."

Apart from the task of tracking down this killer, in the back of my mind I wondered "if Carla and I were ever going to get a chance to sneak away and do what we'd wanted to do ever since I handpicked her to be on my team. That was to have sex till the sun came up, or maybe till the sun went down, like we did in New Orleans. Who knew when we'd see each other again after this case was solved? Carla was actually the type of woman I'd marry if the opportunity ever came up. I didn't see that happening, but who knew? I learned a long time ago to never say never.

Carla and I headed for the runway, checked in with the air force pilots, and were airborne for DC by six p.m. with an ETA of approximately three a.m. East Coast time.

We shined on eating at the base chow hall and just raided the galley aboard the Gulfstream. The pilots did a good job of keeping the plane stocked with tasty frozen entrées you could just heat up in the onboard microwave.

Since we were the only ones on the jet, except for the pilots up front, and even though we knew either one of them could opt to take a restroom break at any time and catch us in the act, we took a risk, anyway, and managed to get in some heavy grinding.

Carla pulled up her dress, took her thong off, and straddled me. When she did that, it was almost more than I could take.

I instantly got aroused, so I unzipped my pants and put my hard cock into her, but not long enough to climax. I'd save that for another time. Maybe later on today after the news conference if we could get some time alone before heading back to Frisco.

She climbed off after a few minutes of hard grinding,

then we quickly put ourselves back together, reclined in our seats, and acted as if nothing had happened, hoping to get some shut-eye before landing.

CHAPTER 5

Briefing With Director Becker

About an hour before landing at Andrews Air Force Base, I called the FBI motor pool and asked that a driver meet us to give Carla and me a ride over to DC headquarters.

It was still early in the morning, so we camped out there using the mini-barracks solely set up inside headquarters for FBI agents who had done redeye flights. These mini-barracks weren't like a hotel room, just bare bones accommodations with a bed, bathroom, and shower meant only to be used for short stays of a day or less, just so agents could clean up, or get a few hours of shut-eye when arriving in the middle of the night.

At around nine a.m., we both met with the director in his office, and he briefed us on the game plan for the news conference with the media.

"It'll be short and sweet," Director Becker told us. "I'll introduce you first, Drake, since you're running the team then, when you're done, you introduce Agent Simmons and she'll fill-in the press on what the FBI thinks the Gaf Killer looks like by showing sketches of the person that broke into Bandfield's condo, giving his height and weight, and also the sketch of the male who bought her drinks that same night, who we'll refer to, for now, as a person of interest, and giving the profile she did of the killer. After you two are done, you'll take questions from the media. Understood? Oh, by the way, I have another thing to add. We think this killer is now linked to eight other homicides, in and around San Francisco, going back about five years."

At first I didn't know what to say to the director, after getting that news. "That's the first time I've heard that, Director. Now it's even more critical that we find him. As far as the news conference goes, no problem, Agent Simmons and I are prepared to take on whatever questions are thrown at us."

I knew that was somewhat of a stretch, but I had confidence in myself and my ability to think on my feet. I knew the director wouldn't stand up well if he got asked a bunch of heated questions from reporters but, for me, it was no problem. I didn't get stage fright, and neither did Carla. Even though both Carla and I were still tired and on the verge of burnout, we still looked forward to addressing the press and were determined to put our best foot forward, in hopes of putting an end to this killer's reign of terror.

For me, just like Becker stated before, "I'd like to see that Gaf sum-bitch fry." The thought of The Gaf Killer being convicted, and then knowing he'd be sitting there sweating it out on death row would be enough gratification for me. I was sure when his day of reckoning eventually came, he'd probably be whimpering and whining like a little girly boy, begging for his life just like all cowards did. But in the end, he'd have his life snuffed out like the victims he'd terrorized and killed.

After the meeting with the director, it was still early, around ten-thirty a.m. so, since the news conference didn't start till twelve noon, Carla and I decided to visit a local Italian restaurant and have a decent meal, without the wine.

CHAPTER 6

News Conference

Carla and I stood just behind Director Becker, while he stood at the podium, outlining to the media why he'd called the news conference.

As I listened to him, I was expecting to be called up to the podium at any minute. Then it happened, my cell phone went off. Director Becker turned around and looked straight at me. If an icy stare could kill, I'd have been a dead man. I quickly looked at my cell, read the short message, and turned it off. It was a text from Martinez saying, *Urgent, boss, please call back ASAP!*

Next the director introduced me to the media. I made my way up to the podium and began rattling off the MOs the team had discovered so far, tying this killer to all three of the crime scenes. I made a point of leaving out the gory details of the navy lieutenant's gruesome death.

I went on addressing the media, while trying hard to see through the flash of cameras rapidly going off in my eyes. I then gave these additional clues to the killer's identity. "So far we have two important clues. Number one—there's a strong possibility this killer's real first name could either be Jeff or Jeffrey, and the second important clue is that the FBI also knows he's referred to himself as Gaf at three of the crime scenes."

I looked out over the sea of reporters and noticed they were all now paying more attention to what I'd just said and were taking notes like Vack did when seeking important inside info from informants.

Next, I introduced Carla and stepped back as she began giving the press the killer's profile and showing the sketch she came up with, including the additional information on the killer's approximate weight and height—one hundred, fifty pounds and about five foot eight—and that he was left handed. She added that this individual might be a cross dresser. She also mentioned the sketch was of a "person of interest," who, for the moment, the FBI would like to talk to.

She then handed out copies of the sketch, which revealed a devious-looking picture of an individual with an apparently demented mind.

After that, I stepped back up to the podium. Now both of us were standing side by side, as we began taking questions from the media.

First question was, "Special Agent Drake, other than the information you've given us so far, are we to assume he's a serial killer, and does the FBI have any idea where he works, or what city this killer lives in, and also why do you believe he's going by the name Gaf?"

I gave a short answer, saying only, "The FBI believes he works for an airline, but based in what city, we don't know for sure yet. And yes, we consider The Gaf Killer a serial killer, killing two victims, and attempting to kill a third so far. At this point, we have no idea why he goes by Gaf."

It was then that I decided to end the news conference,

because the FBI really had nothing more to add. I looked back over my shoulder at Director Becker, giving him a slight nod before we stepped away from the podium, as a cue for him to step back up for any parting words he might have.

As the director came back up to the mic, assuring the media that the FBI would be giving daily briefings as to the progress of this track down, Carla and I exited out the side door to the main hallway and made it back to our temporary rooms. Then we began gathering up our things for the trip back to Frisco. While in my room, I called Martinez to see what the urgency was. I hoped it was good news.

"Thanks for calling boss. Vack is missing. He hasn't been heard from or seen since last night, nor does he answer his cell!"

I knew that wasn't good news. That was not something Vack would ever do. "Okay, Martinez, I'm on my way to the director's office. I'll get back with you, but in the meantime, start looking for Vack now."

After getting the bad news, I hightailed it to the director's office, catching him just before he entered. After informing Becker about Vack's disappearance, we both entered his office where he immediately got on the phone to the San Francisco FBI office, NCIS, and the San Francisco PD, asking that they put every available law enforcement resource immediately on the streets to look for Special Agent Vack.

When he got off the phone, Director Becker told me to get back to Frisco and head up the search for Vack. After pausing briefly, the director looked up at me. "I have a bad feeling about this, and I hope I'm wrong. Good luck, and keep me informed every step of the way."

Now, having this new situation, with Vack missing, it was really becoming a high-stress track down, something

I was sure was weighing heavily on the director's mind. It was also on my mind, because not only was Vack a skilled special agent with the FBI, but he was a person I'd become friends with over the last several years we'd spent together solving many high-profile crimes for the FBI.

CHAPTER 7

Searching for Agent Vack

After leaving the director's office, I informed Carla about the situation, then we hurriedly left, using the FBI motor pool and headed for Andrews. While en route, I called the pilots back to the Gulfstream for a quick trip to NAS Alameda.

While on board, I told the pilots, "There's no speed limit up here, so I want this Gulfstream on full power after takeoff. I wanna make it back to Alameda in record time. We have a team member missing. It's Special Agent Vack. I thought you both should know."

After hearing that news, both pilots now looked even more determined to turn and burn once airborne. Vack had flown with them right from the start of this track down. With that, once we were airborne, that jet began hauling some big-time ass back to San Francisco.

Carla and I did no hanky-panky during this flight. We were too worried and focused on what we had to do to locate Vack. It was a very somber flight. After all, as far as we're concerned, he was more than just an FBI agent.

Vack was a person. He was family, one of us. Every FBI Agent who had ever worked alongside Vack really liked him. What was not to like? He was the modern version of Inspector Columbo, from back in the day.

God knew what time it was when we landed. All I knew was it was still dark as the Gulfstream touched down at NAS Alameda, and even though I only got a few hours' sleep during the flight, it didn't matter. Both Carla and I had one thing in mind, and that was to find Special Agent Vack.

Before we landed, I realized the Seattle trip would have to be eliminated, or put on the back burner for now. I'd just gather up any info on evidence the agents up there collected at that crime scene. I hated doing that. I'd much rather have checked it out in person, but that was out of the question, at least for now.

It was early in the morning and still dark. After stepping onto the stairs leading down to the tarmac, I made a quick call to Martinez to have him meet us at NCIS. I needed to find out if he knew what area of San Francisco Vack was last working in when he disappeared. It was a long shot question, because I knew when Vack was out in the public, knocking on doors, and using the instincts of a seasoned investigator, he didn't have a habit of checking in with me, or anyone else, unless he stumbled on a hot lead.

From NAS Alameda, Carla and I went straight to NCIS and met up with Martinez, who told me he had no idea where Vack had been during the last twenty-four hours. I figured that. I mentioned to Martinez that I wanted him to contact all car rental companies, because I was sure Vack either rented a car or an SUV to get around Frisco.

We checked in with NCIS Criminal Investigator Jacob Barnes and, as I was about to question Barnes to see if he had anything, I got a call from the FBI office in San Francisco requesting that I come over to their office as soon as I was done at NCIS. Special Agent in Charge, Steward Harden, told me on the phone, "We've just received some very important information this morning, and it's nothing I want to talk about over the phone. It has to do with Special Agent Vack and The Gaf Killer. That's all I'm willing to say for now. I'll explain when you get here."

"Okay, Special Agent Harden, I'm leaving now. Thank you."

All three of us hot-footed out of NCIS immediately, grabbed a cab, and headed over to 450 Golden Gate Avenue, the San Francisco office of the FBI, located on the thirteenth floor.

After passing the security check, Carla, Martinez, and I could hardly get that elevator working quick enough to get us all up to the thirteenth floor. Once we entered the office lobby, we met up with Special Agent in Charge, Steward Harden. He directed us to his office then showed us a poorly written message the *San Francisco Examiner* had received from the Gaf Killer this morning.

As I looked at the note, chills ran up my spine. It read, *Hello to you incompetent fools of the FBI, the San Francisco Police, and the NCIS, this is Gaf, I'm The Son of Zodiac. I have your Special Agent Vack, and you'll never find him...ha, ha, ha...he's under my control, he's my hostage, and I'll be using him as a bargaining chip if you squirrels get close to me again. But trust me, that's not gonna happen.*

The note was signed with a circle with cross hairs running through it, just like the original Zodiac serial killer's notes had back in the late 1960s, and early '70s when he taunted law enforcement.

After quickly reading through the short note written on

what looked like a common legal tablet, the three of us, along with several other FBI agents, began searching through the FBI files stored in the basement's evidence locker, looking for anything that would give us a clue as to who Gaf was.

We found plenty of evidence and police reports from the '60s and '70s on the killings committed by the person claiming to be the Zodiac serial killer. He bragged about committing over 37 murders in the Bay Area and parts of Nevada during the late '60s and early '70s. The problem law enforcement had back then was that there wasn't any evidence identifying who that psycho was. On a common thread, The Zodiac Killer loved to taunt the police with notes to newspapers, similar to the one I'd just read. Martinez was particularly interested in going through the FBI files on Zodiac, hoping to find some tidbit of information that could have been missed decades ago. Maybe something on the lifestyles of the various suspects, who the police at that time, had suspicions of being The Zodiac Killer, but could never prove it.

Harden let us know he was sending the note over to the crime lab this morning to have it checked out for fingerprints, the type of ink used, and, if possible, what company made that type of legal tablet, and, if so, what stores it was sold in.

We did have some clues about The Gaf Killer, but our team, including myself, didn't have a clue as to why he called himself Gaf, or why he mentioned he was The Son of Zodiac. If it was true, and he was the son of the Zodiac Killer, just like his father, he'd kill at random, keeping the people living here in the Bay Area constantly on edge, something Zodiac also loved doing.

While still at the San Francisco FBI office, I got on my cell to update Director Becker on what we had. As soon as Becker answered my cell, I knew right away he had already been given the news about the Gaf note the *San Francisco Examiner* received.

"I want that scum-bag, motherfucking, sum-bitch found," were the first words out of his mouth.

I nearly answered back, "At the moment, Director, that's easier said than done." But I caught myself before I opened my mouth. I was no fool. I liked working for the FBI. So what I said was, "Yes, sir. We're doing background checks now, and I'm confident we'll soon have enough info to identify the Gaf Killer. According to Special Agent Simmons's profile, she believes he does live somewhere here in the area, and most likely works for an airline. Simmons is checking with all the airlines as I speak, and we should have a list of airline employees before three p.m. today. With that list, we'll use FBI agents here at the Frisco office to help whittle it down and eliminate those who don't match the profile."

"Okay, Drake, stay all over this. The president is on my ass. Give me a call this afternoon, if you run across anything."

After hanging up, I now knew I had to make it happen and that wasn't going to be easy. I was sure this psycho was out cruising the city streets right now with a plan to kill again. I knew I could be walking down any street in San Francisco, and The Gaf Killer could walk right by me, and I'd never know it.

CHAPTER 8

Son of Zodiac

It was early in the afternoon, around two p.m. Jeffrey Miller had spent the last few hours cruising around the city, then he decided to stop and get a bite to eat at a restaurant called the Bay Diner, over in the Financial District of San Francisco. He grabbed a table way in the back, because he didn't like sitting by windows. He never had.

A good-looking waitress, with what he'd call "An Attitude," strolled up to his table as if she was strolling down a catwalk at a fashion show, acting as if she was doing him a big favor by taking his order for a patty melt and ice tea with a lemon wedge.

When she brought the order to his table, the patty melt was cold, the cheese wasn't even melted, and the ice tea had no lemon wedge. *Now why would she do that?*

It was then, after he told her about it, that she copped the attitude.

She rolled her eyes. "You know what, mister? I don't give a rat's ass whether you like that fucking patty melt or not. I'm off at six p.m., then I'm off for the next two fucking days, and I can forget about this fucking dive!"

He smiled politely at Rachel—her name was sewn on her waitress outfit—and told her, "Okay, it's no big deal to me. It's no problem. Can I please have a to-go box so I can take the patty melt with me, and heat it up later?"

With another sneer on her face, she walked away, came back with the box, and tossed it on the table. Then, with that same sneer, she just walked away again. Now he was pissed off, but he kept his cool, because killing her right here wouldn't be a good idea. So he got up from the table, paid the bill without adding a tip, and left.

He knew when he walked out the front door of the Bay Diner that he had found his next victim. She didn't know it, but she was *fucked*. Later on, he'd come back here and follow Rachel home, just like he had in Norfolk, Virginia, when he followed Sandy Bandfield home from the Flash in the Pan, but that one didn't work out. This time, he was not going wait till she entered her place before he wasted that bitch. She'd never know what hit her.

Sometimes, he thought what he was doing was bad, but then he'd decide that it wasn't *that* bad. After all, that fucking waitress should have been nice to him. Arrogant and rude people thought they were better than him and, to him, that meant they didn't deserve to live. It just wasn't right, the way she talked to him, and now she was going to pay.

After pulling away from the restaurant, he knew he had to get back to his place over on Green Street, near August Alley, and check up on that pig FBI Special Agent Vack, who he had left in the basement of his row house. Vack was chained to a basement wall with his head covered by a pillowcase. Over the pillow case Gaf had duct-taped Vack's mouth and eyes shut. He'd placed the pillow case over that pig's face mainly so that, when he pulled off the duct tape, he wouldn't rip off Vack's eyelids or any facial hair, including his eyebrows. Gaf could kill fairly easy, but he wasn't into torture.

His row house on Green Street had been given to him by his daddy, The Zodiac Killer, and how appropriate it was that it looked like the Bates Motel. His dad never told him how he'd acquired it. But it was not costing Gaf anything to live there, so why should he care? Besides, if he was renting an apartment somewhere, he'd probably have ended up killing the landlord the first time he or she complained that the rent was late. So this place was just fine for his needs. No nosy neighbors who could bother him by knocking on his door trying to borrow something. That would be a big mistake on their part, especially if they borrowed a hammer and didn't bring it back.

While driving back to his place, he thought about the fact that he had lost his job last week as a flight attendant, mainly because his female supervisor didn't like it when he showed up wearing lipstick and dressed in a female's flight attendant's outfit for the flight to Denver. Gaf liked cross-dressing every now and then and didn't think it was a big deal. He'd done it as a joke to see what kind of re-action he'd get.

His female supervisor didn't see the humor in his getup at all, and she'd fired him for arguing with her when he got mouthy.

Well, the bitch didn't know it yet, but she was next. Her days were numbered soon as Gaf found out where the cunt lived. He wanted to see the fear on her face when he showed up wearing his Gaf outfit—and see her com-plain about that while, at the same time, realizing she was going to die.

He loved that look of fear in someone's eyes. It turned him on and, frankly, that was why he did what he did—just like his daddy had done over forty years ago. And so now he was continuing on with that family tradition. It was something he'd been doing for a number of years. He loved his dad. Gaf was well aware of what his dad had been doing in the late '60s and early '70s. He only wished his dad was still around, because he knew he'd be really proud of him now.

It was just lately that he'd let his presence be known by telling his victims he was Gaf. And he had now stepped it up a notch by capturing that FBI pig Vack, the one who'd gotten too close to him when the pig started snooping around and asking all those questions about the navy lieutenant's demise. He'd fucked up by doing that.

All throughout the interior of his row house on Green Street, Gaf had framed photos and oil paintings of his beloved dad. Gaf liked living in total darkness in his row house and, to achieve that, had nailed up black construction paper over every interior window of the house, blocking out all light.

He only used one-bulb light fixtures in the small cramped kitchen and bathroom, whose walls and ceilings were all painted black.

As he pulled up, using the remote to open the ground floor single-car garage door leading to the basement, he thought, *I hope Vack likes patty melts. I'd hate to have to kill him over something that trivial, but I'm sure he will. After all, most pig law enforcement officers love greasy cold food, including stale donuts with those multicolored sprinkles on them.*

No, I'm not gonna warm that patty melt up for Vack, but I'm pretty positive I won't get any complaints from him since he hasn't eaten anything in the last twenty-four hours. Not since I put my long-barrel 44 magnum revolver in his face, as I pulled him from his car yesterday, and relieved him of his Glock revolver and FBI shield. Then zip tying his hands behind his back, duct taping his

mouth, throwing him in back of my van, and driving off,
heading for my place.

Gaf had caught Special Agent Vack totally off guard,
as he sat in his car near the water front eating a hamburger and paying no attention to his surroundings. He had his
head up his ass, totally oblivious and unaware of Gaf as
he walked up on his cheap-looking rental car.

Vack's Glock-19 revolver and FBI shield were going
to come in handy when Gaf tried his hand at impersonat-
ing an FBI agent. He was going to love doing that!

While driving back to his place, Gaf had also thought
about how much he loved his gun—one he'd had to have
after watching those *Dirty Harry* movies from back in the
day. His 44 Magnum had come in handy when he'd used
it to strike fear into the heart of anyone he'd stuck it up
against. Even if he had no plans on killing them, just to
see that look of terror on their face was, for him, always
priceless!

After Gaf removed the pillow case and duct tape from
around Vack's head, Special Agent Vack scarfed down
that patty melt like he hadn't eaten in weeks. He even
thanked Gaf for bringing it to him, telling him he loved
patty melts and didn't mind if it was cold. Gaf liked that.
Maybe he'd let Vack live now—or maybe not. He'd have
to see.

After he let Vack use the bathroom, while holding his
44 to his face, and after Gaf chained him back to the wall,
Vack asked, "What are you gonna to do with me?"

Gaf just looked at the fear in his eyes and got that feeling of being superior. That, for him, was a big high. It
made him feel good, knowing that he was holding hostage a person, a highly trained FBI special agent, who'd
gotten sloppy by asking patrons of a gay bar—the one
Gaf happened to be sitting in—if they'd ever heard of
anyone going by the name of Gaf, because the FBI

thought Gaf might be involved in a navy lieutenant's recent murder here in the community. Gaf had overheard Vack's remark and knew he'd have to do something about it.

The FBI would never find Vack and, even if they did, Vack was probably going to be found dead, if he was found at all.

CHAPTER 9

The Search

The team was now headquartered at the FBI's office in San Francisco in a huge board room meant for training or holding meetings, which now held the forty agents assigned to our team by Director Becker. I started the early morning meeting off by giving those agents a rundown on what we knew at this time.

"As far as tracking down the Gaf Killer, who's now on the FBI's Most Wanted list, the main focus of the meeting this morning is that we now find fellow Special Agent, Vack."

After I filled in the additional agents with the details on what the FBI knew, I instructed thirty of the agents to fan out, look for clues in San Francisco that would help locate Special Agent Vack.

Continuing to address the agents I was sending out onto the streets, I added this additional information. "We do know Agent Vack rented a car from Mavis Car Rentals. It's a small economy car, blue in color, with the license number Cal-1017-44. So start there."

Soon as the agents left, I turned to Carla. "What do you have on airline employees?"

Carla had just got off the phone with several airline hubs located at San Francisco International Airport. "One airline in particular, Docket Air, a high end luxury styled air carrier that only deals with rich business clientele types, or in common language, just the plain rich, had a lead that sounds promising. It left me thinking he could be our man. A recent employee, Jeff Miller, was recently fired by Docket Air. Now we know his name could be Jeff, but actually I was told over the phone, he goes by Jeffrey Miller."

"Okay, find out where he lives, and if he has a record. Maybe he's been fingerprinted. And also check with DMV."

I called Director Becker to give him the update he wanted. "Director, I think we should get this info to the media as soon as Docket Air emails their personnel photo of Jeffrey Miller, who we think could be the Gaf Killer. During this press conference, we'll claim he's a person of interest, which we both know is law enforcement code for the main suspect. I personally think we should do a nationwide broadcast from here at the Frisco FBI office, and throw out all the additional details we now have, and not hold anything back."

"Okay, set it up, David. I'll fly out tonight. Schedule the live telecast at ten a.m. I want all media there, just like last week."

"Okay, Director, will do."

After talking to Director Becker, I got a call from the San Francisco PD about the murder of a waitress who had worked at a place called the Bay Diner and, again, it had the same MO as most of the Gaf murders. The San Francisco Police had found a slumped-over female, who apparently had been shot through the head while just sitting in the driver's seat of her car, parked directly in front of the cottage apartment over in the Mountain Lake area. It wasn't robbery. Her purse was still in the car, along with the tips she made working the day shift that day, but on the driver side window was the name Gaf smeared in blood.

I hung up my cell phone, then Carla, Martinez, and I headed out to investigate that new crime scene in Mountain Lake. On the ride out, I mentioned to both Carla and Martinez, "After we're done at the crime scene, head over to the Bay Diner and interview everyone who worked there yesterday, including the owner, with the hopes someone saw, or heard, something."

It'd be another long day, but, hopefully, we'd get some good leads out of all this chaos. This killing had the Gaf Killer written all over it. I knew it and so did the team. I was hoping any leads we came across here would help in finding Vack. Even though I did feel sorry for the innocent waitress, if a good lead on this murder would help in finding Agent Vack, at least some good would come of this. Right now, that was my main concern, and I was counting on Martinez to, hopefully, come up with something concrete that would lead us in the right direction.

We rolled up to the crime scene in a generic FBI dark blue Crown Victoria four-door sedan—a car any civilian could spot from a mile away, if they were trying to avoid the law. *"I don't understand why FBI agents aren't issued every day, common vehicles like the average American drives, and also why FBI agents are required to wear suits and ties.* It never made sense to me. For me, it seemed to be beyond old school, especially if you were an agent trying to surprise the criminal element. If I was appointed director of the FBI, my first order of business would be to get all FBI agents out of those stuffy-looking suits and ties, so they'd blend in with the public, instead of having to walk up on a potential crime scene, with a more or less stamped forehead saying, "Hello, I'm an FBI Agent."

The police still had the crime scene taped off to keep lookie-loos and the media away. Out of respect for the victim, they had placed a yellow tarp over the roof of the car, covering the front windshield and side windows, hiding the gruesome shot to the head this poor woman received.

We peeled back the tarp and, right off, I knew this was most likely the work of the killer we were looking for. Even though there was a gunshot wound to the head, and it appeared to have had a silencer attached to it, this crime scene had the same MO as the other Gaf killings. The killer had to have opened the driver's door, because there was no bullet hole through the driver's side window. The door was shut and had the word *Gaf* smeared in blood on outside of the window.

I turned to Martinez and had him take photos. And then we all agreed this had to be the work of Gaf. I directed both him and Carla to go over to the restaurant where the waitress had worked and question everyone working there yesterday. "Find out who she waited on and check for any surveillance tapes, especially for customers she waited on. Maybe we'll get lucky."

While I was still checking out the crime scene, I got a call from FBI Special Agent in Charge Steward Harden from the San Francisco office. He told me the *San Francisco Examiner* had just received another note from Gaf, bragging about his handy work, saying, "That waitress Rachel will never be rude to me or anybody else again, and I feel I've done the public a big favor by putting Rachel out of her misery."

When I heard that news, I thought, *What a sick fuck. If*

*he feels this way toward a waitress, I can't imagine what
he has in mind for Vack.*

Harden went on to mention, "We now have a photo of
Jeffrey Miller—who we think is the killer—supplied to
us by Docket Air."

"That's great. Please have the photo blown up for the
news conference in the morning, the one the director will
be attending. I'm sure when the public sees Gaf's photo
we'll get some good leads, most likely from someone
who knows him—that is, if he has any friends. From my
experience, most serial killers are loners with no friends,
so we'll see."

Next I called Agent Martinez and Carla, and told them
to meet me back at the FBI office on Golden Gate Avenue soon as they were done at the Bay Diner, and we'd
put together a game plan for the nationwide news conference in the morning. I also let both agents know we'd all
be staying just down the street at the Embassy, less than a
mile from the FBI office on Golden Gate. I then called
both pilots—something I hadn't done since landing at
NAS Alameda—and let them know I'd just booked them
rooms at the Embassy so they could stay at a class hotel
and remain close if I found out Miller had fled the area,
and we had to take off—or launch as the navy pilots
called it—at a moment's notice again.

At the waitress crime scene, the only evidence discovered were prints of the killer's shoes left in fine dust on
the street, apparently left as he made a hasty retreat back
to his vehicle to flee the area. Actually, our best evidence
was the note he'd left with the *San Francisco Examiner*,
which was now being analyzed for fingerprints. I personally didn't think we'd find any, but who knew? Maybe
we'd get lucky. We could use some luck about now.

The three of us met up at the FBI office that afternoon,
with Carla and Martinez telling me they did have one

promising nugget of information, passed on to them at the diner while interviewing every employee who worked there yesterday. It was a comment about an odd customer Rachel had waited on.

"That waitress told me she had worked the morning shift with Rachel," Carla said, relaying what the waitress had told her. "And Rachel had made the comment she had an asshole customer she was waiting on at table six, located way in the back of the restaurant. Rachel mentioned he bitched about his patty melt and ice tea. Other than that, that's all we have for now. It may be nothing, but who knows?"

"Boss, we checked surrounding businesses for surveillance videos, but none had security video setups," Martinez added. "Most told me they felt they didn't need it, because that area has such a low crime rate. The cashier at the diner told us that the customer paid in cash, but she was only able to give us a vague description of what the customer looked like. The cashier met with Simmons, who is working on the profile and sketch now, and so we can compare that sketch with the photo of fired flight attendant Jeffrey Miller."

CHAPTER 10

Jeffrey Miller is The Gaf Killer

My team went over the sketch Carla came up with and then compared it with the faxed employee photo Docket Air sent of Jeffrey Miller, and we all concluded, including Director Becker, that it was a match and we weren't going to dick around. We'd name him as The Gaf Killer at our nationwide news conference.

During the live televised broadcast, we showed the media the blown-up employee photo of Jeffrey Miller, and we also put his face on the FBI's website, naming him as one of the FBI's Most Wanted. During the broadcast, we also mentioned that Special Agent Vack was being held hostage by Miller, and that locating Vack was the FBI's number one priority for now. While showing the blown-up photo of Miller, we emphasized that if anyone saw anything, or knew anything about the whereabouts of Jeffrey Miller, or where he was holding Special Agent Vack, they should please call the FBI.

"You can remain anonymous and, if your information

leads us to Miller, there's a huge reward waiting for you in the sum of one million dollars." Director Becker ended the news conference by adding, "The FBI wants this killer bad. We especially want the safe return of one of our own."

Of course, the director held back and didn't mention one of his favorite nicknames for Gaf, "Fucking scumbag sum-bitch," because, after all, it was live television.

Later on that day, the San Francisco FBI office was flooded with leads. Some were ridiculous, coming from people just looking for some free reward money. Most said they had either talked to, or seen, Jeffrey Miller, who was hot-footing it to Mexico on a bus. There were a couple of leads stating they saw him driving a van. Those were good, because we never mentioned at the news conference what kind of vehicle Miller drove.

We needed to find Vack before it was too late. Finally, we got a good lead from some old lady who had lived on Green Street for twenty years and swore she saw a man looking like Jeffrey Miller coming and going at all hours of the day and night. But now it seemed like that row house was abandoned. We got the address and my team, along with about twenty other agents, rushed over there to this depressed-looking neighborhood on Green Street, just off August Alley, where the row house was located. I knocked on the door and got no answer, but as I put my ear up against the front door, I heard what sounded like muffled speech coming from deep inside this old-time-looking Victorian town house.

I made the decision to bust the door down, even though we didn't have a search warrant. I knew, from the FBI training manuals that, if it was a life or death situation, FBI agents could do that, rather than wait for some judge to sign off on a piece of paper that would allow us to do a legal search.

Hoping we'd find Vack, I stepped back from the front door and told two of the biggest agents I had with me, "Bust down this fucking door!"

Bam, we were through that door as if it wasn't even there! When I entered, I thought this was some bizarre-looking interior. Nothing like anything any decorator that I knew would have ever put together. Right off, I recognized the framed photos and witnesses' sketches of The Zodiac Killer hanging on every wall of this dark living room. Apparently, they were of Miller's serial killer dad from the late '60s, since Jeffrey looked just like him.

All the windows were covered up with what looked like thick black paper, making this one dark, creepy-looking room, to say the least. The only light came from a single bulb fixture hanging from the ceiling in the drab and dated kitchen.

As my agents hurriedly entered the row house, branching out, looking to shoot anything that moved, we heard the same muffled sounds we had heard before entering, but now once inside those sounds were clearer and louder.

"I recognize that voice," I said. "And it's coming from the basement. I'm sure it's the voice of Agent Vack."

We all rushed to the door leading down to the basement, sprang it wide open, and, in the dim light below, I noticed a figure twisting in chains that were attached to a wall at the base of the stairs.

We all ran down there, with me leading the way, and—even though I was pretty much a hard-core guy and couldn't remember the last time I cried—I nearly did after seeing Vack chained to that wall, barely alive, and hanging on by a thread.

"Cut those fucking chains off of Vack," I ordered. "That motherfucker who did this is gonna pay big-time when I get my hands on him. His ass is gonna be mine!"

We used bolt cutters and got Vack cut loose from that cinderblock wall, pulled the duct tape off from around his mouth, and immediately gave him some bottled water we had retrieved from one of the FBI vehicles parked on the street.

I knelt down beside Vack, as he lay there on the basement floor, and held the plastic water bottle to his mouth so he could once again taste water. Something I was sure he hadn't had for the last couple of days.

"Just hold on," I told him. "We have help coming."

Carla grabbed an old hand towel from the basement bathroom, poured water on it, then ran it across his face in an effort to reassure Vack that we were there for him.

Within five minutes the paramedics were there. Carla and I rode along, keeping Vack alert, letting him know how important he was to our team.

Special Agent Vack spent the next three days in the hospital and pulled through it just fine after getting some good food, hot showers, and a place to catch up on his sleep. Something he really hadn't had for several days, since being caught off guard while sitting in his rental car, eating that hamburger on the waterfront.

CHAPTER 11

Gaf Killer's on the Run

The team was glad to have Special Agent Vack back, including, Director Becker. Becker, who was now back in DC, called me and, in confidence, told me he wasn't sure how much longer he planned to stay on as director, mentioning that he had other things he wanted to accomplish in his life, other than just being the FBI director. And, after spending twenty-five plus years in the FBI, he had already made the decision that after The Gaf Killer was captured, he was done.

"If you can capture this fucking scum-bag sum-bitch soon," Director Becker told me, "I'll appoint you assistant director."

In real terms, that meant I'd take over when he retired as director. That was, if the president listened to his recommendations.

While thinking about that, a funny thing flashed across my mind. If I did take over as the FBI director, I'd get all FBI agents out of suits and ties, so they could blend. Plus

I'd get rid of those drab, generic, and boring-looking blue Ford Crown Victoria's we all drove.

Now back to reality. The chase was on. I let both pilots know to stay nearby and be alert, because we might need to launch at any time if we got a good lead on the whereabouts of Jeffrey Miller. I also notified the Norfolk FBI office that Jeffrey Miller was on the run and to stay on the lookout for this wacko, just in case he planned on traveling back there to finish off Sandy Bandfield. I told that FBI office to send a couple of agents out to Ms. Bandfield's, inform her of the situation, and to also show her Jeffrey Miller's photo to see if it jiggled her mind as far as remembering if he was the same Jeff who bought her drinks that night at the Flash in the Pan.

Until we got something concrete to go on, I'd have my team, including Vack, just sit tight for now, but I wanted them to be aware I could be calling them at any time if we got a hot lead.

In the back of my mind, even among all the chaos that had gone on over the last several days, I was thinking, that just maybe Carla and I could sneak off for some indoor bodysurfing. I needed a good fuck to rid myself of all the stress I'd been under since taking on this challenge, and I was pretty sure Carla felt the same.

Director Becker, had one of his agents, who was more or less a spokesperson for the FBI, handling most media inquiries. That agent put out a press release, informing the media that Jeffrey Miller had fled San Francisco and could be anywhere, possibly even Canada or Mexico.

I was pretty sure Miller wasn't going to risk taking a commercial flight anywhere, because now all airlines in the US and around the world knew his face and name and were on the lookout for this killer.

I thought he'd move into an adjoining state, like Arizona or Nevada, and try to keep a low profile until his urge to kill took over again, or if some poor unknowing waitress serving tables at a truck stop, or a diner—God forbid—poured him a cup of cold coffee.

CHAPTER 12

A Score to Settle

Those FBI morons were thinking Gaf was dumb enough to still be driving around like a fool in that old crappy van his daddy gave him years ago. Man, were they stupid. He'd ditched the van, right after the news conference, by driving it off a cliff near the San Francisco's Bay Trail Road, and now it was on the bottom of the ocean somewhere. He didn't need it to get around, anyway.

He had a way to get around that no one knew about, a motorcycle, or his crotch rocket, as he called it. He pulled it out of the van, just before deep sixing it, then simply got on the bike and drove away. The bike was registered to some other poor motherfucker who he didn't even know. He was pretty sure it was stolen when he bought it off this drug addict he ran into at a bar several months ago. The guy was wandering around the bar in a drunken stupor, looking for a buyer just so he could make some quick cash and probably score some more drugs. Even though Gaf knew the bike was most likely stolen, he didn't care. He got it dirt cheap, and it was a good thing he had it, because now it was coming in real handy.

Soon he'd ditch it too and buy some used piece of crap car, truck, or van for cash. Then he'd be back in the killing business when he left San Francisco and went on the run for good.

He still had a score to settle with that bitch of a boss, Hayes, who fired him. He now knew where she lived— and, man, was she going to get it, and soon. He had a plan in mind, and she was just vain enough to fall right into it. He would take great delight in watching her eyes bulge out of that pinhead skull of hers after she figured out she'd been had. But, by then, it'd be way too late.

Gaf thought he'd pose as delivery person from Welcome Bouquet, delivering her some lovely roses from someone she thought was an admirer at Docket Air. He'd hand her the bouquet then reach out with his clipboard to have her sign for them, and that was when she'd probably figure out he was no Welcome Bouquet employee. That was when she'd realize she was about to die.

What fool would admire that cunt anyway? She was so vain. She thought every employee at Docket Air loved her. One good thing, though, at least those roses wouldn't go to waste. They could be used at her funeral.

He didn't think he'd kill her with his magnum. He wanted that fucking bitch to suffer just like he was doing, now that he was out of work.

CHAPTER 13

Protecting Ms. Hayes

W e still had no clue where Jeffrey Miller was. He could have been anywhere. That was what made this track down even more frustrating, the not-knowing part.

I had Carla notify Janet Hayes, Miller's ex-female boss at Docket Air, who had fired Miller for wearing that wacky outfit to work and had told him, "Go home and change, and also wipe that ruby red lipstick off your face. It makes you look like the Joker character in Batman."

"I'm thinking he's gotta be holding a grudge," Carla told me. "Not only for what Miller probably thinks were insulting remarks on his freedom of expression, but also, being fired limited his access to potential victims across the US. In his demented mind, Jeffrey Miller thinks everybody picks on him for no reason at all. We'll have to protect Janet Hayes, at least until Miller is found."

We put four FBI agents on it—two inside her residence, and the other two outside in undercover FBI vehicles.

I had the agents working twelve hour rotating shifts, so they could stay fresh and alert. I advised Ms. Hayes to take a leave of absence until we arrested Miller, which she arranged through Docket Air. It was in her best interest, because I had a gut feeling that if he had a chance, she was going to be his next victim, and the FBI didn't have the man power to provide twenty-four-hour protection both at home and work.

In a way, I kinda hoped Miller did come around Ms. Hayes's residence, looking to take out his revenge. We'd be waiting, and would happily blow him away, doing it without an ounce of regret. We wouldn't be concerned with reading him his rights. We'd shoot first and ask questions later. I was on the side of Director Becker with this one. Low-lifes like Miller didn't deserve any rights.

Now we were on the third day of the stake out, and there was still no sign of Miller. But that was no reason to let our guard down. If we did, it'd probably be the time Miller showed. That was, if he hadn't left the area already. That was the hard part—having to keep our agents there on constant alert for the unknown.

CHAPTER 14

Some Raw Dog

In the meantime, while the team and I waited for something to happen, Carla and I finally were able to sneak away. Not at the Embassy, where we had separate rooms, but at a little bed and breakfast place located in a little sleepy town just north of San Francisco, called Sonoma. I booked it for the weekend. It was known for its wine vineyards and old-time feel. Of course, I paid cash and registered under a bogus name—and, surprisingly, I wasn't asked for ID. When you paid cash, "money talked." It was a good thing, because I didn't want to leave a paper trail and have Director Becker, or anyone else at the FBI, putting two and two together.

The place was called The Sonoma Retreat. Located in a wine vineyard on the outskirts of Sonoma, it was the perfect location, with no one around within miles of the place.

For two glorious days all Carla and I did was "Get Drunk and Screw," just like the Jimmy Buffet song said. Problem was, two days of fucking doggie-style wasn't enough for either of us. But under the circumstances, we made the most of it. Carla loved it doggie-style, nearly as much as I did. Heck, we never left the room. I ordered room service for the entire weekend. It was great being there for only one thing, and one thing only—to fuck our brains out.

Soon the weekend was over, and late Sunday we got into separate cars and cruised back south to the Embassy Hotel and back to the task at hand. When I got back to my room, I put my things away then went next door and paid both agents Martinez and Vack a visit to see if anything had come up while I was gone that I should be aware of.

"Nothing boss," Vack said. "Neither one of us have had a call from NCIS, the local FBI, or the SFPD, over the weekend."

"Okay, thanks and, by the way, I want the team to meet with me tomorrow morning at the hotel café at eight a.m. for a meeting. I wanna go over a plan I'm thinking about implementing in the hopes of forcing Miller's hand."

With that, I went back to my room and called Carla, letting her know how much I enjoyed the Raw Dog.

"Not half as much as I did," she said.

With that good news, I crashed, wondering when we'd be able to have another lover's rendezvous.

CHAPTER 15

The Sting

It was Monday morning, and the FBI had been on the stakeout at Ms. Hayes's residence, for going on five days now, and still no sign of Miller. We couldn't afford to let our guard down, though, when we still didn't know where he was.

I met with my team in the hotel cafe and went over the plan I'd be suggesting to Director Becker as soon as our little meeting was over with. "I have a plan to bait, or should I say, do a sting and, hopefully, trap Miller into coming out into the open from whatever hole-in-the-ground he's living in. My plan is simple. The FBI will run a bogus story in the newspaper, the *San Francisco Examiner*, the same one Miller uses to taunt law enforcement. The story will go something like this. We'll state that the FBI is no longer focusing on the San Francisco area and has moved its resources to Nevada, a place we believe The Gaf Killer to be hiding out. I'll pull the two agents from the street in front of Ms. Hayes's house and move Ms. Hayes to a safe house temporarily. We'll still have two agents in the house, with one female agent posing as Ms. Hayes. Moving the agents off the street will give the impression we are no longer protecting his ex-boss and, hopefully, Miller will take the bait. What he doesn't' know is we'll also have agents in both homes on either side of the Hayes's house. We only have to put one homeowner up somewhere, paying them a pretty good chunk of change for use of their house during the stake out. The house on the right is empty and is in foreclosure, so we'll contact the real estate company for entry and we'll use it, also.

I went on to mention, "Be ready. This is gonna happen as soon as I get the director's okay. I'll be calling him as soon as we're done here, say within the next ten minutes. I don't see a problem there, since the director wants this crime solved ASAP, making him look good, which in turn will get the president off his ass."

"Who do you plan on using as Ms. Hayes's look-a-like?" Carla asked me.

I had a pretty good idea where that question was going. Carla probably was going to volunteer as the Ms. Hayes look-a-like, and that's exactly what she did.

"I'll give it some thought," I told her.

Now the pressure was on me to come up with a good reason for not using Carla, simply because I had feelings for her, and not because I thought she couldn't do the job. I knew she could. Vack wanted to be the second agent on stakeout and, for me, that one was a no-brainer.

If Miller did show, Vack could get some payback and, hopefully, make Miller suffer a little before being cuffed, arrested, or shot dead.

Either way was fine.

I got the okay from Becker and the sting was now going ahead as planned. We ran the bogus press release and got the one homeowner to move out temporarily. Also, the real estate company let us use the empty house next door.

I did end up caving to Carla's request. It was something I hoped I didn't regret doing, but if I didn't grant her the request to pose as the Ms. Hayes look-a-like, I knew I'd never hear the end of it. I was in a no-win situation on that issue.

I did feel a little better about granting Carla's request, though, knowing that Vack would have her back. After all, we were a team. Now, we'd just have to wait and see if Miller took the bait.

CHAPTER 16

They Sound Like My Kind of People

Gaf didn't totally buy into the FBI story in the *Examiner*, so before he went knocking on the bitch's door with a bouquet of roses and wasted her, he'd cruise by her place on his crotch rocket and scope out the street and her house first.

His helmet had a dark shield covering his entire face, so he knew he wouldn't be recognized coming or going from his rat-hole motel room on St. Francis Place. At least not until he went there to put that bitch out of her misery. Then the law would realize it was him.

So before he went through with his original idea of delivering the roses to the vain bitch, he had a better idea—something the FBI would never have thought of. They didn't know he had all kinds of electronic devices, most of which were now sitting on the bottom of the ocean, along with the van he'd dumped, except for the one he'd kept—the one thing he knew would probably come in handy as he dodged the law.

It was a law-enforcement, wireless, electronic, cryptic-decoder recording device used by all cops, including the FBI. He'd stolen it right out of a squad car last year as this fat slob of a cop was busy inside a donut shop, stuffing his face on glazed donuts, and never realized what Gaf was doing right under his pig nose. Gaf had always had a distain for cops, any kind of cop.

When he cruised by the bitch's place, he'd have the cryptic de-coder turned on and, if there were FBI agents in the house, their chatter would be picked up, including cell numbers and all text transmissions they made, and stored in the decoder's memory, which he'd check when he got back to the rat-hole dive motel he was staying in.

If he got a hit on the decoder, he wouldn't go back. He'd can his original idea of the fresh flowers and just hit the road, probably to some hick town in Tennessee—most likely Nashville. Then he'd change his appearance and maybe become a country singer. He liked singing about trucks, booze, and bad romances anyway, especially after a fresh kill. Yeah, he could hear the FBI news flash now. "Be on the lookout for a hillbilly singing serial killer, going by the name of Gaf, and not Garth." He snickered. Sometimes he even creeped himself out.

It was now ten-thirty a.m., and he was riding his crotch rocket down the bitch's street, just behind a couple of cars, as he neared her house. He didn't look directly at it when he zoomed by, but he had the cryptic decoder turned on, hoping to pick up sounds coming from inside. If he didn't pick up any FBI chatter, he'd come back in a couple hours, do the dirty deed, then head out of California for good.

When he got back to his rat-hole motel and began playing the decoder back, he noticed that someone inside the house had sent a text to some pizza place and ordered a pepperoni pizza to be delivered. He knew right then that there had to be law enforcement inside the bitch's place, because he knew, for a fact, the cocksucker who fired him didn't eat pizza. She was one of those god-awful tree-hugging vegetarians and would have never ordered a pizza. At least the cunt had one good trait.

But even if he didn't get his chance now, it didn't mean he wouldn't be back. He hated her guts. She was going pay for firing him, no matter how long he had to wait. She'd need to sleep with one eye open for the rest of her life. He could show back up at any time.

He packed up what little belongings he had, including the cryptic recorder, Vack's Glock-19 revolver, his FBI badge, and left San Francisco with plans of heading for the East Coast, knowing he'd be making several stops along the way. He'd definitely be using Vack's Glock and FBI badge during his time on the run. It'd give him the look of being legitimate when he just walked up on his next victim and flashed the badge. They'd be at a lost as to what kind of trouble they were in. That, of course, would be for him to decide.

One good thing was that he did have a duffle bag full of cash, so money wouldn't be a problem at all. The only problem he'd have would be avoiding the police and FBI and figuring out who his next victim would be. Preferably, it'd be someone who pissed him off for some reason or another, and it very well could be either a man or woman. Gaf didn't care what gender, because he wasn't really that picky. He sometimes wondered why some people disliked him and caused him to waste them. He thought he was actually a very nice person as long as people treated him with respect. But if they didn't, they were all his.

He finally walked out of his rat-hole motel room with his helmet on and strapped his backpack—which contained, along with his meager belongings, Vack's Glock revolver and FBI badge—to the rear fender. He cranked up the crotch rocket and headed East on Interstate 80, towards Salt Lake City.

He'd never been to Utah, but he'd heard it was a state where those Mormons loved to congregate. In the past, he'd had negative feelings about Mormons, mainly from what he'd heard from non-Mormons, but after watching the TV show *Mormon Mafia*, he gained a whole new respect for them, realizing they weren't as rigid as he'd once thought when it came to religion. Actually, they sounded like his kind of people. He thought he was going to like his stay in Salt Lake City. Maybe, he'd even break down and go to church, or—as Mormons called it—the temple. Yeah, sure, like that was going to happen. That'd be a cold day in hell.

There I go again, cracking jokes to myself.

On his way out of town, he dropped a note into one of those blue, free-standing mail boxes. It was addressed to the *San Francisco Examiner* and asked, "Which one of you FBI fools ordered the pizza today?"

That was all it needed to say. He grinned, knowing they'd be scratching their heads, trying to figure out how he knew that. Then they'd spend time finding out who ordered it. Man, were they going to get an ass chewing.

CHAPTER 17

The Gaf Killer, Six. The FBI, Zip

Sometime Tuesday morning, while at the FBI head-quarters in San Francisco, I was informed by Special Agent in Charge Steward Harden that the *Examiner* had received another hand-written note from the Gaf Killer, mentioning, in so many words, he was onto the sting the FBI had set up.

My first reaction was, "What do you think this means, Hardin?"

"Drake, did either of your agents, on the stake-out, order food to be delivered? If they did, that was a big mistake."

"I don't know, but I'll find out."

I called Vack at the Hayes's house and found out he ordered the pizza. He told me, at the time, he didn't see the harm in it. If it had been anyone besides Vack, I would have come down hard on them.

"Okay, Vack, hand your cell over to Simmons. I've got something I need to tell her."

"Sure, boss, no problem."

"Carla, I'm shutting down the sting. Vack messed up by apparently placing a call on his cell to a pizza shop. Somehow, Miller found out about it, or else he probably would've shown up yesterday." I explained about the note sent to the *Examiner*. "I want both of you to head back here and meet up with me and Martinez at headquarters. We need to re-think what we're doing. So far, what we've done isn't working. Right now, it's the Gaf Killer, six—the FBI, zip. There's one attempted homicide, three murders, an FBI Agent who was held hostage, and a sting operation that went nowhere."

"Miller's probably long gone from San Francisco by now," Carla agreed, "since the note to the newspaper was probably written nearly twenty-four hours ago. We need to work on where we think he's headed. And, by the way, we should find out what he's using for transportation. I'll bet he's dumped that van he used when he surprised Vack and brought him back to the row house."

"You're probably right. Well, I'll see you both back here shortly."

"Okay, boss, we're on our way."

It felt strange, having Carla call me boss, especially since we were fuck buddies again.

I called the safe house, informed Ms. Hayes of the situation, and told her I was calling the sting off. "You can move back into your house." I encouraged her to go back to work, but to be careful. "The FBI will be watching your house until we're certain of Miller's whereabouts."

That definitely didn't put Ms. Hayes at ease. "So what am I supposed to do in the meantime?" she asked me. "Be constantly in fear for my life, not knowing if this lunatic could just show up unannounced at any time, and kill me?"

She had a right to be nervous but, under the circumstances, that was all we could do. I knew that's easy for me to say, because I wasn't a target of Jeffrey Miller's anger.

☙☙☙

We four—Carla, Vack, Martinez, and I—huddled in a small office at FBI headquarters on Golden Gate Avenue.

I began by saying, "This Jeffrey Miller is playing us for fools, so we're gonna take another approach. I want you, Simmons and Vack, to head out to Docket Air and question any employee who came in contact with him during and/or after work. Maybe there's something we've missed, some little tidbit of information that might shed some light on this killer's traits, or his psyche. Someone at Docket Air might know if he had another means of transportation other than the van he used to kidnap Vack."

I turned to Martinez. "I want you to map out a radius of just where Miller might be. Figure it's been about twenty-two hours between the time he mailed the note and now. He's been driving approximately ten to twelve hours, so allow the remaining hours for gas stops and sleep. Other than that, Miller is traveling at a minimal speed of sixty to sixty-five miles an hour on average, possibly more, but figure less." I broke out my calculator, did some calculations, then glanced up at Martinez, "You'll be looking at a radius, out from San Francisco, of somewhere between six hundred to seven hundred eighty miles. You've got an hour to come up the routes he may have taken using those parameters. Understood?"

"Yes, boss, I understand, I'm on it."

Glancing over at Carla and Vack, I nodded. "Okay, you two, head over to Docket Air and get back here soon as possible. Then we'll go over the new pro-active game plan I have in mind." I reached down under the conference table, pulled up a duffle bag that had four new cell phones in it, and handed one to each team member. "These new cell phones are cutting edge and only send out cryptic coded transmissions. And the good part is that the transmissions can't be picked up by any kind of recording device. The CIA has been using this type of cell phone for years and, thanks to Director Becker, we've gotten an okay from the president to issue them to all FBI agents on this case. But even though wireless transmissions from our new cell phones won't be picked up, I want to impress upon everyone sitting here at this conference table that these cell phones are meant to be used strictly for FBI business."

Agent Vack didn't need to apologize again. The expression on his face said it all.

"Okay, with that, this meeting is over," I continued. "Now, let's catch this low-life bastard before he kills another innocent victim."

After the agents left, I called Director Becker and gave him an update. He wasn't pleased, mainly because he was a results guy and was only interested in success. Anything less wasn't an option.

One thing that was not helping my situation, as far as getting the director off my ass, was that President Anderson was probably calling the director daily, wanting to know why we hadn't caught the Gaf Killer. Like the saying went: "It all flows downhill."

In the meantime, I had decided the team should pay another visit to Miller's row house on Green Street and give it the once over again, looking for anything we might have missed the first time. Then we'd fly up to the Seattle crime scene—the one we'd never made it to. I called the pilots and told them to make sure the Gulfstream was gassed up and ready to launch for Seattle tonight.

Martinez got back to me in forty minutes with a detailed map, plotting the radius out from San Francisco, as if Miller had been on the road since mailing the note yesterday. I thanked him and reiterated that our plan from this day forward was to be pro-active in tracking Miller down.

From now on, the team wasn't going to be just sitting around, waiting to be informed that Miller had struck again. I directed Martinez to send out an FBI memo—okayed by Director Becker—to all FBI offices located in major cities in the US, instructing them to download Miller's FBI Most Wanted poster and distribute it to all night spots—including gay bars—gas stations, and convenience stores in their respective cities.

"The team is through fucking around," I told him. "We're done with being taunted by this scumbag. We're gonna give Miller a good supply of heat now and, hopefully, box him into a corner. Then we'll come down on him with extreme vengeance."

Right after and I got through talking to Martinez, Vack called. "Boss, apparently, he didn't socialize with fellow employees. They all said they rarely even spoke to Miller and that he was pretty much a loner. He liked to keep to himself. In fact, no one even knew where he lived. Most thought he had a house or apartment in the Castro District because he had told them he was bi-sexual but, other than that, that's all they knew about him."

"Yeah, Vack, it figures. That's a trait most serial killers have, for some reason. Okay, head back here pronto. We've got some work to do out at Miller's row house, then we'll be leaving for Seattle right after that."

I began to get impatient, mainly because I knew the team needed to make some real progress that resulted in Miller's arrest.

Soon both Carla and Vack were back. The team

packed up their things for the flight up to Seattle, before making it back over to the Green Street row house, Miller's last known residence.

When we pulled up and, as I was in the process of parking the Crown Victoria, I glanced over at the row house. It just seemed to give off a bad vibe, just like the old Bates Motel did in the movie, *Psycho*. As I got out of the car, I looked at this two-story structure, feeling there was something evil about the place. I wondered how many murders had been committed by the Millers over the years that they lived here. We now knew that Jeffrey Miller was the son of the Zodiac Killer, a serial killer from the late '60s, so who knew what went on back then? I couldn't even imagine.

Inside, we started scouring every square inch of the place, with Vack checking out the garage and the rest of us each taking a room, starting with the bedrooms upstairs. When we got done there, I'd know, at least in *my* mind, that we'd done everything we could in looking for clues, something that hadn't been done after Vack was rescued. I'd left that to the police and a handful of other FBI agents—a mistake that wouldn't happen again as long as I was in charge of this track down.

While upstairs in one of the bedrooms, I heard Vack yelling, "Hey, boss, can you come down here? I want you to look at this."

I ran downstairs to see what Vack had found.

"Look at these things," he said. "They look like old motorcycle license plates, both with different years printed on the small stick-on labels. One label has the year 2010, and the other has the year 2011. I bet these are stolen plates, boss."

"I think you're right, Vack. Call those plates in right now and have them checked out. I'd bet a week's pay that those motorcycle bike plates *are* stolen and, if they are, they'll give us an idea how Miller is getting around."

"Yes, indeed, these plates were stolen," Vack told me when he hung up the phone. "And both were off motorcycles that had similar paint schemes of black and silver. They're called crotch rockets, boss. Do you know what I mean by that? You know, those fast bikes that look nothing like a Harley?"

"Yeah, Vack, even though I'm no biker, I know what crotch rockets are. All right, thanks. Now we have a good idea of how Miller's getting around, unless, of course, he could have ditched the bike. By the way, where in the garage did you find those plates?"

"Oh, they were in plain sight, nailed to one of the two-by-four studs on the back wall of the garage."

I was at a lost as to why these plates weren't discovered when the police supposedly did a thorough search of the row house after the Vack rescue. I called Director Becker to let him know what we'd found, and Becker immediately put out a news flash stating, *The FBI has good reason to believe the Gaf Killer is using a silver and black crotch rocket—a fast motorcycle—to get around on now.*

To me, that wording sounded rigid and strange. I figured the director had no clue what a crotch rocket motorcycle even was. Just from the tone of the bulletin, it sounded like it came from someone who was real old school FBI. I'd bet Director Becker went online and Googled crotch rocket.

Nothing else was discovered at the row house, so we packed up and drove out to NAS Alameda, met up with the pilots, launched the Gulfstream, and headed for Seattle, Washington.

CHAPTER 18

Mormon Town

Gaf drove straight through to Salt Lake City, taking uppers all along the way, which helped keep his eyes wide open and his heart thumping strongly so he wouldn't have to stop and spend the night at a motel, taking the chance of being snitched on by a motel clerk.

That would be bad news for the poor soul who made the mistake of snitching Gaf out. He'd surely have to kill that person, teaching them a lesson that snitching just wasn't right. Why did people do that? He'd never snitched on anyone nor, for that matter, had he gone out of his way to piss off anyone. He just didn't understand why people thought and acted that way. Couldn't they be normal, like Gaf?

As he rolled into Salt Lake City, he was beat. Even though he had taken uppers all along the way, he hadn't slept for the last forty eight hours. He needed to find a place to crash, or else he knew he'd start hallucinating from lack of sleep.

Sitting there, on his bike beside an old asphalt road, he contemplated his next move. He wondered if the heat was onto his location, so he broke out the Tracfone he'd bought at a swap meet, just to monitor CNN for any updated news they might be putting out on his whereabouts etc. After listening to the latest CNN broadcast, which included a news bulletin from the FBI indicating they believed he was now getting around on a stolen black and silver crotch rocket, he knew he needed to ditch the bike. He was shocked to hear that those FBI fuckheads had figured that out. Maybe the FBI was a lot smarter than he thought they were.

Now he really had to lay low, and that was going to be hard to do, seeing as how he only had a quarter of a tank of gas and needed to fill-up so he could find something else he could buy for cash to get around on. Whatever he ended up with, he knew he wouldn't be registering it with DMV, and he also knew it wouldn't be another bike. This time, it had to be either a used car or truck that someone had looking to unload for some quick cash. Then whatever he bought, he'd keep until the tags expired, then he'd either steal some new plates, like he did with the bike, or just dump it and buy another car or truck.

Looking both left and right, up and down I-15, he decided to take a left and head north up, toward Willard, about thirty-five miles away. He got off at the Hwy 315 exit and was now in the middle of nowhere, cruising, looking for some mom-and-pop type convenience store selling gas and food. He definitely wouldn't be stopping at a 7/11, with its video cameras sweeping inside the store and the outside parking lot. While he was there, he'd go old-school and buy a copy of the local newspapers. Maybe he could find someone who didn't use the internet for everything and who was looking to unload a used car or truck.

As he zipped up Hwy 315, he kept a close eye out for anything that remotely looked like a cop car while, at the same time, keeping a lookout for some unscripted gas-station-store combo. Then a funky hand-painted sign, just a little down the road, caught his eye. It had big, red capital letters, reading, *GAS HERE*, painted on what looked like a sheet of white plywood nailed to a big oak tree growing near the gas pumps. Now, this was his kind of place. It even had one of those old newspaper stands, the kind you dropped fifty cents in, popped open the lid, and grabbed a paper. He hadn't seen one of those in years.

He pulled off the road, rolled onto the graveled area surrounding the gas pumps, shut off the bike, and read the note on the gas pump, *CASH ONLY, NO CREDIT CARDS!* After glancing at the note, he looked up. That was when he heard the shuffling sound of someone dragging their feet, as they walked toward him on the coarse graveled driveway.

"Yes, young man, how you doing this great day in the morning? You lookin' to fill-up? Bet that bike of yours isn't gonna take more than three gallons. Don't blame you for using a bike to get around on these days, you know, with the price of gas and all."

Gaf couldn't believe it. The old man, who looked to be in his eighties, actually grabbed the pump's hose handle and started filling up the bike's tank, kinda like they did back in the '60s when you could get your windows cleaned and your floorboards swept while getting gas. Man, things had changed.

The old man did all this with a constant grin on his face, as if he enjoyed his work. That was refreshing, and, to say the least, Gaf was impressed.

"Okay, young man, that'll be twelve dollars even, although the pump reads twelve dollars and nineteen cents, I don't like collecting and making change, so I just round it off. It's generally in the customer's favor most of the time. Nineteen cents isn't gonna change my life one way or another and, besides, I've found if you treat a paying customer right and show your appreciation, they'll be back."

Gaf thought maybe this old guy was still living in the '60s, but he had to admit he agreed with the old man's philosophy. He held out his hand to thank this old timer for treating him right. "Hey, by the way, old man, what's your name? Sorry, didn't mean to call you old man."

"That's okay, young man, I don't know your name either, that's why I called you young man. Ha, ha, ha. My name is Jimmy Watkins, but you can just call me old man, if you want. It's no problem, because I am old. I just turned eighty-five last month. Man, does time fly."

"Thank you, Jimmy. It's been a long time since I've run into a business man who treated customers right. I really appreciate that and, oh yeah, my name is John Zoddie." While shaking the old man's hand, Gaf gave him that bogus name on the spot. It came from a combination of an uncle of his from back in the day named John, along with a play on Gaf's daddy's tag name, the Zodiac Killer. "Hey, Jimmy, I noticed you have one of those old-time newspaper stands there by the front door of your store, so I'll need change. I wanna check the want ads for a used truck."

"Well, John, the reason I still have the newspaper stand is because it has the latest addition of the Salt Lake News in it and, actually, it's mostly for my old-time customers, who still read newspapers. Frankly, I quit watching TV and reading the *Salt Lake Dispatch* after my wife Gladys died last year. I'm pretty much old school when it comes to modern technology. But, don't worry, about the paper. I'll just give you a copy. But even better, I can save you time reading, because I have a pickup truck with a camper shell that I've been trying to sell for a while now. I'll tell ya what. I'll give you a good deal on it if you're interested. It's out back behind the store."

"Sure, I'm interested, because I planned on taking a trip to the East Coast, and that would really come in handy, seeing how I wouldn't have to waste money on motels. One other thing, Jimmy, I planned on sticking around here for a short time and was wondering if you knew of anyone who had a place I could rent cheap, say for maybe a month?"

"Ah, okay. Well, I have a little old house out in the boondocks, not too far from here, that I no longer live in. Actually, I hadn't thought about renting it out. I was gonna just sell it because I've been living here in the back of the store since my wife died. How much can you afford to pay, John?"

"I don't know. Why don't you just give me an idea of how much you want?"

"I could let you rent the house for a short time, and say, charge five hundred for the month, including utilities, with no deposit fee, as long as you promise not to trash the place."

"Okay, that sounds good," Gaf said. "After we go in the back and look at the truck, do you have time to show me the place? I'll pay ya in cash, by the way, hundred dollar bills. I don't believe in using credit cards, never have."

Of course, Gaf didn't mention the reason why. He walked his bike to the back where Jimmy showed him this old 1992 Ford F-150 with a camper shell in the bed. "It runs like a Timex Watch," Jimmy told him. "'Takes a lick'n and keeps on tick'n.'"

That *was* old school. Jimmy clearly thought he was being hip, bringing up that old catch phrase.

"Well, John, what do you think? Do you like it?" Before Gaf could answer, the old man pointed to the trucks tags. "Oh, yeah, there's one other thing, John. You'll notice the tags are good for another couple of months, so you'll save money. You won't have to reregister it right away."

For Gaf, that was a plus, because he was actually never going to reregister the truck and put it in his name, anyway. He got into the old truck, and it cranked right up, so now all he needed was the price.

"I'll let you have this rig for only three grand, John," Jimmy said.

Gaf wasn't going to nit-pick the price, because he knew it was a good deal, since this older truck was in excellent shape. The truck looked way better than a lot of the newer ones did. "Okay, I'll take it. Now all I need is the title, and I'll peel off the thirty, one hundred dollar bills. Do we have a deal?"

Old man Watkins's eyes lit up. "Sure, this truck is yours now."

While standing there next to the truck he now owned, Gaf asked the old man, "Can you show me the house now?"

"Sure, let me go inside and put up the close sign with a note on it, letting customers know I'll be right back."

"Okay, Jimmy, that sounds good, but first if you don't mind, I'd like to pick up some groceries from your store, so I can just bring them with me and not have to come back to pick up something later."

"Yeah, that's no problem, John."

With that, Gaf bought enough food to last him a while and, from the look on Jimmy's face, after ringing up over two hundred dollars for the food, he was surprised. Gaf thought the old man's eyes were going to pop right out of his head. Surely, he hadn't done this much business in one day since his wife died.

After that, Gaf loaded his crotch rocket up in the camper shell, and they headed out to the old house, with Gaf following behind the old man as he drove his old antique Jeep, that looked like an old World War Two relic.

Now, in the back of his mind, Gaf knew he'd be this old man's protector, just because he wasn't some money grubbing prick business owner who was out to scam the public like most businesses did. The old man seemed to genially want to help Gaf out.

From his encounter with the old man, Gaf knew that as long as he was staying nearby, he wouldn't have any problem snuffing out anyone who did Jimmy wrong. Gaf felt good about himself, knowing now that he did have a conscious. He'd be doing some real good if anyone fucked the old man over.

The old house did look just like a shack, as if like it hadn't had any remodeling done to it in at least thirty years, if not longer. It had an old weather-beaten salmon-colored stucco exterior with peeling white trim. When the old man let Gaf in the house, he felt like he'd been sent back to the '70s.

The interior furnishings looked like something from the *Brady Bunch* house. But Gaf didn't mind. The place was really clean.

"If you watch TV, I have one in that closet over there," Jimmy told him, pointing to what looked like an entry closet where people hung their coats.

Gaf liked that, because now he could monitor news broadcasted on CNN and not have to use any lousy Tracfone. "Okay, Jimmy, here's $500 upfront for the month I plan on staying here, and if I do decide to stay on longer, I'll fork up another five hundred dollars. No problem. Okay, well, I guess that's it for now, and I appreciate you renting the shack to me. Now I'm just gonna put some of my things away and maybe wash some clothes.

Yeah, that's what I forgot to ask. Does this place have a washer/dryer?"

Gaf knew he was pushing his luck. But if this shack had a washer/dryer setup, he could hang out here, totally avoiding the public by not taking the chance of being spotted by a snitch who was looking for some easy reward money.

"Yes it does, as a matter of fact. You see that little storage shed behind the house? Well, there's an old washer & dryer in it you can use."

"Excellent, Jimmy, that's perfect." Yeah, it was perfect for Gaf, because now the only time he'd need to leave the place was to maybe go back over to Jimmy's store to buy more food if he ran out, or to fill-up just before he decided to head east out of Mormon Town.

With that, he and the old man shook hands.

"If you need anything, just drop by the store," Jimmy said.

"No problem, Jimmy. I think I'm set. Now all I wanna do is take a hot shower and take a nap for a few hours."

The old man left, and Gaf commenced to do just that. When he was done with the shower, it came back to him just how good a hot shower felt, and he followed that up by scarfing down some chow then jumping into bed to get some much needed sleep.

While lying there flat on his back, looking straight up at the dingy ceiling, he began thinking. *Man, I nearly feel normal.* But he knew he wasn't. It was just a matter of time before he ran across someone who rubbed him the wrong way, and he was forced to put them out of their misery, like the bitch who got him fired from Docket Air. He hadn't given up on wasting that bitch. He knew it wouldn't happen tomorrow—but one day, just when she thought she had nothing to worry about, bam. He'd be there in her face! She'd probably drop dead of a heart attack when she saw his face, realizing it was him, Jeffrey Miller. *I'm gonna love that*!

He was pretty sure that he wouldn't stay cooped up here in this shack for an entire month. After a couple of weeks he knew he'd get itchy feet and hit the road. But before he did that, he'd change his appearance, by letting his beard and hair grow.

While he was stuck here, he'd be constantly monitoring all the media news outlets and only leave Mormon Town when things had cooled off. One thing, he was sweating was that even though Jimmy said he didn't watch TV or read newspapers, Gaf figured his face and name had most likely been plastered all over the front pages of most newspapers across the nation. And that did worry him, because he'd hate to have to kill Jimmy. Gaf liked the guy. The old man had been nice to him.

On the good side, Gaf was sure the FBI hadn't a clue where he was at, or else they'd have been busting his door down right now. Oh, those incompetent fools. He loved ragging on law enforcement. It was one of his favorite things to do, other than wasting people who had done him wrong, or people who seemed to be rude, or just plain annoyed him—like that waitress Rachel at the Bay Diner. She was a little of both. Gaf was pretty sure she never liked patty melts, but he loved them. It was one of his favorite foods.

CHAPTER 19

Seattle, Washington

Before leaving Frisco, I called the Seattle FBI office and spoke to Special Agent in Charge, Gloria Meyers, letting her know the team would be landing at the Seattle-Tacoma International Airport shortly, and then we'd head straight to her office to get a rundown on the crime scene before we analyzed it in the morning. Meyers told me that she was sending out an agent from the office to pick us up.

After landing, I had the pilots park the Gulfstream in an area of the tarmac that was normally reserved for high profile individuals, just so we could depart the Gulfstream without a whole lot of fanfare. I didn't want to alert the public that the FBI was here in Seattle to check out another of Jeffrey Miller's crime scenes and create a wild media frenzy.

Now it was about seven p.m. and dark outside. As we waited for our ride, I noticed it felt damp and misty, like it was going to rain. I'd always heard it rained a lot in Washington State, and that was the reason this state had one of the highest suicide rates in the nation. I didn't know about that but, on the good side, I imagined that most of the vegetation up here was a bright green so, for me, that seemed like a good thing, but then again, I didn't live here.

We met up with Meyers at the FBI office located on East St. John Street, then proceeded to an empty conference room, and went over all the crime scene photos. The team also viewed some video shot by an FBI agent who was sent there by Director Becker to assist the local PD. During the investigation, it was determined that this crime scene had the same MO as the Sandy Bandfield break in, in Norfolk, Virginia and, with that, Director Becker had the Seattle FBI office takeover.

"Special Agent Drake, I assume you'll wanna check out the crime scene first thing tomorrow morning," Meyers said.

"Yes, we do, first thing early in the morning. Even though it's a stale crime scene, I still think it was important to have my team fly up here and give it the once over. Like they say, a fresh set of eyes will sometimes catch things that weren't noticed the first time around."

"You bet, Drake, no problem there."

While listening to Meyers, and thinking to myself at the same time, there was one thing that had been bugging me since the Sandy Bandfield break in Norfolk, and that was, "How does Miller manage to gain entrance into these 'supposedly secure' locations." I had my theory, but I was keeping that to myself for now, at least until my agents and I went over the crime scene.

"Okay, Special Agent Drake, if need be, you can have use of a squad car while you're here, say, for the next forty-eight hours. I'll also have one of my top agents, Special Agent Thomson, follow you over in a separate car and give you a run-through of the crime scene as we saw it a couple weeks ago. After that, your team can do their thing."

"I appreciate your help with the squad car, Special Agent Meyers, and with that I think we now have enough to go on. The team would like to grab some chow and catch up on some much-needed sleep. Tomorrow morning is gonna be an early wake-up call. As for grub, we'll just hit the twenty-four-hour snack bar here in the FBI building and not spend time looking for an open restaurant. I've heard they cook up fantastic tasting charbroiled hamburgers. Oh, one other thing, I'd like to have the team crash here for the night, if you don't mind. We'll just camp out in the Red Eye Rooms and book out of here, say, no later than seven-thirty a.m. in the morning." I glanced over at my team and could have sworn I saw Carla roll her eyes. *There I go. Now, no sex for a month.*

"No problem," Meyers said. "Follow me to my office, and I'll give you keys for the rooms. Then you can put your bags away and hit the snack bar. And, by the way, those burgers *do* taste fantastic. You're gonna love 'em.'"

I looked back over at Carla, saw the expression on her face, and realized there'd probably be no sex for the next two months.

⍥⍥⍥

Before heading out to the crime scene the next morning, I gave Director Becker a call to see if any good leads had been generated since the FBI sent out that press release with Miller's photo and the description of the silver and black crotch rocket he most likely used to leave the San Francisco area.

"I thought I'd give you an update," I told him. "The team's rolling out to the Seattle crime scene to size it up, being that it's the only crime scene we haven't yet viewed. I'm calling to see if any concrete leads have come in since we sent out the press release."

"Nothing yet, David. I'm sure that sum-bitch is laying low somewhere within a thousand mile radius from San Francisco. I'd lay odds Miller didn't head north up the West Coast. I'm thinking, he would have headed directly east, stopping somewhere along the line when he thinks he's found a safe haven to hide out in for a while."

"I absolutely agree with that, Director. So unless we get a hot lead before we leave Seattle, we're gonna fly back down to Frisco, rent cars, and head east, canvassing every city along the way for leads as to Miller's whereabouts."

"Okay, David. We need to do something. It's only a matter of time before that sum-bitch will get the urge to kill again."

When we rolled up to the female victim's condo, located in the Evergreen Point section near the shores of Lake Washington, I was shocked to see how similar this building looked in comparison to the Sandy Bandfield condo complex in Norfolk, Virginia. We gained entrance via the onsite manager and, while walking through the front door and into the lobby, I noticed there was a laundry room located just beyond the main entrance. It was in a similar location as the one at Bandfield condo. I made a note and continued on into the unit, with the four of us following in behind Special Agent Thomson. After a quick glance around the living room and kitchen areas, I saw that this condo had pretty much the same dated floor plan as Bandfield's did.

With Thomson again leading the way, we headed into the victim's bedroom.

"Well, this is where it all happened, Drake," Thompson said. "Other than the name Gaf and the smiley face smeared in blood on the mirror, we didn't really find any other evidence at all. Unfortunately, there was no DNA discovered here, other than the victims, and nothing was taken from the condo.

"This was a coldblooded killing, pure and simple," Thompson continued. "We checked out anyone she knew, and they all had alibis. Her ex-husband lives in Austin, Texas, moving there two years ago, right after the divorce, and never returned to Seattle. He's clean. We checked him out thoroughly. She did have an off-and-on-again boyfriend, a cop with the Seattle PD, and he also had a solid alibi. He was on TAD—temporary assigned duty—with the military, working undercover and posing as a navy man dealing drugs aboard an aircraft carrier."

I turned to Martinez. "What do you think? Does anything here in the bedroom stick out? So far, we really have no proof that this is Miller's the work, other than what was smeared in blood on the dresser mirror."

"Nothing sticks out, boss, but, for me I'd like to examine the lobby area, and see if we can figure out how he gained entrance."

"I agree," I said. "I don't think we're gonna really learn anything new here inside the condo, so let's head downstairs. I also wanna check out that laundry room on the first floor. I've got a theory on how he gained entry, both here and Bandfield's condo."

"I second that," Carla chimed in. "There's nothing here in this condo that's telling us anything new. We already know who did this, it was Jeffrey Miller."

"Okay then," I said.

"I agree with Simmons. Let's head back downstairs and check out that laundry room," Vack said and shuffled in behind us, while making notations in that small spiral note pad of his.

Just as we got to the elevator, Vack put the pad and pencil in his suit jacket's right side pocket, similar to the way Columbo would have back in the day. The only difference in his appearance was that Vack didn't wear old, matted trench coats or smoke cigars. But other than that, they were clones of one another.

Back downstairs my theory got shot down because the laundry room's window was way too small, plus it was positioned only one foot from the ceiling. Just to be on the safe side, I asked Thomson if the FBI had dusted the window for prints.

"Yes we did, and found none."

"Okay then. How do you think the killer gained entry?"

Thomson pointed to the rear entrance to the laundry room. "He most likely entered through the back door that leads out to the patio and pool area, but he'd have to be good at picking locks, because when that door is shut, you'd need a key to get back into the lobby we're standing in."

After hearing that, I turned to Carla and Martinez and tossed this out there to both of them. "Now, if the access door to the pool was left open for some reason, then Miller would have had no problem getting into the building. But the question is, how did he enter the front door of the victim's condo? That's the sixty-four thousand dollar question. I'm beginning to believe Miller probably has had training in picking locks. Vack, do me a favor. Get on your phone and check that out. Maybe at one time he worked for a locksmith or took one of those blue collar vocational classes at a community college in the bay area."

"Okay, boss, I'm on it. You mind if I go out to the squad car and make the calls?"

"No problem, Vack. Go ahead. We'll be out there in a few minutes. We're leaving here shortly. I just wanna check out the pool area out back."

We all walked out the rear door leading to the patio/pool area and gave it the once over.

"Martinez, what do you think?"

"I'm betting that, to avoid being seen coming in the front entrance door of this complex, Miller climbed up that tree there on the other side of the far back wall then stepped onto the top of that stuccoed wall and just jumped down, landing on the soft ground cover in what looks likes planting mulch."

"Was that area checked for foot prints?" I asked Thompson.

"Yes, it was, and there were none. And, if there had been foot prints left there to start with, the heavy rains would have washed them away."

"Okay, I've seen enough. Let's hat up and head back to the office. We're flying back to San Francisco ASAP." I called both pilots on the way back and told them to gas up the Gulfstream and do a preflight, explaining we were heading back to Frisco shortly.

On the way back to the FBI office, I turned to Vack and asked him what he found.

"Jeffrey Miller did work part-time for two years at AJ Locksmiths while in high school, boss, and continued working there for three more years full-time after graduating. After that, the owner told me he quit when he got the flight attendant's job with Docket Air. That was about fifteen years ago. Miller was very good at what he did and was an expert at picking locks and safes. I think that explains how easily he's been gaining entrance to these residences."

"I agree, Vack. Good work."

"I'm not really surprised," Carla said, knowing what we know now about Miller. He may be a deranged serial killer, but his profile tells me that he has a high I.Q. It makes me wonder what else is there that we don't know about him."

We gathered up our things from our Red Eye Rooms, then I made it back over to the snack bar and picked up a bag of charbroiled burger but, this time, with Swiss cheese. I met the team out front, and we all climbed into our loaner squad car, drove out to Tacoma International Airport, climbed aboard the Gulfstream, and took off, heading back South to NAS Alameda.

After gaining altitude, I brought out the huge grocery size bag of burgers and told the team that the burgers were on me.

At first, I didn't think Carla appreciated my generosity, then she surprised me by thanking me for picking up the burgers. "That's awful nice of you." But she said it in sort of a condescending way.

I began to wonder if this would be the end of our sex rendezvous, but I quickly got over that thought, because I knew we wouldn't break up over a hamburger. But then again, it was hard to know what a woman was really thinking. I knew I loved those burgers, but the only thing that was missing for me were jalapeño peppers. I loved jalapeño peppers. If I were sitting on death row, that was what I'd order for my last meal—a charbroiled burger with cheese and jalapeños catered from the San Francisco office of the FBI's twenty-four-hour snack bar.

Not knowing, at the time, that Miller had a thing for eating at diners and ordering patty melts with iced tea with a lemon wedge, I'd be recommending that gourmet delight to Miller after we tracked him down, and he ended up sitting there on death row, contemplating what his last meal should be.

Being that NAS Alameda was 680 air miles south of Seattle and, with the Gulfstream having a cruise speed of 550 knots, it only took about an hour and twenty minutes to get the team back to San Francisco. That was the advantage of having access to the Gulfstream. If the team had to fly commercial, we'd all still be traipsing around San Francisco International Airport like four trolls in a slow-moving line, wondering how many more hours would it be before we took off.

☙☙☙

After landing, I had the other three agents de-board the jet while I went up to the cock pit to give the two air force pilots a little pep talk. "I know it's not easy being on call, but your help in flying us agents around the country is vital, and necessary if we plan on catching Miller before he strikes again. I just wanted both of you guys to know that what you're doing for the FBI is greatly appreciated. By the way, how did you like the burgers I brought aboard?"

Both the air force pilots just smiled and gave me a big military thumbs up on the burgers.

"I have one other thing I wanted to mention," I said, then I went over the team's plan of now renting cars and heading east, hitting every city between San Francisco and Salt Lake City, in the hopes of scoring some good leads that would put us hot on Miller's trail, ending with his arrest. "What I'd like to have you do now is to fly to Hill Air Force Base in Salt Lake City and sit tight for a few days until you hear from me on what our next move will be."

"No problem, Special Agent Drake. We'll just gas up the Gulfstream, do another pre-flight walk around, fill-out a flight plan, and take off for Hill Air Force Base."

I shook both pilots' hands and thanked them again, then I met up with my agents on the tarmac, and we all headed for Hertz.

Within the hour, we each had our rental cars and began caravanning, heading northeast out of San Francisco up I-80, with a plan to make our first stop in Vacaville, about sixty miles up the road. That's where we'd chow down and then scour the area for leads before continuing on. After that, our next stop would be Dixon, then Davis, and Sacramento, and so on until we'd reached Salt Lake City. I wanted the noose to tighten around Miller's neck. If he'd been in any of those cities we were hitting, he was going to panic after finding out we were on his trail, and that was when I hopped he'd make a mistake and show himself. If he did, Miller was done. The team would be all over him like a cheap suit.

CHAPTER 20

The Shack

T he next morning, Gaf woke up wondering how long he'd actually end up staying in this shack of a house old man Watkins let him rent. He thought he'd just hole up here until the dust cleared. He was sure he wouldn't be staying the full thirty days. *Yeah, I don't see that happening. Here it is only the second day, and I'm already getting cabin fever.*

He dragged his ass out of bed and fried up some bacon and eggs on the old gas stove while, at the same time, he looked for a coffee pot in this dump. There had to one here somewhere in the 1950s-style kitchen. He did like the dining room table, though, with its green Formica counter top and chrome legs, making it look like the same kind of table he and his daddy used to sit at for dinner on many occasions, when they both lived in the row house, back in the day.

Gaf flipped on the tube and checked out CNN for any news the pigs might have fed to the media recently in hopes that some civilian would snitch on him just for the reward money. He had to admit that one million dollars was a tidy little sum. He wondered if he'd get that reward if he turned himself in. Well, that thought quickly came and went. "What moron would do that?"

CNN didn't even mention his name, and that kind of upset him. Was he becoming old news now? He'd have to mail another note, maybe this time to CNN, just to let them know he was here, hiding in plain sight, but where, no one knew. He liked that. It gave him a rush, a feeling of being superior by playing the FBI and media for the fools they really were.

One thing he'd been thinking about was that, although he might be bi-sexual, he still liked getting a good piece of female ass every now and then. And lately, he'd had a hard-on for some good, old-fashion doggie-style pussy. But he knew that if he did go out carousing the bars, looking for ass, it would be risky. It was something he just might do, anyway, especially if he decided to stay here another three or four days before he moved on.

Sex could make you take risks. Too bad some of his victims didn't understand that equation. If they had, they'd be alive now.

Enough with the daydreaming. He snapped out of it and wolfed down his bacon and eggs while washing it all down with some good strong unfiltered cowboy coffee. *Man, that's good. I think I'm gonna order some cowboy coffee the next time I stop at a diner, and God help the waitress or waiter that gives me a hard time like that bitch Rachel did at the Bay Diner.*

"Would that really be asking too much, to just order something off the menu, like some cowboy coffee? I don't think so."

All he'd ever wanted was to be treated with respect, nothing more, and nothing less. Most of the time, he only put people out of their misery if they've talked down to him. And the other ones he'd wasted simply because they were uppity or just plain snooty and annoying—the ones that came across as thinking they were better than him. He couldn't stand those types. They could piss him off without ever saying a word.

For him, they didn't deserve to live. Sometimes he thought he'd missed his calling. He should have been a psychiatrist, because he was an expert at reading people. But the problem was that they read *him* wrong, and that was how some end up sliced and diced.

Okay, enough of that. Now I think I'll wash some fucking clothes just to have something to do. Maybe I'll hang my clothes up outside on that clothesline that I see out the kitchen window. Thinking back to his childhood, he remembered that, for him, there was nothing like the fresh smell of clean, breezy, air-dried laundry brought in after hanging out on a clothesline all day.

CHAPTER 21

The Pursuit

After the second day of being on the road with my team, we had hit five cities and talked to numerous employees working at convenience stores and gas stations, showing Miller's photo to all of them, in the hopes that it would jog their memories. I knew Miller had to have stopped for gas somewhere along I-80 if, in fact, he had headed east like the director and I both presumed he most likely did.

We're now in Sacramento, the capital of California. It was about ninety miles east of San Francisco and spread out over hundreds of square miles, so we certainly weren't going to cover the entire Sacramento area for leads.

As we caravanned into western Sacramento, I radioed the team members, letting them know we'd stop for some lunch at the first diner we spotted, then I'd discuss our game plan for this area. After I got off the radio, I spotted one of my favorite places for lunch, a little diner chain that was unknown outside California. It was called The

Broiler Café—a classic-rock themed deli/diner with great tasting food. I instantly thought of Carla saying to herself, "Oh my God, not another hamburger joint."

We all parked in the front, went in, and sat at one of their vintage tuck-and-rolled red vinyl booths. While waiting on our orders, I started off by going over the plan. "Okay, you guys, obviously we're not gonna be scanning an entire city of this size, that would take us several days to do, so we're only gonna hit gas stations and convenience stores all along I-80, including any on the outskirts heading out of town. As soon as we're done with lunch, I want us to start leapfrogging one another up I-80, stopping and questioning every employee working at every convenience store and gas station as to whether or not Miller has been in their store. Also ask permission to have our FBI Most Wanted poster of Miller plastered prominently on their store's front windows, closest to the main entrance. That's the plan. It's a simple one, but one I think will work and should save us time."

"Only thing I'd add, since I am a profiler," Carla said. "I'm thinking we should also hit all the delis and diners along I-80, including the one we're sitting in right now. I'm beginning to think one of Miller's quirks is that he has a thing for deli and diner food. I'd bet he has a habit of ordering patty melts with ice tea and a lemon wedge, like he did at the Bay Diner in San Francisco. And if it isn't served to him the way he likes it, he sits there fuming. But I'm pretty sure the waitress probably did say something that pissed him off for some reason."

"Thank you, it's a good observation," I said. "It's something I hadn't thought of. That's one of the reasons I recruited you, Agent Simmons. I'm no profiler, and I probably wouldn't have given that fact a second thought." Of course I left out the part about my sexual attraction to her as being one of the other main reasons I recruited her. But we both knew those feelings were mutual and had been ever since our little sex romp in New Orleans a couple years ago.

ᥫᥭᥫᥭ

As we moved swiftly up I-80 toward the end of the day, we got lucky. Vack got a response from an independent gas station owner at the edge of town, just before the Sacramento city limits. Other than pumping gas at his station, the owner specialized in repairing only foreign vehicles. His name was Jake Barley, and he wasn't the typical shyster BS'n car mechanic, and certainly not some butt-crack hillbilly mechanic who spat chew while looking to rip you off on repairs. So, for me, what he told Vack carried a lot of weight.

After Mr. Barley viewed the wanted poster, he told Vack, "Yeah, I remember that guy. He stopped here a couple days ago and filled up his motorcycle, one of those fast bikes, and it had a two-toned silver and black paint scheme, the kind you mentioned here on your poster. After filling up, he paid me in cash and then asked if I had a car I'd be interested in selling him for cash. I thought that was odd, so I let him know we're not some used car lot. We make our money repairing high-end foreign vehicles and, with that, he didn't say another word, just frowned and drove off into the sunset, heading north up I-80."

Vack thanked Mr. Barley, gave him his card, and told him if he ran across Miller again, to call the FBI immediately.

Frankly, I didn't see that happening, but you never knew. Now we had a point of reference, knowing that Miller had headed up Interstate 80, and we also knew he had enough fuel to take him another one hundred and eighty miles, and if he had a modified tank holding four gallons, he'd have a range of about two hundred and twenty miles. With that information, there was no need now to have the team stop at every little one horse town within that range.

I called Carla and Martinez and had them meet up with Vack and myself at the Barley garage to discuss our next plan. I knew we were now on Miller's trail, and whether he knew it or not this pro-active search was going to pay off. I could just feel it.

After Carla and Martinez made it up to Barley's, we gathered outside around my rental car. I broke out my i-Pad then brought up Google Maps. "Now let's look for the town that's farthest up I-80, but within his bike's range, considering it has a regular stock three-gallon gas tank. If the crotch rocket he's riding does have the standard size tank, and that's the most likely scenario, he'll have to stop and fill-up in Fernley, Nevada, before going any farther." I pointed to the i-Pad's screen and told my agents, "See Fernley, Nevada there on the screen? From where we are right now, it's one hundred and sixty eight miles farther up I-80. So the plan is we'll drive straight through to Fernley and poke around with the hope that someone there has seen or talked to Miller. Any questions? Do we all agree?"

I looked around and saw the agents were all nodding in agreement. "Oh, there's two other things I wanted to bring up. We may just spend the night in Fernley and then continue on with this in the morning. I'm sure we all could use some dinner and rest, and to show my gratitude for the hard work everyone here is doing, I'm gonna spring for dinner tonight." Looking back down at my i-Pad screen again, I pointed to it, telling my agents, "Look there on Google Maps. There's a Dairy Queen right across from the twenty-four-hour truckers truck wash and restaurant. Man, I haven't eaten at a Dairy Queen since I was just a kid!"

None of my agents seemed to have the enthusiasm I had about the possibility of chowing down at a Dairy Queen. After that dumb suggestion, I looked around, and all I got were blank stares.

"Hey, no problem, that was a stupid-ass idea anyway." So with a big grin on my face, I came back with, "But okay, you guys, if you would rather chow down at the truck stop, we can do that instead." I looked over at Carla and saw that she didn't seem to see the humor in that suggestion either. Not a hint of a smile was coming from those luscious red lips of hers. With the thought of being cut-off forever by Carla, I knew I'd have to come up with a better dinner plan if there was ever gonna be a chance of me getting some more. Maybe I'd suggest some Chinese once we get there.

Picking places to dine out had never been my strong suit, and it was mainly because my job with the FBI didn't give me much time to date. Besides that, when I'd dated females outside of law enforcement, this question always came up. "What do you do for a living?"

Then when I told them I was an FBI agent, they tended to scatter like rats in a barn, never to be seen or heard from again.

We filled-up all four of our rental cars before leaving Jake Barely's gas station then began hauling-ass up the road, paying no attention to the posted speed limits. We cruised ninety miles an hour all the way to Fernley, NV, and in a funny way I nearly felt guilty that we were breaking the speed limit, but that quickly passed after we reached Fernley in record time. Actually, I wasn't surprised that we didn't see any highway patrol vehicles on the way up. It was probably because this part of I-80 was one desolate stretch of road.

While racing our way to Fernley, I was able to call Director Becker, relay the eye-witness account we had received on Miller, and then suggested that he leak bogus info to CNN and all the other news media organizations, stating that the FBI believed Miller had fled the US and was now in Canada. "Sir, we want this maniac to relax, and have him think he has nothing to worry about now," I said, explaining my reasoning for doing that. "And I believe he'll do exactly that if he thinks we're up north trolling around in Canada. If he's hiding out somewhere along I-80, maybe he'll get foolish and step back out into the public, and I believe that's when someone will spot him again. Then *bam,* he'll fall right into our trap."

The director agreed, but went on to warn me that if this didn't work, and we didn't find Miller, he'd never recommend to President Anderson that I become the next director of the FBI when he retired sometime later this year. After hearing that, I thought, *Isn't that the way government always works? It comes down to politics. You scratch my back and I'll scratch yours.*

I wasn't worried, though, because I knew we were hot on Miller's trail, and felt sure his days of being free were numbered.

It was a short trip to Fernley, Nevada. We made it there in less than ninety minutes, so now it was only seven p.m., giving us plenty of time to find a decent place to spend the night, put our things away, and scope out somewhere to have the dinner that was on me.

After getting off of I-80, I had already begun scheming on the sleeping arrangements Carla and I would have. If I can rent her a room right next to mine, one that had a Jack-n-Jill adjoining door on the common wall to our rooms, then we could have one of our all night long fuck-a-thon sessions, without Martinez or Vack having any idea of what we were doing. Carla and I hadn't had an all-nighter since our weekend getaway in Sonoma. I was thinking that once we both got all hot and bothered, I'd probably have to crank up the volume on the TV, because sometimes Carla tended to be a screamer. Man, just thinking about that nearly caused me to rear end the rental car Martinez was driving. Now I had to focus. I needed to calm down and look for a suitable place to camp out for the night. *That's right, most men, when it comes to women, think with their cock, and I'm no different.*

We all stopped at the twenty-four-hour truckers' truck wash and restaurant to fill-up our rental cars. While standing there pumping gas under the fluorescent lit overhang, I motioned for the other three agents to gather around my car.

"Okay, I think I have a good idea. While I scope out a decent place for us to stay tonight, I want you to check out the main drag and look for a place you'd like to have dinner tonight. Whatever place you decide on is okay with me. I just wanted, in a small way, to show my appreciation for the tireless work you've all put in since we began this quest, without complaining about the hours. I figured rather than eating at the Dairy Queen, I'd let you three select some restaurant where we can all enjoy a good meal together, and maybe a few good libations just to loosen up a bit. What do you all think?"

I looked around and saw nothing but smiles, especially from Carla. I think she realized I had an ulterior motive for doing this, and it wasn't because I wanted the agents to select a nice restaurant they liked.

Now, what I had in mind is that while the agents were busy scoping out a place to have dinner, I'd be checking out any nice looking motels that had two adjoining rooms, with that Jack-n-Jill access door separating our two rooms.

Of course, those two rooms would be for Carla and

myself, and neither Vack nor Martinez would know any-thing about that convenient amenity.

I was sure Carla knew I had an ulterior motivate for suggesting that I look for the motel the team would stay at tonight. Again, I was getting all hot and bothered just thinking about viewing Carla's naked ass.

Martinez suggested we eat at a Tex-Mex Restaurant not too far up the main drag from the truck stop. I liked that suggestion, and I liked Mexican food. In fact, I'd eaten at several Taco Bells, but I found my suggestion of eating at Taco Bells didn't go over well with Hispanics agents. I don't think that type of fast-food qualifies as Tex-Mex, at least that was what I'd been told. My idea for tonight was to wolf the Mexican food down then get Carla back to the motel and really enjoy the rest of the night.

Soon, but not soon enough for me, the dinner at the Tex-Mex finally came to an end after the team only con-sumed a couple of margaritas each, during the two hours we were there. I didn't like tequila and settled for a cou-ple of cold beers.

We all got back into our rental cars and drove the short distance to the motel I had selected before meeting up at the restaurant. Personally, I couldn't get back quick enough because sleep definitely wasn't on my mind.

As soon as we all got to the motel and entered our rooms, Carla came through the Jack-n-Jill door, and we immediately commenced to doing an all-night doggie-style sex romp, humping and pumping as if we had never fucked before. I started by fucking her doggie-style, along with slapping her on the ass at the same time. If I died doing it, that was the way I'd choose to go out.

Carla had a great looking ass, and what I really liked is that she liked me slapping her on the ass as I thrust away at that shaved tight pussy of hers while she looked back over her shoulder. "Fuck me harder baby, and spank me more! I love it when you spank me. It makes my pussy shoot like a man's cock."

She was right about that. There was no wondering if Carla did cum or not. With her, there never was any of that orgasm faking stuff going on when we fucked, the kind I'd heard other women talk about. Carla loved sex, just like I did, but for now we had to be somewhat discrete.

I knew one day I'd ask Carla to marry me, and then we could have sex when and wherever we wanted without having to sneak around. That would be one great day.

Carla and I got about two hours of sleep last night, but you wouldn't hear me complaining. At seven a.m. I rousted the agents from their rooms and told them to meet me over at the truck stop for breakfast, so we could go over our next move.

While waiting for the other agents to show up, I grabbed a table at this greasy spoon truck stop restaurant that was full of what I would call, ex-hippie-looking truck drivers with gray beards and long straggly hair. Most of the truckers were wearing clothes that looked as if they hadn't been washed in some time. In the meantime, I ordered some coffee and asked the waitress if I could speak to the manager.

"Is there a problem, sir?"

I pulled out my badge, and she glanced at it. "No, miss, don't worry it has nothing to do with the service here, it's a law enforcement matter. I just wanted to inquire about a customer who we believe may have eaten here."

You could see the stress on her face just fade away.

"Yes, sir, I'll send her right over, no problem. By the way what are you ordering?"

"I'll have coffee for right now, but I have three other

agents joining me for breakfast, who should be showing up any minute now."

Before joining the FBI, I'd done a bartending gig while living in Palm Springs, and I depended on getting good tips, so after telling the waitress I had three more joining me, I could see her mind working like a Vegas slot machine, calculating the tip money she'd be collecting from this table.

"Hello, I'm Mindy, what can I do for you?" the manager said when she arrived at my table.

After showing her my FBI Shield, I pulled out a copy of the Most Wanted poster with Miller's face on it and asked the manager if she recalled seeing this person in here within the last week.

She held the poster up close to her face, scanning it through her horn-rimmed glasses, and handed it back to me. "Yeah, I saw this guy in here last week, and, in fact, I waited on him because we were shorthanded that day. This person you're looking for ordered a patty melt and ice tea, but the odd thing was—and the reason I remember this character—is that he emphasized, making it very clear to me, to make sure that his patty melt's cheese was melted and that his ice tea was freshly brewed, and that it came with a lemon wedge. He wasn't smiling, either, when he said it. He just sat there with this grim look on his face, as if to say there would be no problems from him as long as he didn't get a cold patty melt along with instant ice tea with no lemon wedge. Yeah, this guy here on your wanted poster, Jeffrey Miller, gave me the creeps. I knew the sooner I could get his order to him and have him chow it down and leave, the better I'd feel. I made damn sure that patty melt was steaming hot and that his ice tea was brewed and came with two lemon wedges, just to be on the safe side. I do have to say though, he really appreciated the fact I took good care of him, telling me he loved the patty melt, and gave me a five dollar tip on just a seven dollar tab."

I really appreciated her thorough report. "One other thing. Did Miller mention where he was staying or if he was just passing through, and if so, where he was headed?"

"No, like I said before, the sooner he chowed down and left, the better I'd feel. We really didn't converse at all, but I do remember looking out our large picture window, and seeing him get on his motorcycle and speed off, north up I-80."

I leaned over the table and handed her my FBI business card. "Here's my card, Mindy. I want to thank you for the info, because what you've told me has helped. In fact, I now know Jeffrey Miller was here, and I also know now where he headed after leaving the truck stop. If Miller does, for some reason, come back here, please give me a call."

"No problem, I'll do that, Agent Drake."

"Now can you send over the other waitress please, and we'll order breakfast, I see my agents have just walked in through the front door. Thank you again for your help."

"I'm starved," Was the first thing Vack said after sitting down in the booth. "That Mexican food last night just didn't fill me up. No offense, Martinez, but tacos and guacamole just aren't my thing. I will agree that restaurant was full of great aromas, but it wasn't Italian—the kind of food l like the best. I didn't complain, because I was trying to be nice. Anyway, the boss was buying and, usually, when the food is free, it somehow just tastes better."

Martinez just let Vack's remark bead off his back. He liked Vack and, apparently, knew he was an old-school Italian and meant no harm by it. "No problem Vack, next time we'll do Italian."

I relayed what Mindy the manager had just told me. "Okay, I talked to the manager here. Miller did eat here last weekend and then headed East up I-80. I have a feeling he's not gonna try hiding out in a small town like Fernley where everyone knows everybody else's business. I say we head straight to Salt Lake and hit that area hard. I'd bet he's hiding out somewhere there in Salt Lake, or in the outlining suburbs. So let's wolf down our grub, get the hell outta here, and find Miller. Salt Lake is 486 miles up I-80, so we'll have to gas up one time after leaving. Then we'll get rooms again and start canvassing the Salt Lake City area for tips."

I glanced over at Carla and noticed she had a grin on her face, clearly assuming if I got the chance, I'd book us adjoining rooms again, so we could do another all night sex romp.

Vack, Martinez, and, of course, Carla all nodded yes in agreement as they chewed away at their ham and egg omelets that came with side dishes of cheesy grits. Even though I wasn't from the south, I had to admit I loved cheesy grits. Even Vack liked them, and that was something, because we all knew he was Italian.

Before leaving, and while still at the table, I gave Director Becker a quick call to update him on Miller, letting him know what the truck stop manager had told me.

"David, we haven't had any good tips at all on Miller now for over a week. He's hiding, keeping a low profile, but I'm sure he's somewhat more relaxed now that he thinks the FBI is searching for him in Canada. I'm sure he's gonna fuck-up and take for granted no-one will spot him if he ventures out into the public, and that's gonna be that sum-bitch's down fall."

"I agree totally, Director, and, in fact, I've decided the team will head straight to Salt Lake and search that entire area. I have a strong feeling he's camped out somewhere there."

"Okay, David, I like your idea. The FBI has to catch this scumbag sum-bitch, before he kills again and I end up having to listen to President Anderson give me another ration of his shit."

"No problem, Director. We're doing everything we can to catch Miller, and now I feel we're getting close."

"Okay, but remember that you getting named director of the FBI after I retire will totally depend on how soon you catch Miller. The sooner the better. It'll get the president off my ass. Understood?"

"Yes, sir, I sure do."

There's the politics raising its ugly head again, but I've learned that's the way it is when you work for the government.

We finished eating breakfast by eight a.m. and tore out of Fernley, again breaking every speed-limit law known to man. I led the pack and had the pedal to the metal, averaging 85 mph all the way to Salt Lake, making it there in less than six hours, even after we all stopped once to fill-up again, after leaving Fernley.

CHAPTER 22

A Friendly People Person

Now it was nearing the end of the first week of Gaf's self-imposed exile of being cooped up in this small old house in the middle of nowhere that old man Watkins had rented him. He was beginning to feel the need to get out. Why should he have to hide here like a common criminal? After all, regardless of what the public thought of him, he considered himself a friendly people person, as long as he was treated with respect.

Maybe he'd scope out Mormon Town tonight. He knew there was less of a chance of him being recognized when it was dark outside. First, he turned on the tube to see if there was any news updates from CNN on the hunt for Jeffrey Miller.

As soon as he flicked on CNN, he listened to Norman Croft do a news alert. "...the FBI has now confirmed it is targeting the town of Winnipeg, Canada, claiming that a reliable source there has come forward who has actually talked to Jeffrey Miller at a combination gas station and diner, what we call down here in Atlanta, Georgia, a truck stop. The FBI believes this to be the one hot lead they needed, because it's the type of place where Miller likes to eat."

The news alert didn't mention the identity of the person who'd spotted him, just saying it was an anonymous tip.

That's it. Tonight, I'll be trolling bars, looking for some hot chick I can fuck. I'll wait till around eleven p.m. before I head out. I know from experience that's when you'll have a better chance of hooking up and getting laid by female lounge lizards. By that time, they would have had enough time to throw back a bunch of drinks and be good and loose when I arrive on the scene. That's just my type—a drunken lounge lizard woman. Screw the formalities, and all the posturing. All I wanna do is bring her back here and pound that pussy of hers. I hope she doesn't end up being a complainer after I bring her back to the shack. I hate complainers. That would not be a good move on her part, but I'll try to keep an open mind, as long as she doesn't say anything negative about me while we're in bed. I'm a friendly people person. Why can't people see that in me?

After showering and chowing down, Gaf put on some classic rock and went to Google Maps on his lousy Tracfone in search of local beer joints. He wasn't sure if he'd find any, being that there didn't seem to be many beer-joints or bars in the area, at least that he'd noticed as he rolled into Salt Lake City the other day. He mostly saw Church of Latter Day Saints buildings everywhere he looked. That wasn't a good sign, but who knew? Maybe everyone living in the Salt Lake area wasn't Mormon, and they liked to throw back and get loose on the weekends.

Oh, man, did he get lucky. There was a place called

Larry's Roadhouse Bar & Restaurant, just seven miles north of the shack in Brigham, and it had classic rock bands playing on the weekends! He guessed not everyone living in Utah was a bible thumper. Okay, now he'd crank up the truck and look for some ass. He was getting horny just thinking about what he might run into. He was gonna try and stay positive, because he wasn't looking to start trouble. He just needed some female skin rubbing up against his body. Was that asking too much?

He rolled up to what looked like some hillbilly redneck bar with a huge Confederate Flag flapping away on the roof mounted flagpole. From the parking lot, while trying to find a place to park, he could hear that twang music blasting. He stepped out of his old truck with the hopes this beer-joint hick bar would be full of lounge lizard drinking crack whores looking to get laid.

When he walked through the front door, his eyes scanned the room like a radar beacon on a navy cruiser. He was pleasantly surprised with what he saw. This place was full of loose-looking women, who were letting their various body parts all fallout. He was sure they were the suppressed types. After all, this is Mormon Town, USA. Maybe these women were looking for some non-religious fun—the kind they normally didn't get at home, even if it was for only one night. He could accommodate them because that was exactly what he was looking for. He was here looking for a one night stand with no clingy attachments. All he wanted was a slam-bam-thank-you-mam, and he'd be on his way.

He grabbed a stool at the bar, ordered a draft beer, then swung around and looked over the room again. And what he saw, after his eyes adjusted to the dark barroom, were mostly old chain smoking hags, except for the one bored, fairly-good-looking female, sitting at a table way in the back, all by herself.

Well now, I'm the one person who can rid her of bore-dom and stress, by giving that pussy of hers a good workout. He'd used this old come-on technique before, both when he was rump-ranging and also when he was looking for a female piece of ass. He had the bartender send her over a drink on him, along with a hand written note on a bar napkin reading, *Hello, my name is John, I'd love to have the next dance with you!*

He really didn't want to dance at all. The only dance he wanted to do was in bed, where she could dance on his hard pole all night. That was the kind of dancing he liked.

He watched as the cocktail waitress delivered the drink and bar napkin note, looking closely for any kind of positive expression on her face. After taking a sip of the Jack and Coke he had sent over, she looked up from the table smiling, and that's when he nodded at her, waving and grinning wide like Alice's Cat Dinah. He always looked harmless, and he was sure that's why she made a waving motion with her hand for him to join her.

Man, that's a good sign! Now I have my foot in the door, and that means I'm one step closer to getting my dick in that pussy of hers.

He put on his Rico Suave impersonation, as he strolled over to her table. He acted suave, but not too suave, not as if he was some kind of know-it-all needy prick. He just played the nice guy that he'd been all his life. After all, he was mostly harmless, as long as he wasn't disrespect-ed. And that wouldn't be a good thing. It made him be-come enraged for some reason.

When he sat down at the table, she mentioned her name was Robin and thanked him for the drink. For him, these were always awkward moments, at least until he got a buzz on and loosened up somewhat.

After that, he wasn't not so shy. He ordered a couple of tequila shooters to get his buzz buzzing, and it worked.

Within a few minutes, he could feel it. Then he opened up, as Robin and he scoped each other out.

She told him right off the bat that she was married to a bible-thumping Mormon and was just here looking for fun, with no strings attached. "You know, maybe a *fuck buddy* of sorts. A man I could meet once or twice a week and get the hard pounding I'm not getting at home."

After hearing that, he thought, *Oh, my God, I think I've just died and gone to Mormon Town Heaven! How did I get this lucky? I guess it was just meant to be.*

"I'm not very good at dancing anyway," he told Robin. "So why don't we just drink up, shine-on this hick joint, and head to my place. I don't live far away, and I have booze and music there, plus I think I might still have one joint left we can toke on before we fuck each other senseless."

Neither one could drink up fast enough and bail. On the way to his place, Robin gave him a blow-job, deep throating him as he was driving, nearly causing him to run off the road as he cummed in her mouth.

That night, after smoking a joint and throwing back several cold beers, Robin and he tit fucked and did a sixty-nine, followed by a sweaty doggie-style session with him driving his cock deep into that tight pussy, then finished off the night by doing some anal fucking, which Robin told him she liked the best.

He liked it also. This fuck-a-roma made him think about the fact that he went both ways and wondered, *Where have all the Robin's been in my life?*

If he had discovered someone like her earlier in his life, maybe he wouldn't have turned out the way he did—but, then again, maybe he was just thinking too much.

He knew he was a serial killer, just like his daddy was, and as they said, "The apple doesn't fall far from the tree."

His problem was he had no conscious, and killing was what he did best.

Soon they both began to pass out from lack of sleep and sheer exhaustion but, before crashing, he already knew this would be his last night in this dump. Tomorrow morning, he'd be moving on to parts unknown. He might ask Robin if she was interested in coming along for the ride but wouldn't give her the reason why he was leaving. Then again, he wasn't so sure if he wanted or needed the added baggage because, so far, he'd been able to avoid the FBI traps very nicely on his own, thanks to their total ignorance.

If he did invite Robin, it could become a big problem for him, being that she was married, and he didn't need that crap. He'd probably have to waste her husband before they left the area, and he wasn't sure how that would go down with Robin. After going over all the pros and cons, he realized she was just a one night stand and, really, that was the only reason he invited her to his place. But he was glad he had, being that she was a female sex machine.

One other thing he thought about before his eyes slammed shut was that if he did tell her who he really was, and she found out there was a huge reward for his capture, would she end up snitching just for the reward money?

So he'd pretty much talked himself into going solo. It had worked for him so far. Besides, if he did spill his guts and told Robin everything and she freaked, he'd probably be forced to kill her instead of her husband. He'd have hated to do that to her, because she seemed like such a nice girl. And, so far, she hadn't disrespected him at all like the other bitches he'd fucked in the past.

He got worked up every time he flashed back about women who had played him for a fool or disrespected him, like Rachel the waitress did at the Bay Diner, not to mention that bitch Ms. Hayes, his ex-boss at Docket Air who fired him. Now he was really getting worked up. That bitch, Ms. Hayes's day of reckoning was coming soon, and he was sure she had no clue what he had in store for her. It'd be joyous revenge and satisfaction on his part as he killed her. He'd love seeing the fear in her eyes as she realized she was going to die a slow painful death.

As he lay there in bed, he was thinking he might just double back to Frisco from Utah and put the cunt Ms. Hayes out of her misery. He knew if he did, it'd throw the FBI way off, leaving them scratching their asses, wondering, how they could have let him sneak back through like that.

CHAPTER 23

Raid on The Shack

It was about two-thirty p.m. when we rolled into Salt Lake, so I had the team stop briefly at a Starbucks, where we grabbed a table, some iced java, and deli sandwiches, then I laid out my plan as we munched away.

"Okay, you guys, first, I'm gonna call the director right after lunch and get his permission to contact TV stations in the Salt Lake area to have them broadcast Miller's wanted poster over the air. I'll make sure the stations mention that the FBI now believes Miller has re-entered the US, and he's now hiding out somewhere in the Salt Lake City area. As a profiler, Simmons, what's your take on that?"

Carla seemed to really perk up when I asked for her opinion in the area of expertise she specialized in. "I believe he's managed to escape capture and is just laying low, boss, which I know sounds obvious," she said. "But Miller's probably hiding out somewhere in the boondocks of Salt Lake, not anywhere where there's a heavy concentration of people stirring around who might spot

him. I don't think he's anywhere near the main part of
Salt Lake. Only thing is, the team is now going to be
bombarded with bogus tips from people looking to score
the million dollars in reward money. We'll have to cherry
pick and follow up only the tips we think are legitimate
leads, and then have the team pouncing on them full-
force."

"No problem, Simmons, we'll knock down doors
without a search warrant if we think Miller is inside. My
thinking is the 'end justifies the means.' We're not gonna
sit around for hours waiting, while someone finds a judge
to sign a search warrant. Okay, team, any thoughts on
that?"

"No, boss," Martinez said. "Let's just do it, and arrest
Miller by whatever means are necessary."

Looking around the room, I saw that all of us were in
total agreement. After all, I knew the director had my
back on this one, and he wouldn't give a fuck about some
stinkin' warrant if we brought in Miller.

I got the okay from the director to contact the local
FBI office and give them the order to call the local TV
stations and have them broadcast a local news alert showing our Most Wanted poster on Jeffrey Miller, making
sure it was emphasized that, although Miller sometimes
came across as an unassuming, likeable person, everyone
should be aware he was a dangerous, psychopathic killer
with no conscious.

I broke out Google Maps and, while pointing across
the table, I told Martinez, "You and Simmons move south
on I-15, hitting every gas station, 7/11, and diner along
the way. Vack, you and I are heading north up I-15, and
will do the same. What I'm hoping for is that by noon,
our time, we'll be getting leads from someone in the area
who may have seen Miller, or even better yet, has talked
to him. I'm thinking Miller probably watched that last

news alert CNN did on him, because he's a current events junkie, especially when it concerns him. I'd bet he's still thinking we're still up in Canada looking for him, so most likely he'll let his guard down, thinking no one in this area would know who he is, even if he ventured out into the public. I know it's a long shot, but we have to stick to our game plan and that is by staying pro-active, keeping the heat on Miller, in the hopes he'll fuck-up, believing he has nothing to worry about. At least that's what I'm thinking.

"Before we get out there and start shaking the bushes for Miller, I have one other thing I need to relay. It's a quote that comes from the very top. Now what I'm about to say isn't meant to scare anyone sitting at this table, including myself, but Miller's capture or non-capture will be the defining moment in our FBI careers. It could be great for the remaining years we'll be spending with the FBI before we retire, or it could be bad. It's our choice. As the director put it, we're in charge of our own destiny. So let's find Miller before he gets the urge to kill again."

Especially my destiny. Capturing Miller will put me in the director's vacancy when Becker retires later this year. I want Miller bad.

As I got up from the table, it dawned on me that I had nearly forgotten all about the air force pilots who I'd sent on to Salt Lake ahead of the team last week, telling them to land and just sit tight till they heard from me. I placed a call to the pilots as I walked out of Starbucks, letting them know the team was here now in the Salt Lake City area and that we'd begun a hard search for Miller. I went on to tell them to continue hanging loose near Hill Air Force Base and to make sure the Gulfstream was fueled up and ready to take off on a moment's notice, just in case we had to hotfoot it out of here.

I got the word from the Salt Lake FBI office that all

the local TV stations, all three of them, had agreed to broadcast locally, a news alert at three-thirty p.m., where they'd break into local programming to announce this important news worthy event.

Most likely this news alert, unlike the other ones these stations normally put out on a weekly basis announcing cakewalks at the local Latter-Day-Saints chapels, would certainly be the biggest news story or current event to ever hit the Salt Lake City area in decades.

The team split up and hit the road in groups of two as planned, heading north and south, up and down I-15, looking for anyone who might have come across Miller. I was hoping we'd get some solid leads after it aired at three-thirty p.m.

As Vack and I worked our way up I-15, hitting gas stations, a couple of truck stops, and a few deli's, I got a call from the Salt Lake FBI office, telling me it looked like a solid lead was called in right after the news alert aired. The office gave me the address and phone number of a Jimmy Watkins, owner of a gas station/convenience store, who believed he knew where Miller was living. With that info, I called Carla and Martinez and told both to meet Vack and me at the gas station address ASAP.

Watkins's gas station was only fifteen miles north of our present location on I-15. Agent Vack and I both put the pedal to the metal in our rental cars and raced up the double-lane highway—again paying no attention to posted speed limits—getting there in only ten minutes. I pulled off I-15 onto the wide graveled driveway leading up to the gas pumps.

As soon as we rolled to a stop, Carla and Martinez drove in behind us and parked. Then we all seemed to jump out of our cars at the same time, with all four of us looking to our right, noticing a rather elderly man walking out the convenience store's front door at a rather quick pace and heading straight for us. I presumed this was Mr. Watkins, but just in case, I kept my hand on my Glock-19. This person seemed to be all excited and worked up as he began waving and yelling in a weak raspy elderly voice, "Are you all with the FBI?"

Vack, Carla, Martinez, and I all whipped out our FBI shields at the same time, with me doing the talking. "Yes, sir, we are the FBI. I'm David Drake, special agent in charge and these are Special Agents Vack, Simmons, and Martinez, who are part of the taskforce team in search of Jeffrey Miller. The FBI believes Miller is the Gaf Killer."

I put my shield back in my left-front-suit-coat pocket. Vack pulled out his trusty spiral note pad and licked the point on his pencil, just as Detective Columbo would have done, as I prepared to begin questioning Mr. Watkins.

The old man was practically out of breath by the time he had hobbled all the way over to us. I asked him if he'd mind if we stepped inside his air-conditioned convenience store, where we could have a seat as I interviewed him.

Mr. Watkins agreed, so we entered the store and sat at what looked like a homemade picnic table Mr. Watkins had built by hand using some old scrap and faded two-by-four studs so his customers could eat their microwaved hot dogs and hamburgers inside, rather than outside in the hot, blazing sun.

"Mr. Watkins, tell us why you called the FBI office?"

"Okay, for starters, I normally don't watch much TV. But I can tell you this. For some unknown reason, I decided to turn on my old black and white, the one sitting over there behind the counter, and started channel surfing while I pondered whether I'd close early or not, since I hadn't had a paying customer all day. Then I happened to land on a local channel, where a special news alert broke in while I was watching my favorite TV show, *Mayberry RFD*. I was pissed, until I saw what the news alert was all about."

For some reason, when you got older, like Mr. Watkins was, you liked to gab a lot but, like Sergeant Friday on *Dragnet*, all I cared about were the facts. "Okay, Mr. Watkins, please continue."

"Well, when I saw the FBI's Most Wanted poster displayed on the screen, showing that photo of who you say is Jeffrey Miller, I nearly had a heart attack. Agent Drake, here's the deal, and I hope I'm not in some kind of trouble for doing so, but I'm now 100% positive I rented my old shack last week to the person you're looking for. I even sold him my old truck with the camper shell, because he offered me a fair deal for it, in cash, a deal that was way too good to refuse. This guy, who you're calling Jeffrey Miller, told me his name was John Zoddie, and that he was thinking about staying in the area for a while and needed a place to rent, so I brought up the fact that my old shack of a house has been sitting empty ever since my wife Gladys passed away last year, and that was when I moved out to live here at the station. Anyway, I rented my old home to whom I'm now sure is Jeffrey Miller. Man, Agent Drake, he seemed like such a nice young man."

I had a feeling right then that this was the lead we'd been looking for. I immediately called the Salt Lake FBI office and requested any and all local agents, plus SWAT to meet me at the gas station and we'd form a plan to do an overpowering raid on Mr. Watkins's old house.

Wanting to console the old man somewhat, I reassured him he had nothing to worry about. "Psychopaths, or sociopathic people, all come off that way, Mr. Watkins,. Don't worry about it. It's not your fault. Most psychotic killers come across as being very smooth, someone who you thought wouldn't harm a flea. Unfortunately, in most cases, their victims find out way too late what kind of person they are really dealing with. I can tell you one thing. You can count yourself lucky if this person does turn out to be the Gaf Killer. Now as soon as the other FBI agents arrive, I'll need you to ride along and show us where the house that you rented to this John Zoddie is located."

The old man's eyes were now the size of silver dollars, probably because he'd realized how lucky he was to still be alive, plus the fact that he'd never, in his wildest dreams, figured he'd ever be caught up in something like this. I did manage to calm Mr. Watkins down, somewhat, when I mentioned that if his tip led to Miller's arrest, he'd be in for a good chunk of the reward money, now totaling one million dollars. It was amazing, the calming effect that had.

As Vack finished jotting down Mr. Watkins's statement, we all turned toward the front door, when we heard the blazing, screaming sound of sirens coming from out front. At least ten FBI squad cars rolled in, accompanied by the SWAT vehicle I'd requested just in case Miller didn't come out of Mr. Watkins's house voluntarily. That was, if he was still there at all. For now, I'd assume Miller was holding up there. I had to think positive.

All of us headed outside, where I met up with the Salt Lake City FBI agents and clued them in on my plan, telling them this would be without lights or sirens, because we didn't want to tip Miller off that we were coming for him.

I opened my car door and told Mr. Watkins to jump in the back seat, tighten his seat belt real tight, and hold on. After Mr. Watkins cinched himself in, I laid rubber out of his parking lot, slinging dust high into the air, with all the other agents doing the same thing, as they followed close-

ly behind. While speeding along, I listened to Mr. Watkins barking directions loud and clear from the rear seat,
and not in that old, weak, raspy voice like he did when
we first met. I wrote it off as Mr. Watkins having an
adrenalin rush. I was sure this was the most excitement
he'd ever had in his entire eighty-plus years of life.

We were a racing caravan of FBI agents, with all of us
leaving rooster tails of dust, as we all headed to Mr. Watkins's house, in the hopes of finding Miller there and arresting him.

About a half mile from the rental house, I stopped the
caravan and had everyone put on their FBI logo'd Kevlar
bullet proof vests, including one for Mr. Watkins, then I
went over my plan for the raid.

"I want all the squad cars, including our rental cars, to
do a half moon circle around the front of the house, with
the SWAT vehicle and their men centered directly on the
front door. Then I'll get on the bullhorn and, if I get no
response within a reasonable length of time, we'll gas the
shack, make entry, and clear it."

I looked everyone in the eye, and asked them, "Any
questions?" Everyone shook their heads, no. "So are we
clear?" I continued. "I'll be giving the orders. Don't
make a move or fire on the house, unless I give the order.
"Then I looked at the agents again and, without me saying another word, they all gave me a big thumbs-up.
"Okay, let's lock and load."

"Special Agent Drake, what about a chopper, is there
one coming?" the SWAT commander asked just as we
started heading back to our vehicles.

"Yes, and thanks for bringing that up. But I don't
think we'll actually need the chopper. If Miller is in the
house, he'll have no escape. If he tries to exit out the back
door, to make a run for his truck, we'll shoot the tires out.
If Miller manages to get in the truck, and it starts rolling,

then we'll fire on the truck and shoot Miller. Lethal force will be used. We'll shoot first and ask questions later." I saw a few eyebrows raised when I made that statement. "I'm not gonna have this serial killer get away with taking down any FBI agents, SWAT, or special taskforce team members on my watch. I'll waste the dirt bag myself before I allow that to happen. Okay, let's hat up, and remember, be careful and don't put yourself or anyone of us here at risk."

My little pep talk was echoed by, "Yeah, let's do it," from several of the agents who I knew are itching to capture and put an end to Miller's crime wave. With that, we all got back into our vehicles and headed the short distance up the road to Old Man Watkins's house or, as it was sometimes referred to, the shack.

While en route, I told Mr. Watkins, "When we pull up to your house, get on the floorboard in the backseat and stay there unless I tell you to get up. Trust me, it'll be safer there."

I'd thought Mr. Watkins's eyes got big earlier when I clued him in on who John Zoddie really was and how much reward money there was for tips leading to his capture. Now, after he'd heard how things were going to go down, along with me telling him to kiss the backseat floorboard and not get up, his eyes looked like they were literally going to bulge right out of his head.

Man, will Mr. Watkins have something to really gab about when this is all over.

We all slowed down when we came within sight of the shack. Going stealth, with no lights or sirens, we slowly rolled up to within one hundred feet of the front door, and I put my plan into action. SWAT was on point, and the other ten squad cars, plus our four rental cars, formed a half-moon circle, covering both the front and sides of the house. After opening our squad car doors, we drew our weapons and crouched down behind the opened doors. I knew then that we were ready.

The SWAT commander handed me the bull-horn, I clicked on the volume button to full volume and made my demand to anyone listening in the house. "This is the FBI. Come out with your hands up. You are surrounded on all sides, and we have a chopper overhead."

I glanced up momentarily and noticed that the two-man, local police department chopper had just arrived on scene and was circling some five hundred feet above the shack.

I paused for a short time then put the bull-horn back up to my mouth and shouted loud and clear, "There's no escape. You have sixty seconds to obey my command."

Even if someone was sleeping in the house, I was sure that, with all this commotion going on outside, they had to have heard the chopper and the loud demand I've just made.

After thirty seconds had gone by, I turned to the SWAT commander and told him, "Get ready, I'm sending you in to clear the house if no one comes out within the next thirty seconds."

"Yes, sir, we're ready Special Agent Drake. Just pull the trigger and we'll go in and take care of business."

That's what I liked about SWAT. They didn't fuck around when it was their turn.

"Okay, get ready, SWAT. I'm gonna bark the same order again, then I'll give whoever is in the house an additional thirty seconds and, if we get no response again, charge the house and bust that door down." I click the bullhorn to full volume again. "Hello, whoever's in the house, come out immediately with your hands in the air, and no harm will come to you. You have thirty seconds to comply, then I'm sending SWAT in."

For a moment there was no movement, then all of a

sudden the front door creaked open and out stepped a female with a bath towel wrapped around her chest down to just below her hips. When I ordered her to raise her hands high in the air, the towel fell to the ground.

Now, standing near the front door, was a completely naked woman with her hands high in the air. I got back on the bullhorn. "Turn around, backup ten feet, kneel down, lay flat on your stomach, and put your hands behind you. Do it now. If anyone else is inside the house, come out now with your hands in the air!"

Nothing happened. No one came out.

"Okay, SWAT, I want that placed cleared and, Simmons, you follow in behind SWAT, cuff that female, then bring her to one of the squad cars, and throw her in the back seat. While you're at it, get her one of our spare windbreakers and a blanket from the trunk to cover her up. I'll question the female after SWAT clears the house."

"Okay, boss, no problem."

"Be careful, Simmons. Remember, shoot first and ask questions later if you feel threatened in anyway."

She smiled at me as SWAT stampeded through the front door. She followed right behind the fifteen well-trained and well-armed officers. I wasn't worried about Carla's safety, because I knew those SWAT goons were bad assed, and the last thing they'd do would be to let any harm come to her.

Within minutes, the house was cleared, with no sight of Miller. I was pissed. I went back over to my car, stuck my head in the driver's side window, and told Old Man Watkins he could now get up from the floorboard. He sat up in the back seat, looking white as a sheet, but the color soon came back to his face, after I told him, "It's over, Mr. Watkins, we didn't find Miller." Pointing with my hand toward the squad car where the female was sitting in the back seat, I said, "Climb out of the car and follow me over there. I want you to have a look at the woman we cuffed and tell me whether or not you recognize her."

I had Watkins stand back about ten feet from the squad car, just far enough so the female couldn't see what I was doing, but close enough so Mr. Watkins got a good look at her face.

"Yes, sir, I know who that is, it's Robin Osborne. She comes by the station every now and then to fill up, and she's also been in the store to buy snacks. I know she's married to some weirdo I don't care much for. She brought her husband with her one day and introduced me to him and, man, is that guy arrogant and bossy. If this turns out to be a one night stand, I wouldn't blame her for it."

"Well, Mr. Watkins, let's hope for her sake that this was a one night stand and she didn't, as in your case, have a clue who this John Zoddie, aka Jeffrey Miller, really was."

Before I started questioning the woman, I had the crime lab dust inside the shack for fingerprints, and we found some. While we were still on scene, they transmitted those latent prints, via an app on our encrypted cell phones, back to headquarters to have the lab check them out on IAFIS, the Integrated Automated Fingerprint Identification System. We got a hit right off the bat. I wasn't surprised those were Jeffrey Miller's prints.

I walked up to the squad car's window—the one Robin Osborne was sitting in—looked at her, and said, "Young lady, for starters, I'm Special Agent in Charge David Drake." I flashed my shield, and she only glanced at it. While informing Ms. Osborne who I was, I pointed over to Carla, Vack, and Martinez who were standing nearby, and mentioned, "I've formed a taskforce of FBI special agents, under the direction of the FBI director in

Washington, DC, to track down, capture, and arrest a serial killer who goes by the name of John Zoddie. But his
real name is Jeffrey Miller. Do either of those names ring
a bell? Before you answer the question, I'm gonna read
you your Miranda Rights."

I'd always hated doing that because I thought it gave
criminals the edge, or in other words, the easy way out of
not talking.

"Okay, do you understand your rights? And do you realize that lying to a federal officer is a serious crime, pun-
ishable by some serious prison time? Is what I just said
crystal clear in your mind?"

"Yes, sir, I understand. I've watched a lot of crime
shows on TV. Man, what is this all about?"

"Well, miss, first, this is no TV crime show. This is
the real thing. And, secondly, I'll ask the questions here.
For starters, what's your name? And don't lie to me, unless you wanna end up in the slammer tonight."

"Okay, no problem, I'm Robin Osborne."

"That's a good start, Robin, because, young lady, I already knew who you were. Since you're wondering what
this is all about, I'm gonna tell you in a minute. What I'm
wondering right now is, don't you watch the news on
TV?"

"Yes, I do occasionally, but I had no idea this was the
person you were looking for. He told me his name was
John Zoddie."

Next, I pulled out the wanted poster and handed it to
her. "Do you recognize this person?"

"Oh my God, that's the guy I spent the night with!"

"Well, for your information, Ms. Osborne, that man's
real name is Jeffrey Miller. He's the psychotic serial killer we've been looking for. He must have really liked you,
for some reason, because if he didn't, you wouldn't be
talking to me right now. You'd be dead. Where did you

meet Jeffrey Miller, and how and why did you end up spending the night with him in this house?"

She told me the entire story of how Miller bought her a drink and she invited him over to her table at Larry's Roadhouse Bar & Restaurant and, being that they were both looking to get laid, they decided to come back here for some sex.

I didn't see any reason not to believe her, but I followed up with one more critical question. "Ms. Osborne, where is Jeffrey Miller? Before you answer my question, I should tell you I've already had you checked out for possible warrants. The answer you give me is gonna determine whether or not you go to jail for that outstanding warrant you have for a traffic violation in Salt Lake last year. If I find out you've lied to me, I'll have you arrested for aiding and abetting a fugitive, who's a serial killer at that. I've got news for you, if you think a traffic warrant is bad news, you don't even wanna think about how much prison time you'll do for making the mistake of not telling me the truth. Do you understand?"

I was feeling like Special Agent Vack, using one of the techniques he'd bring out when leaning on informants for information.

"All right, please," she said. "I'll tell you anything you want to know! I'm not a bad person, and I'm surely not going to lie for someone I don't even really know, much less a killer. Goddammit, why didn't I just stay home last night? All I know is he got up early this morning…oh, I don't know around four a.m., nudged me, and said something about leaving the area, and that he wouldn't be back. I was still very hung-over and dead tired, so I barely comprehended what he was saying, since I had crashed only a few hours earlier, probably sometime around two a.m. this morning."

"Okay, where did he say he was going?"

"I was still in a slightly drunken fog, but I did make out him saying something about being bored staying here in the shack and that he had some kind of unfinished business to take care of in Frisco. I swear that's the truth. That's all I know, and I have no clue where Frisco is. Now that I think about it, there was one other thing that I did just before he walked out of the bedroom. I grabbed a piece of scratch paper off the night stand and jotted down my cell number, and handed it to him, telling this John Zoddie, if he came back to the Salt Lake area, and wanted get back together again, here was my cell number. He just nodded, as if to say sure, then put it in his billfold, turned around, walked out of the bedroom, and left without saying another word. Also, he never gave me his cell number, and I forgot to ask. Now that's all I know!"

It was at this point that Ms. Osborne began to tear up, so I backed off and walked over to Carla, telling her, "Get Osborne out of the squad car, uncuff her, and take her back inside the house so she can get dressed and gather up her things. Then I want you to drive her home and, after that, meet the team back at Hills Air force Base. We're flying back to San Francisco. Before I forget, here's my FBI business card." I handed it to Carla. "I want you to give Ms. Osborne my card and tell her to call me immediately if Miller does try to contact her. We need Jeffrey Miller's cell number, even if it's under a bogus name."

I then turned and got the attention of Martinez, telling him to call the San Francisco FBI office and inform them about what Miller told Osborne, and that I was requesting an around-the-clock guard on Ms. Hayes for her safety.

"You got it, boss, I'm on it!"

I also let Martinez and Vack know I'd be giving Mr. Watkins a ride back to his place and that I'd meet everyone back at Hill Air Force Base, and we'd take off back to Frisco as soon as possible. While I was in route to Watkins's place, I decided I'd inform the director on what had gone down and send a copy of Vack's transcribed notes to him after we got airborne. I called Vack on his cell. "Vack do you have all the notes you took today?"

"Yes, boss, you know I do."

"Yeah, I know, so after we get airborne transcribe them to a PDF doc, using the one of the onboard laptops, make copies for the team, and send one to the director."

"You got it boss."

I always left that to Vack He loved doing that kind of stuff.

ఈఎఈఎ

Meanwhile, Carla walked over to the squad car, opened the door, and asked Ms. Osborne to get out. Carla uncuffed her then informed her that the two of them were going into the house so Ms. Osborne could get some clothes on, gather up her things, and get a free ride back home.

"I know Special Agent Drake made it clear what will happen to you if, indeed, you lied to him," Carla said. "And I'm telling you now, for your own sake, that I hope what you told Special Agent Drake is the truth because, if not, I'll personally come back here and arrest you myself. Is that understood?"

"I haven't lied. Please, just let me get my things and go home. I think I hate that motherfucker I married, even more now than I ever have, because if he wasn't such an asshole, I never would have gone out last night, and none of this would have happened."

"Okay, come on. Let's go into the house so you can get your clothes on, and then I'll drive you home. By the way, there's one million dollars in reward money for information leading to the capture and arrest Jeffrey Miller. A good chunk of that could be possibly be coming your way if, indeed, we do capture and arrest Miller in San Francisco."

"Fucking A! That would be sweet! Then I could divorce that looser I'm stuck with!"

They both had a laugh over that one.

"By the way, Ms. Osborne, the news isn't all good. Here's some possible bad news."

Right then Robin Osborne's facial expression turned from happiness to concern.

"I don't know how to quite tell you this," Carla continued. "So I'll just say it. Jeffrey Miller is bi-sexual, so I'd recommend that you get an HIV test right away."

"Fuck me! I didn't think this day could get any fucking worse, and now you're telling me it's possible I could have contracted AIDS! You know what? After hearing what you just told me, Special Agent Simmons, I could save the FBI a whole lot of time and trouble by killing him myself if he were standing here in front of me."

Carla gave Ms. Osborne Drake's FBI business card and told her it was imperative that she called him if Miller contacted her. Then she gave Ms. Osborne a ride home, dropping her off just down the block from her house. That was what The woman preferred. Carla wished her luck, telling her, "I'll be in touch on the reward money," and, with that, she headed out to Hill Air Force Base for the flight back to the FBI office in San Francisco.

ᴄᴐᴇᴐ

Before leaving for Frisco, and being who I was, I felt the need to talk to the SWAT commander and all the other FBI agents who had helped, even if we didn't find Miller. "We missed Miller, but not by much," I said. "But we did come across good Intel that just might help in saving the life of a potential victim in the San Francisco area, and that's where I and my team are headed now. Thank you all very much. You did a great, 'By the Book' job!"

SWAT ate up that comment.

When I'd taken Mr. Watkins back to his gas station—and the old man was really relieved to be back where he knew it was safe—I had informed him again that there could be reward money coming his way if we did capture Jeffrey Miller. Mr. Watkins, like before, had liked the sound of that.

By five-forty-five p.m., we had all boarded the Gulfstream and begun jetting the six hundred miles back to San Francisco. The first thing I did, right along with the other team members, was to get a shower, change into a fresh set of clean clothes, followed closely by chowing down. We were all starving, since we hadn't eaten anything since this morning. Having access to the Gulfstream was critical to the team. Without the jet, we'd all still be wandering around Salt Lake City International Airport for hours in search of a flight out of town.

It was a short flight, lasting less than an hour and a half. Soon the team was back at FBI headquarters, on Golden Gate Ave, with all of us huddling in a conference room, as I laid out my game plan to catch Miller before he could create any more havoc in this city.

CHAPTER 24

Unfinished Business

Gaf hoped Robin enjoyed their little sex romp. He knew he did. Enough to nearly make him think about going straight. And who wouldn't, if they had a chance to fuck a woman with an ass as fine as hers? He was kind of thinking he wouldn't mind doing some more slam bam with Robin and, next time, being the nice guy that he was, he might even spring for dinner, just like he would do on a real date. If they did go to dinner, he wouldn't order a patty melt with an iced tea and wedges, because he wouldn't want anything to fuck-up their romantic interlude if it happened to be served to him cold. He was thinking he and Robin probably hadn't seen the last of each other.

Even though he did like being with Robin, there was something he just had to get out of his system. He had to come back to San Francisco and pay Ms. Hayes a little visit, because of some the unfinished business he had with her.

Even though he was still half drunk and dead tired

when he left Mormon Town, he was glad he left the
shack at four a.m. He'd made good time, being that it was
now only twelve-thirty p.m., and he'd already made it to
the outskirts of San Francisco. He was looking forward to
making a fresh kill. It was something he hadn't done in a
while. But a special kill indeed. He was getting an adren-
aline rush now, just thinking about wasting that cunt Ms.
Hayes.

For now, he just wanted to find some nondescript
place, maybe a campground on the outskirts of Frisco
where he could hide out while he put together his plan to
eliminate Ms. Hayes. It was all about getting even.

Yeah, she'd never know what hit her. That bitch was
going to pay big-time for firing him for no reason at all,
and if she thought he had forgotten about what she did to
him, she was dreaming.

So what? He crossed dressed once in a while. Big
deal. He'd just sit there and enjoy every minute of it as he
watched her beg for her life. Or maybe Ms. Hayes would
give in and beg him to put her out of her miserable pa-
thetic existence.

First, he'd tweak her nipples with the Vise Grip pliers
he always carried around with him. That should really
smart. Either way, she was a dead woman when he located her. He wasn't sure, but he didn't think she was stupid
enough to be living in the same house, knowing that he
was still on the run and with the law not having a clue
where he was.

But her house would still be the first place he'd check,
because maybe she was more of an air-head than he gave
her credit for. The exciting part of this whole thing, for
him, would be seeing the look of fear on her face when
he broke into her house late at night, and they came eyeball to eyeball. That look of sheer fright would be a turn
on.

Before he started looking for that bitch, he was going to check out Craigslist for someone who was hard up, who'd sell him a used car or van for some quick cash, and do so without asking him a whole lot of goofy questions. Then he'd deep-six this truck Old Man Watkins sold him, just like he did with the van. He'd be looking to buy something with updated tags, and again, he wouldn't have to bother with registering it in his name for months, which was something he'd never do anyway. When the tags expired, he'd just dump it and buy another set of wheels. He was pretty sure that was one of the reasons the pigs could never track his daddy, down. And Zodiac taught his son well.

CHAPTER 25

Going Undercover

Before I laid out my plan to Carla, Vack, and Martinez, I let them know we were not going to notify the media and let them know we thought Miller had returned to the San Francisco area. In fact, the less they knew now, the better off we'd be in having my plan work.

I stepped out of the conference room briefly and called the director in Washington, DC, to have him sign off on the plan I was about to unveil to my team.

"Do whatever it's gotta take to catch that cocksucker," the director said after I ran my plan by him. "This may turn out to be our best chance at reeling him in."

"Okay, Director, I'm going back into the conference room and, hopefully, Simmons will agree. Then we'll start instituting the plan tonight."

"Okay, David, keep me informed, and make it happen so I can retire on a good note."

"Will do, Director."

Then I hung up and headed back to the conference

room, fully knowing if my plan worked, I'd be appointed the new FBI director before the end of the year. For me, that was a strong motivator, besides the fact that I wanted to see Miller end up on death row where he belonged.

Back in the conference room, I did something I didn't normally do. I asked Vack and Martinez to step out for a minute, because I had something I needed to discuss with Carla.

"No problem, boss," they both replied. "We'll be just outside the door."

I could tell Carla was somewhat taken aback, realizing that from the start of this track down there hadn't been any secrets between the team members—except, of course, the sex she and I had both enjoyed having.

"Okay, here's the main part of the plan, which involves you playing a big part in the capture of Miller by going under cover and posing as Ms. Hayes."

There wasn't any reaction right off the bat from Carla, as if she was taking in what I had just said, then she sighed. "You must be crazy? How would that work?"

"Okay, Carla, bear with me for just a minute. I'm gonna explain everything to you when I call Vack and Martinez back in. What I *can* tell you is that you'll be in no danger whatsoever. You can take my word on that. You know how we feel toward one another, and you should know by now that I wouldn't ask you to do this if I thought any harm at all would come your way. Just say yes, and I'll invite Vack and Martinez back in and explain how the team is gonna lay the trap for Miller that'll result in us arresting this scumbag."

There was another sigh and long pause from Carla, then she reached over the conference table, placed her palm on the top of my hand, then slowly slid it off and stood up, wearing that short red mini skirt—the one I liked—turned around, and patted herself on the ass. "You better be fucking right, or else your cock will never get a piece of this ever again."

For a moment, I lost my train of thought and got somewhat aroused by that display, but I also knew Carla always kept her word. Now the pressure was really on me. I definitely wanted more of that.

As she strutted toward the conference room door to let Vack and Martinez back in, she looked over her left shoulder and gave me that sexy half-smile, obviously knowing what that look did to me. It was the look she gave me while standing there completely naked, just before she slipped into the shower after we'd spent most of the night bodysurfing in bed.

After Vack and Martinez sat back down at the table, I laid out the plan to have Carla go undercover. "First of all, at my request, the Bureau is sparing no expense in putting together a trap to capture and arrest Miller, and here's the plan. We've made arrangements to have one of the top makeup artists in the country, Carmon Simone, who runs that division at Wave Breaker Studios, come here tonight. And, in fact, Agent Simmons, she's due to arrive within the hour. Also coming shortly to our office will be Ms. Hayes herself. When Ms. Simone arrives, you and Ms. Hayes will sit side by side so Ms. Simone can start her transformation, turning you into, as close as possible, a near exact copy of Ms. Hayes. As far as Ms. Hayes's facial features go, you both are approximately the same height and weight, so other than the facial transformation, you'll only need to pick-up on a few of Ms. Hayes's mannerisms. Match them as closely as possible, because if Miller is in the area, I'm sure he'll most likely be looking to scope out Ms. Hayes's house, by using some type of high powered binoculars, so he can peer through windows before he makes his move.

"When the makeover is complete, probably somewhere around midnight tonight, you'll drive to Ms. Hayes's house, and the sting will begin. There'll be FBI agents set up in adjoining bedrooms of the of house, plus it'll be wired with micro-mini video cameras throughout. The monitored cameras, called Big Brothers, will be checked constantly by a special FBI van sitting about one block south of the house. We're also installing high-intensity lighting, the kind used by the Bureau on these types of undercover operations, something the naked eye wouldn't catch in daylight hours and, in a dark room, they'll never be seen. If Miller takes our bait and breaks in, he'll never get closer than the bedroom door, the one Agent Simmons will be in, pretending to be asleep. At that moment, all the high intensity lighting will be flipped on by remote control from the FBI van, and every room in the house will light up like a Christmas tree. The agents in adjoining bedrooms, who, by the way, will be you two, Vack and Martinez, will bust out, along with SWAT coming through the front door, plus the another agent hiding in your bedroom closet. We'll all have our weapons drawing down on Miller."

I looked back again at both Vack and Martinez and added a serious tone to my voice. "Vack and Martinez, I want you two and the other agent hiding in the closet—and including Simmons, who'll also be armed—to just blow him away if you see that he has a weapon, or even if you just *think* he has a weapon, without saying 'Freeze,' like they always do on those goofy TV crime shows. Trust me, Miller will have no escape, and if he does decide to challenge us, he's a dead man. I'm hoping, and so is Director Becker, that Miller doesn't make that fatal mistake. The FBI wants Miller to just give himself up so we can bring him in and question him. Yeah, and that's after we inform him he's under arrest for multiple felonies, including first degree murder."

"There's one other thing, Vack. When we do arrest Miller, I'm gonna give you the pleasure of slapping the handcuffs on him," I said, knowing this was something he would enjoy hearing, "as payback for the time you spent chained to the wall of that row house basement. Other than that, I'm sure you'll have some choice words for this psycho while you drag him out the front door and throw him in the back seat of squad car for the trip down-town."

A big smile came over Vack's face when he heard that from me. "It's Karma, bitch. What goes around comes around.'"

I acknowledged that comment from Vack and briefly continued addressing the team with some advice that I was sure they'd heard before and, most likely, were aware of. I did it because I wasn't the type who took things for granted. "One other thing. This entire operation has a chance of failing if we have underestimated what we think Miller's plans are. But from what Robin Osborne told us, I'm sure we're on the right track. It may take one day, or it may take several days. We're in it for the long haul. Everyone—from the director on down, including everyone here—wants Miller behind bars. We'll have to be patient because, at this point, like I said before, we really don't know for sure what his plans are. I'm betting, along with Director Becker, that Miller's looking to get even with Ms. Hayes for firing him. Okay, that's the plan. As soon Ms. Simone arrives, the plan goes into effect. Any questions?" Everyone shook their head, no. "Okay, let's hat up."

I pulled Carla aside. "One other thing. Don't worry, you won't be driving out to Ms. Hayes' house all alone. They'll be a well-armed FBI agent crouched down, hiding behind the driver seat on the floorboard, plus several undercover FBI squad cars following along, shadowed by plenty of nondescript police undercover cruisers along the entire route. They'll all be watching for anything that looks out of place. You'll be well protected, so there's nothing to worry about."

"Yeah, that's easy for you to say, but regardless, I'll take your word for it."

I didn't say anything about that comment. She knew I wouldn't let any harm come to her. I failed to mention that the FBI agent who'd be crouched down behind the seat of the car she was driving, would be me. I wouldn't have it any other way.

Right after the meeting, the FBI van, transporting Ms. Hayes, rolled up and parked in the underground parking lot. Then four, heavily armed agents escorted Ms. Hayes into our conference room so Ms. Simone could start working her magic.

Carla seemed surprised after she realized I'd be the agent who'd be protecting her, hiding out on the backseat floorboard, just in case something went down before she reached Ms. Hayes's house. I could tell she became a little more at ease after hearing I'd be the one covering for her.

ᏮᏜᏮᏜ

Carla and I pulled up the darkened driveway of this 'seventies-looking ranch house, opened the garage door using the remote, then drove in and clicked the remote again, closing the garage door. It was then that I was able to finally get up from my cramped position on the rear seat floorboard and proceed to enter the house ahead of Carla. I slowly opened the garage access door to the kitchen and, before I completely entered the house, called out, "Vack, Martinez, it's Drake and Simmons."

As edgy as I knew they would be, I didn't want them

firing off rounds at us. Vack and Martinez exited the bed-rooms with their weapons drawn, but soon put them away after making sure it was us. Both Carla and I also hol-stered our Glock-19s and then commenced to set the trap.

By choice, I ended up being the lone agent stationed in the bedroom's closet and, after having Carla slide the doors shut, I thought, *How appropriate. This will be the first time Simmons and I shared a bedroom and haven't had the pleasure of sleeping together.*

We all settled in for the first night in Ms. Hayes's house. Not surprisingly, nothing happened. Being an ex-perienced FBI agent, I knew that even though Miller didn't show the first night, it was definitely not a reason to relax and let down our guard. We really didn't know whether Miller was planning to hit the house during the daylight or nighttime hours and, for all I knew, Miller could just wait it out and do a daytime ambush, thinking Ms. Hayes would, at some point in time, drive off in her car. That scenario wasn't in my plans. It was something Carla wouldn't be doing. I was putting all my money on Miller striking at night, just like he'd done on all his other assaults. My career plan on becoming the next FBI direc-tor depended on the team capturing and arresting Miller. We knew what Miller's modus operandi was and, as with most serial killers or felons, they were like cats. They didn't like change.

CHAPTER 26

Delbert Mitchum & His F-250

Gaf did find a campground in a deeply wooded area called Nature's Campground, which had a wide fresh water stream running through it. The good thing about this place was that it was only ten miles from the Frisco area.

At the campground check-in shack, there wasn't one of those Smokey the Bear goofy looking park rangers checking people in—just a big giant sign that read, *First Come, First Serve & No Swimming or Bathing in the Fish Stream.*

He drove around a bit until he found a spot he liked, and backed the camper-shelled truck in. This space was perfect, because it had large over hanging oak trees and was surrounded on both sides of the graveled parking space by heavy brush. He knew this was the spot where he could stay hidden until he decided to unload his camper-shelled truck on some hick fisherman. If a hillbilly bought his truck, he or she would probably think they were style'n, because now they could not only fish night and day at that stream over there, but could then turn around and crawl into the camper shell while smelling like a dead carp, crashing until the next morning. They would be in fish scale heaven.

He figured he should be doing stand-up, because he sometimes even cracked himself up, as he just did. But then again, he was a little demented. After all, he was a serial killer, and killing was what he liked doing best— not fishing and then having that messy job of scaling and gutting those poor helpless fish just to eat them. He was satisfied with just being served the perfect patty melt and iced tea with a lemon wedge, which would always be his favorite type of diner food.

No one was going to know he was headed back to the San Francisco area, except for Robin Osborne, and she didn't know who he really was. Plus, the last he'd heard on CNN was that the FBI was up in Canada on a wild goose chase and, most likely, be following up on hundreds of bogus tips up there. Every time he thought about that, he had a good laugh at how inept those FBI buffoons really were.

They had no clue where he was, or what he was about to do, and that was to rid the earth of that bitch, Ms. Hayes. Yeah, when he was done with her, she'd be history.

He decided he'd go by the name Jimmy Watkins, since the title to the truck was still in Old Man Watkins's name. And if Gaf did decide to sell the truck, it'd be no problem signing off on the pink slip.

He'd hang low at his campsite space for a few days, giving himself just enough time to unload Watkins's old truck and find himself another one he could buy for cash. Maybe he'd get lucky and find someone at the campground who was looking to sell their truck. When he did, he'd ride out to Ms. Hayes's house and check her neighborhood for any cops that might be lurking around, then he'd go back one night to do his dirty deed.

On the first night of living out of his truck, he thought about Robin Osborne. What a fine piece of ass she was. He knew in the back of his mind that, as soon as he was done here, he was going back to the Salt Lake boondocks and look her up. If he had to waste her loser husband, just to be with Robin again, he'd have no problem with that.

The first night at the campsite, he broke out a Coleman portable propane gas stove, a cast iron fry pan, and some cooking utensils Old Man Watkins had apparently forgotten about when he sold the truck.

On the way back to Frisco, Gaf had planned on scoping out a campsite, so he already had picked up a bag of ice, a couple of steaks, some bacon, eggs, and a loaf of bread at a mom-and-pop supermarket along the way. For now, he was good, as far as food went. He didn't plan on staying here in the woods more than a couple days, anyway, before he made his move.

Right after he fired up the Coleman, some hillbilly fisherman, waving a flashlight, came through the thick brush, walked up on him while he was cooking, and shined his fucking flashlight directly in Gaf's face. That was a near fatal mistake on his part. That hick clown was a fool for sneaking up on him like that. It was a good way to get yourself killed, something Gaf specialized in.

While the man stood there, still shining the flashlight in Gaf's face, this Smokey the Bear Wanna-Be began rattling off the campsite campground rules. "Hey, Mr., I'm Delbert Mitchum, and no I'm not related to that great actor Robert Mitchum, although people do tell me we sort of look alike."

This stupid hick, dressed in Farmer John overalls, annoyed Gaf even more with that dumb comparison, claiming to look like that great actor. To Gaf, he resembled one of the gay hicks in *Deliverance* and, to make it worse, he smelled like dead fish.

"What I wanted to inform you about and, oh by the way, first, what's your name?"

"It's Jimmy Watkins."

"Okay, well, Jimmy, since I don't think I've seen you here before, and I would know because I'm one of those full-time campers staying here. Yeah, I camp year round. This campground is my favorite one for the pure enjoyment of just kicking back and fishing. What I'm getting to, Jimmy, is there are rules and regulations that have to be adhered to, and apparently you don't know the rules, because I'm noticing you're cooking food after six p.m. That's not allowed in the park, because of the bear population. If they smell that steak you have frying up there on your old Coleman, those bears will come snooping around, and we can't have that, especially since my campsite is only about thirty yards from yours."

Just the fact that this self-appointed campsite cop pig kept calling me, "Jimmy," as if he had known me for some time, was really beginning to rub me the wrong way.

"Do you have a California fishing license, Jimmy?"

"Yes I do," Gaf lied. "And who are you to ask me if I have a fishing license?"

"Oh, don't get me wrong, I'm not a park ranger, I'm just letting you know that park rangers do come around periodically, and when they spot someone fishing, they always ask to see their license. Also, if they notice that you're fishing, say in that stream over there, they'll not only wanna see your fishing license, but the park rangers will look at the type of hook you're using. You see, you aren't allowed to use a barbed hook."

"What kind of dumb-ass rule is that? How are you supposed to catch a fish without a barbed hook?" *Man I have already had enough of this Delbert dude.* "Okay, Delbert, are you done? Frankly, right now, I'm starved, so I'm gonna finish frying up this steak here and eat, bears or no bears."

He finally shut the fuck up with the bullshit rules and left, then GAF was able to enjoy his top sirloin along with some beers he'd had on ice since leaving Salt Lake City. After eating, he put the stove and utensils back in the truck, then crawled into the camper shell and laid there thinking about his plans for tomorrow.

He woke up early the next morning thinking about Robin Osborne, and not about Ms. Hayes. He was now beginning to think that getting revenge on his ex-boss might not be such a good idea. He'd much rather be between Robin's thighs, pounding that pussy of hers.

He climbed out of the camper and began making a pot of coffee on his site's picnic table that sat on a patchy bit of grass just off to the side of his campsite. Then that stooge, Delbert, showed up again. Gaf decided he'd play it cool and not let the man get to him.

"Hey, friend," Delbert said. "I'm cooking some bacon and eggs at my site, if you'd like to join me. We can eat and shoot the breeze."

Gaf figured, *what the fuck, why not?* Maybe this Delbert dude knew someone here in the campground Gaf could sell his truck to. "Yeah, sure, Delbert, but are you sure the bears aren't gonna show up?"

That was a sarcastic joke on my part and, lucky for him, he took it in stride. While chowing down at Delbert's site, Gaf couldn't help but notice Delbert had a bitchin', older model Ford F-250, which looked about ten years old. Gaf figured he'd interject his truck into their chit-chat session, mainly because he was tired of hearing him drone on about the fish that got away.

Bored with the fish talk, Gaf stood up from the picnic

table and pointed toward Delbert's two-toned blue F-250, which when he looked close, he could see the lightly blue shaded ghost flames just under the dark blue paint job on the front end of the hood. "Delbert, that's a sweet looking paint job on your truck." Gaf figured he'd eat up that complement and get the fuck off his fish tales.

Sure enough, Delbert smiled, got up from the picnic table, and motioned for Gaf to walk over with him and check his truck out.

"Hey, let me show you something, Jimmy. If you think this custom paint job is something, take a look-see at the interior. I had it all done in a light beige, one hundred percent real leather, and those seats there are trimmed out with dark brown accents. Also take a look at those gauges there on the dash. A speed shop custom made them for me in the form of old-school, flat-faced gauges. Those gauges are one of a kind. No other F-250 has gauges that are remotely similar to what I have here." After they looked at the interior, Delbert walked around to the front of the truck and popped open the hood. "See that engine there. It puts out over five hundred horses at 6000 RPM. I could probably lay rubber for one city block if I put the pedal to the metal."

Okay, now Gaf was thinking, *How can I get my hands on this primo looking truck of his?*

Delbert continued to run his mouth about the truck's engine. That was when Gaf decided to feel him out on whether or not, for the right price, he'd part the F-250.

Now with both of them back at the picnic table, and Gaf finishing off his cold bacon and eggs, he asked, "Delbert, would you consider selling your truck to me for the right price?"

"Jimmy, what kind of fool do you take me for? Even if I had a price in mind, I can tell you wouldn't be able to afford it anyway."

That remark really pissed Gaf off. It was the way Delbert said it, with that look on his face, as if to say Gaf was some kind of penniless drifter.

He looked at Delbert and didn't say a thing but, in the back of Gaf's mind, he thought, *Well now you just fucked up by disrespecting me like that. Price or no price, I'll be taking your F-250 regardless of how I do it. No one puts me down like that, and gets away with it. Now Delbert the hick is on my list, a list you don't wanna be on.*

"Okay, man," Gaf said. "I'm going back to my site. Thanks for the grub Delbert."

This hick fisherman had no idea what Gaf planned on doing to him before the sun rose tomorrow morning if he didn't change his mind and sell Gaf the F-250. If he didn't, the only thing Gaf was sure of was that Delbert would never see the sun rise again.

As he walked back to my site, Gaf had decided he'd call Robin and make arrangements to meet up with her tomorrow night in Mormon Town if she could get away from her old man.

He'd pretty much decided to kill the idea he had of wasting Ms. Hayes. He'd let her live for another day, at least for right now. There he went again, cracking himself up over that line, *Kill the idea*, again thinking for a second that maybe he'd be good at being a stand-up comic, but then again maybe not. If people didn't laugh at his jokes and disrespected him in that way, he'd have no other choice but to make them pay. He wasn't a bad guy. In fact, he considered himself rather likeable. But making fun of him wasn't something he'd advise someone to do.

He called Robin, who seemed surprised and very happy that he had called—most likely because she probably figured he looked at their night at the shack as a slam-bam-thank-you-mam, one night stand, thinking she would never hear from him again. Robin happily agreed to meet up at the Lazy Day Motel, telling him it was only about five miles from the shack we spent the night in.

Before leaving to find a Western Union so he could wire Robin money for the motel room, Gaf mentioned to her that he should be getting there no later than five p.m. tomorrow afternoon and told her to call him back with the room number they'd be staying in. She sounded almost as excited as he was at knowing they were going to have two days of uninterrupted humping and pumping. After he hung up, he felt good inside, knowing that someone of the opposite sex liked him, and it was one good-looking woman with one fine-looking ass. He could hardly wait to get some more of that.

Now he'd have to deal with Delbert tonight. One way or another, Gaf wasn't leaving there tomorrow morning without that truck.

CHAPTER 27

The Hayes Stakeout Ends

M y team and I were now on the third day of the stake-out sting operation at Ms. Hayes's house, with initial high hopes of drawing Jeffrey Miller into our trap, and arresting him.

About mid-day on the third day, I got a frantic call from Robin Osborne, who was practically yelling over the phone with excitement and talking so loudly and fast that I could barely understand her.

The one bit of information I did catch was exactly what the team had been waiting for. Miller had called Robin and he planned on coming back to see her again. He was wiring her money to get a room at the Lazy Day motel.

Now I was excited. "Pick up the money at Western Union," I told her. "But don't book the room, I'll call the owners of the motel and take care of that. We'll be jetting out to Salt Lake immediately, arriving between two and three p.m. this afternoon, your time. Our essential meeting, Ms. Osborne, won't be at the motel. I'll call you back when we're in the air and let you know where to meet us after we land."

"Okay, Special Agent Drake, I'll be waiting for your call. I'm very nervous about doing this. It's a first for me."

"You did the right thing by calling, Ms. Osborne. Don't worry. You'll be well protected by the FBI. No harm will come to you. You have my word on that."

As soon as I got off the phone with Osborne, I got the team together briefly and told them the good news. All of us were ecstatic, knowing this could be it. I then called the surveillance van parked a couple blocks away and the San Francisco FBI's office and let them know I was calling off the sting. Right after that I called Director Becker and gave him the good news. He was overjoyed, feeling just the way I did. "That bastard is ours now, as long as he shows up."

All four of us then ran to the waiting squad cars and drove out to the NAS Alameda hanger, where the Gulfstream had been parked since returning here.

On the way out there, I called the air force pilots and informed them they needed to pre-flight the Gulfstream, make a flight plan back to Salt Lake, and have the engines running when we arrived, say in about thirty minutes. "We're gonna be literally running from our squad cars and up the gangway," I told them. "Then taking off as soon as we get the passenger's door secured."

I could feel the energy in the pilot's voices, both of them probably feeling this could be the one flight they'd be remembering for a long time—second only to the return flight back to Frisco headquarters with Jeffrey Miller cuffed and under arrest to face justice.

As soon as we were airborne, I called Osborne to let her know we were in the air and should be landing at Hill Air Force Base no later than two-fifteen p.m. "Meet us in the parking lot of the old boarded up Piggly Wiggly, Ms. Osborne. It's about one mile from the Lazy Day. We'll meet there first so I can go over our plan for the motel surveillance with the other FBI agents, then we'll all head on over there. By the way, I had Special Agent Vack call ahead to set up a short meeting with the owners, a retired couple, to explain what's going down."

I figured those motel owners were probably thinking, "All we wanted was to just retire together from the school district and live a simple life. Now look what we're all mixed up in."

Well, for them, that was pretty much out the window. On the good side, they'd also be eligible for some of that reward money.

While on the phone with Ms. Osborne, I could feel that she seemed really overjoyed, probably because she'd stand to nab the majority of the million dollar reward money when we either arrested or killed Jeffrey Miller. Heck, I couldn't blame her. If it were me, my mind would be spinning like a Vegas slot machine, just thinking about coming into that kind of money. If I were that lucky, and that did happen, both Carla and I would retire and forget about the FBI. We'd be throwing back Hurricanes at a New Orleans blues bar as soon as I got my hands on the loot.

Ah, well, I can always dream, I thought as I looked out the porthole window of the Gulfstream, which was making record time. Those air force pilots up front were as amped as my team, knowing that this time there was a good chance this motherfucker's days were numbered.

After landing, we hurried down the gangway and met up with the other eight FBI agents waiting outside their cars on the tarmac. I quickly introduced the agents to my team and thanked them all for their assistance in helping us, hopefully, bring down Miller. "We don't have a minute to spare, so let's hat up and head for the abandoned strip mall where Ms. Osborne is waiting for us."

As I rolled into the deserted parking lot, I saw that, sure enough, Osborne was there, pacing back and forth next to her car with what looked like a case of nervous anticipation. When she noticed us rolling up, a huge smile came over her face.

After doing the introductions for the agents she'd never met, I informed Ms. Osborne that the FBI would be occupying all the Lazy Day Motel's rooms. And after check in, we'd start setting up the surveillance recording equipment. "Special Agent Vack, here, has confirmed to me that the owners of the motel have already lit up the 'No Vacancy sign,' and the last remaining occupants have checked out, so the motel is all ours now. Okay, Ms. Osborne, we're gonna head over there, so I want you to leave your car here, and ride along with Agent Simmons and myself."

Just before leaving, I turned to speak to the other FBI agents. "Oh, one other thing, Agents Simmons, Vack, Martinez, and I, along with Ms. Osborne will be the only ones going into the motel's rental office. I'll be paying for the rooms and picking up the keys to all twelve rooms, and after that we'll get to work setting up video cameras in and around room eight, the room I've selected as the one Miller will think he's gonna have that rendezvous in tomorrow night. Any Questions at all?" No one spoke. "Okay, no questions. Let's go."

When I pulled up to the Lazy Day, I noticed this motel was an L-shaped, ranch-style structure, with a red tiled roof and old-school white slump stone exterior. This motel was way off the beaten path, about one mile east of I-15, among rolling sand dunes, surrounded by very tall Palm Trees.

I walked into the motel's rental office with Carla,

Vack, Martinez, and Osborne. We flashed our shields and introduced ourselves to the older, white-haired retired school teachers. They seemed really nervous, so I had to put them at ease, something, I had to admit, I was good at doing. "Mr. and Mrs. James, the FBI really appreciates your cooperation in our efforts to catch this fugitive, Jeffrey Miller, who's been on our Most Wanted list now for the last month." I pulled out and unfolded a copy of Miller's Most Wanted poster and laid it flat on the office's green Formica counter. "Just for your information, Jeffrey Miller is someone we desperately need to get off the streets before he commits anymore heinous crimes against the public." I didn't mean to scare the couple, but I figured I'd better be up-front and not sugarcoat anything. "Jeffrey Miller is bad news to anyone who's been unlucky enough to cross his path and happens to tick him off for one reason or another. Don't worry, you're both safe. We have a total of twelve agents here, who know how to take care of business if it comes down to that. I'd like to pay for all twelve rooms now and take care of that first. By the way, just like Special Agent Vack mentioned to you on the phone, that'll be all twelve rooms for two days at one hundred dollars a day for a total of $2400 cash. Right? You do take cash, don't you?"

I noticed barely controlled grins coming from both husband and wife. I thought this retired school teaching couple was going have a coronary when I laid out twenty-four crisp one-hundred-dollar bills on the counter. When Mr. James gathered up the bills and started counting them, his hands were shaking like the leaves of an oak tree on a windy fall day.

"Thank you, Special Agent Drake. It's all here. I can tell you one thing. We've never had the motel completely booked up since we bought this place after retiring three months ago. For that, we are grateful."

"No problem and, by the way, you'll both be eligible for some of the reward money for your help here. How much, I'm not sure, but I can tell you one thing, just like I've told Ms. Osborne here. I'll be the first one to put in a good word for the both of you after this goes down and we have Miller in custody."

From the couple's body language, I could see they liked the sound of that. Like Osborne did when Carla informed her of the same fact after the raid on Old Man Watkins's shack several days ago.

"Okay, thanks, Special Agent Drake," Mr. James said after counting the money. "Here're the keys to all twelve rooms."

I picked the keys up from the counter and started to head out the front door of the motel's office. Then I looked back at the couple, for one last comment. "Oh, for your information, they'll be no need for cameras here in the office. Miller will have no reason for entering the rental office, hence the *No Vacancy* sign should be lit up outside. And, even if he does come over to the office, we'll have this front door secured shut with deck screws. If I need you, I'll call you on my cell. I'm doing it this way, Mr. and Mrs. James, because I don't want any chance of you two having any direct personal contact with Jeffrey Miller. It's way too risky. So there's no need to stress. You'll never come into direct contact with Miller. He is totally unaware the FBI is here, lying in wait and ready to pounce the minute he drives up and steps out of his vehicle."

I saw relief on both their faces after my last comment. With that, we left the office and, after stepping outside, I told Osborne to call Miller back and let him know she'd be in room eight. "Just be calm," I said. "I'll be listening in with my clip-on mic, so don't act nervous."

"I don't get nervous, Special Agent Drake. I only do

that when I get pulled over for a traffic ticket."

We both laughed at that comment.

The phone call went great. Osborne remained calm. Miller didn't seem to have a clue I was listening in. After she got off the phone with Miller, I had one other thing I needed to clear up, concerning the money she picked up today from Western Union.

"One other thing Ms. Osborne, I'll need your Western Union wire receipt and the money Miller sent you. All two hundred dollars of it. I'm sorry about that, but it'll be needed as evidence."

She wasn't' pleased with that, probably thinking she'd be able to pocket that money since the FBI had already paid for the room.

"Don't fret. You'll be able to retire and never work again after you receive your share of the reward money."

That news wiped the frown right off her face.

Before starting the pinhole video camera set-up, I brought all the FBI agents together, including my team, for a short meeting in my room, room number nine adjacent to the room Miller thought Osborne would be in. Most of the agents didn't sit. They stood in this '80s scantily decorated motel room with its dated, dark-wood-grained paneled walls.

I got right to the point. "Okay, there's just a couple of other things I wanted to bring up. After Miller exits his vehicle, I'll give the signal to charge and take him down to the ground. I want Vack here to be the only FBI agent cuffing of that son of a bitch. It'll be, even as slight as it might be, a little payback revenge for the days Vack spent chained to that wall in the basement of Miller's row house on Green Street. If this were happening back in the day when criminals didn't have all the ridiculous rights they have now, I'd be allowing Vack to slap Miller around for a while before he gets thrown into the back of a squad car."

After hearing what I had to say, all the agents gave me a big smile along with a thumbs up. I wasn't sure if it was for the fact that Vack would be doing the cuffing or if they felt the same way I did about criminals' rights, especially being that Miller was a known serial killer.

As I gestured towards Agent Martinez, I had another comment to make. "Martinez, here, is not only an expert at crime scene analysis, but he's also been trained in setting up pinhole video surveillance equipment and has been a big help to me at several crime scene locations we've worked on together around the country. He will be assisting and giving suggestions, where needed, on the placement of those cameras inside room eight and all the other various exterior locations around the motel, but not inside the motel's office. We'll conveniently have the door to the office locked and screwed shut. I've decided, and have told both Mr. and Mrs. James, we're not gonna put them at risk like that. I wanna control Miller's movements from the minute he rolls up to the Lazy Day."

I then looked over at Martinez and could sense that he liked what he'd just heard. I was sure he was thinking, he was relevant again, being that there hadn't been a crime scene to break down lately, other than the raid on Old Man Watkins's shack. We'd just missed Miller there by a matter of hours but, on the good side, we ran into Robin Osborne. That was the yin and yang of doing detective work."

"There's one more thing to clear up," I continued. "Even though we are wiring room eight, no way are we gonna let Miller enter that room. Just like I've mentioned, we'll take him down the minute he exits his vehicle and, if he somehow did enter room eight, which he won't, Simmons will be the one on the inside waiting for him, not Ms. Osborne. If Miller so much as flinches, Simmons's laser beamed Glock-19 revolver will drop him like a bad habit." That was something that I hadn't told Robin Osborne yet, but I was sure it was something that would lower her stress level a bit.

"Are we all clear?" I looked around the cramped room, noticing that the agents' body language was telling me they were all anxious to get to work. "Okay, we know what we have to do, so let's get to work."

Other than Martinez, I and the rest of my team shuffled out the door. I knew now that our plan to catch this homicidal manic was in full swing. As soon as we got the motel wired up, that piece of the puzzle will be complete and our trap to catch and arrest Miller will be in place. All we'd have to do then was to be patient and wait for Miller to show up tomorrow afternoon. Sometimes, that was the hardest thing for me to do. Being patient wasn't in my DNA.

Outside the room, I thanked Carla again for agreeing to act as Robin Osborne. The only minor technicality I had thought about, as far as Carla having room eight all to herself, was of course that I would have loved to have been able to share that room with her, but that wasn't possible, under the circumstances. I knew that day would come after we had Miller in custody, then I'd plan a week long romantic rendezvous with Carla. Where? I had no idea.

CHAPTER 28

Back To Mormon Town

W hen Gaf got back from Western Union after wiring Robin the $200 for a two-day stay at the Lazy Day Motel, Delbert Mitchum was standing out in the front of Gaf's campsite space, waving his left arm and smiling from ear to ear. He moved out of Gaf's way, only after he started backing in Old Man Watkins's truck, pulling up to a stop next to his site's weather-beaten picnic table.

Gaf figured there was some kind of emergency, the way this hick fisherman came right up to his driver's side window, and began jabbering in a muffled incoherent rant, which Gaf couldn't hear because he hadn't rolled down his window yet.

As he rolled down the window and opened his driver's side door, Delbert backed away from the truck, then Gaf climbed out and stepped onto the graveled driveway.

"What is it? What'a ya want?" he asked Delbert with a strong voice.

"Hey, Jimmy, I'm sorry about what I said this morning when you asked me if I'd consider selling you my F-250."

Gaf didn't say anything right away. He just gave Delbert a sneering half grin, like Clint Eastwood did in his *Dirty Harry* movies. Gaf didn't really think the hick was sincere at all. "Why the change, Delbert? Frankly, this morning I came close to beat'n your ass for insinuating that I was some kind of penniless drifter who couldn't afford your truck." He followed up in a sarcastic, joking manner. "Frankly, I've killed for a lot less disrespect."

This hick had no idea he was serious.

Delbert started rambling again. "Man, I'm sorry about that. I shouldn't have put it that way. Anyway, after thinking about what you said, I'd be inclined to sell my F-250 at the right price. I'm not interested in gouging you at all and, like I said, after thinking about it, I'd definitely entertain a fair offer for my truck. I'll take that money and start building me an old-school '32 Ford hotrod. Something I've always wanted to do. What'a you think, Jimmy? Did you have a price in mind for the truck? Something you'd be comfortable with?"

To Gaf, Delbert's BS sounded like more mumbo jumbo. Just like the crap you'd hear from shyster used car salespeople working at a dealership offering up a bunch of worthless old cars and trucks they had displayed on their crumbling and faded asphalt lots. Those used car salespeople liked to pressure customers into buying after getting them to step inside their old, rather ratty-looking, trailer that was being used as their sales office. A trailer the car lot owner probably picked up cheap from a junk-yard.

Delbert had no clue that Gaf's plan had been to just kill him and take his truck. Now, since the man had sort of apologized to him, Gaf started thinking he might do this all legit like and spare Delbert, as long as the hick accepted the offer, otherwise he was a dead man and the truck was Gaf's, anyway.

"Before I make an offer, Delbert, what price range were you thinking about?"

"Oh, maybe twenty-five?"

"I'll tell you what, Delbert, I have twenty grand, all IN hundred dollar bills, right here in my truck, that's where I'm at."

Delbert hemmed and hawed around while rubbing the stubble on his chin as he paced back and forth around the picnic table. Then he came back with some more BS. "Jimmy, I like you and so I'm thinking we'll meet half way at, say, twenty-two fifty. I think that's a fair price, after all, I have thirty-five in the truck."

"Yeah, but, Delbert we both know customizing vehicles isn't normally done for profit. If you flip a car or truck that you've customized, you'd be lucky just to break even on the re-sale. I'm surprised you don't know that. Tell you what I'll do. My final offer is twenty-one grand and that's it, all crisp hundred dollar bills, and, on top of that, I'll throw in my 1992 Ford F-150 with the camper shell. You can just keep the truck or sell it, and probably get at least two grand for it. That's my final offer."

Gaf really didn't give a shit what Delbert did with his truck, as he was going to abandon it soon, anyway, because the tags were expiring in a few months.

"Well, Jimmy, I like that deal for sure. But do you mind if I just step away for a few minutes and run it by my wife Mabel."

Gaf had no idea this redneck was married. That was the first time he brought up his wife Mabel.

It's a good thing I didn't decide to just kill Delbert and take his truck, Gaf thought. *His wife would've filed a missing person's report and the police would be on the lookout for anyone driving his F-250.* Gaf had only known a few Mabels in his life and they were all butt-face ugly. He figured that came with the territory of having a name like that. *I wonder where he met her. Maybe it was at some drive-in swap meet where she was pitching household junk that should've been in a dumpster headed for a landfill somewhere in Macon, Georgia.*

Shortly after Delbert left Gaf's campsite to call his wife, he was back again. With the same goofy grin on his face that he'd greeted Gaf with, Delbert told him what he really wanted to hear.

The look he gave Gaf was the look of someone who'd just won the super lotto jackpot. Gaf had often wondered why hicks from the South gave off that less-than-intelligent expression when showing looks of extreme enjoyment, or excitement—like they did after spending a week's pay, playing the coin toss at the local town carnival. If they did get lucky, they'd win a cheap, overpriced stuffed toy, then turn around, and brag about it to everyone they knew.

"Yes, sir, we have a deal," Delbert said. "The boss, being Mabel, gave me the okay."

Gaf thought that was strange, Delbert having to call his wife to get permission to sell his truck. That was one of the reasons Gaf had never married and, if he was ever to marry, no woman was going to pussy-whip him like that. "Do you have a pink slip on the F-250, Delbert?"

"Yes, I do." Delbert had the pink slip to the truck folded up in his front shirt pocket. Still smiling like a chimpanzee gone wild, he pulled the neatly folded document out of his front shirt pocket, unfolded it, reached out, and handed to Gaf. "There it is, Jimmy. It's all legit, and in my name. You'll have no problem transferring title. By the way, Jimmy, what about the title to your 1992 Ford F-150? Is it clear?"

"Now what do you think? Sure, it is." Gaf had the pink slip in his billfold in anticipation that this was a done deal. Only thing left now would be to sign off on each other's pink slips, and make out the bills of sale, so that Delbert didn't get suspicious.

Gaf couldn't believe how easy this fraud was. He'd just have to remember that right now he was Jimmy Watkins. Sometimes he ended up using several aliases and forgot which one he was going by at the time. Like the dumb-ass clerk at Western Union. Gaf was surprised that she didn't say anything to him after he'd already told this dizzy broad he was Jimmy Watkins, and then when she ask to see his driver's license, he showed her my bogus California license in the other name he often used, John Zoddie.

"Okay, Delbert, let's have a seat here at the picnic table and do this thing."

"I'm ready when you are, Jimmy. You have the money, don't you?"

"Delbert, don't get your thong all wadded in a knot. I got it all. And I got it in cash."

Gaf leaned down and pointed under the old picnic table. "See that duffle bag under the table? There's way more than enough cash in that bag to cover this transaction. I'll hand it over to you soon as you sign the F-250 over to me."

That greedy hick couldn't click his blue inked, ball-point pen fast enough to start signing the truck's pink slip over to him. Gaf did the same, then they both exchanged titles, and Gaf forked over twenty-one grand in cash.

As he watched Delbert walk away, carrying the cash in a brown paper bag, Gaf had thoughts of raiding his tent tonight and taking back the money he'd just given him. What made him nix the plan was that Delbert's wife Maple knew Delbert was camping here, not to mention the fact she now knew who he was selling his prized truck to. If he didn't show back up at home, she'd report him missing. It wouldn't take long for the pigs to put two and two together and then be on Gaf like white on rice.

Now the only thing for him to do was to transfer his things from Old Man Watkins's truck to the F-250, hit the road, and get back to Mormon Town.

He decided just to leave for Mormon Town now and show up unexpectedly late tonight at the motel. He was sure Robin would be thrilled when he showed up a day ahead of time. Yeah, that's what he'd do, but he'd still call Robin, anyway, when he was about half way between there and Salt Lake City. He wanted to make sure she was there when he showed up with his hard throbbing dick, a cock that was looking to stay rock hard for hours, as he pounded away all night long, fucking all her holes. He was sure she'd be pleasantly surprised. Why wouldn't she be when he told her he'd be there tonight instead of tomorrow?

Right now he was beginning to feel like a Born Again Headasexual.

He got his things all loaded up in his new ride, with its ghost flames and all, then tore out of the campground and headed east again, back up I-80 toward Salt Lake City.

He was making excellent time. This fucking truck did haul ass. Delbert wasn't lying to him when he'd told Gaf, in so many words, "It's got power to burn."

Gaf remained conscious of the fact that he needed to be on the lookout for the "man" along these desolate stretches of endless highway, winding through the hot and dusty Nevada desert. He didn't have a bogus Delbert Mitchum driver's license yet, so that would be a big problem if he got pulled over for speeding and had to explain why he was driving someone else's F-250.

Before long, he was nearing the town of Fernley, Nevada, and since he'd eaten there last week at the twenty-four-hour truckers' truck wash and restaurant and liked it, he decided he'd make that place his first stop. He didn't want to waste time going inside to eat, so he called in a to-go order and, while there, he'd also fill up this gas hog.

"Hello, I'd like to talk to Mindy. I have a to-go order."

"Sir, I can take that order for you."

"No, I'd rather not do that. Please let me talk to Mindy."

Now he was starting to get a little uptight. He had to take a deep breath and calm himself down. He didn't want to end up having to kill another waitress over a patty melt and iced tea order, at least not tonight. After all, he was in a hurry to get to Mormon Town.

"Okay, sir, I see her. I'll ask Mindy to come to the phone."

"Thank you, ma'am."

Even though he didn't particularly care for truck stops, truck stop food seemed to be decent and not overly priced, and they did make his patty melt and iced tea just the way he liked. That was why he insisted on talking to Mindy, that same waitress, again.

ᴄᴏᴇᴏ

After going inside and paying for the to-go order, he walked outside to the pumps to fill up. While standing there, he decided he'd call Robin and give her the good news. Letting her know he was in Fernley, Nevada, and headed her way with an ETA of six hours, so he should be rolling up there around midnight. He was sure she'd be overjoyed, knowing he was coming a day ahead of time. He wished he could be there just to witness the surprised look on her pretty face when he sprang that news on her.

After he left the truck stop and got out of this one horse town, he'd only have one more gas stop to make, then it was straight through to Mormon Town and the Lazy Day Motel for some nice primo tail.

CHAPTER 29

The Set-Up

It was getting late here at the Lazy Day. The sun was just beginning to set over the Wasatch Mountains, leaving the desert landscape drenched in a reddish golden glow. It made you feel, if only for a short time, tranquil and somber, even under the stressful situation I and all my other agents found ourselves in, as we prepared for the show down with Miller tomorrow afternoon.

Setting up our video surveillance camera equipment was coming along nicely, considering the circumstances. That was, until Robin Osborne came running up to me, looking like she'd seen a ghost.

"Agent Drake," she said in a panicked voice. "He's on the way now!"

Hearing that made the hairs on the back of my neck stand up. "Did Miller just call you? Where is he?"

"Yes," she said, almost yelling. "He just called and told me he's leaving Fernley, Nevada, right now and should get here around midnight!"

I first thought, *Fuck Me!* Then I got my game face back on and my act together. Not wanting to show any concern, I told Ms. Osborne, "Not a problem. I'm just glad Miller called, giving us that warning. Now that we know he's coming tonight, we'll be ready."

She looked mystified and, at the same, time relieved to hear me tell her that.

I went on to reaffirm, "I'm just glad we got the warning. So don't worry, Robin, when that psycho shows up. Like I said, we'll be ready."

I knew in the back of my mind that if Miller hadn't called and just unexpectedly showed up here in the middle of the night, he would have caught all of us off guard, and this planned take-down would of have gone south for sure. There's no telling what would've happened. Only thing this meant to me was that we'd have to swing it into high gear now, knowing we only had—give or take—about three hours to finish. That'd give us a cushion of a couple hours before Miller showed up.

It wasn't two minutes later, just after Robin turned and headed back to her room, that Mindy, the restaurant manager from the truck stop in Fernley, Nevada, called me in a panic. "Special Agent Drake, your serial killer, Miller, the one you showed me on your Most Wanted poster, has just left the truck stop after picking up a to-go order and gassing up. I didn't call while he was here. There wasn't enough time. He was only inside the restaurant for a few minutes, and I was extremely nervous at the cash register, as he handed me the money for the order, as that's when I realized who he was."

"No problem, Mindy. You did the right thing." I knew she probably watched Miller as he left, by looking out the restaurant's huge store front window. I was hoping she saw what type of vehicle Miller was driving before he headed out of Fernley.

"Now, think for me, Mindy." It was at this time I asked her a critical question. "Did you get a look at what Miller was driving?"

"Yes I did. It was a truck."

"Could you tell what color and make it was?"

"No, I'm sorry, Special Agent Drake. I was way too nervous to remember those details."

"No problem. Thank you for calling me. You did good, Mindy."

"Mr. Drake, do you think he'll head back this way? I feel like I'm gonna throw up, knowing I've run into who you're calling a serial killer."

That sounded funny to me. No one had called me Mr. Drake in years. It only occasionally happened before I became an FBI agent.

"No, I don't, Mindy. Thank you again for your help. But maybe you should go home now and get some rest. I'll be in touch. Oh, yeah, there'll be some reward money coming your way, because of the tip you just gave me, after we take down Miller."

That news seemed to sooth her anxiety just a tad. Yeah, it was funny how coming into an unexpected non-taxable windfall affected most people. Almost similar to winning the Lotto, I guessed.

After talking to Mindy, I pulled all the agents together and gave them the news. "At least we got a warning that Miller is on his way now, so we'll need to step it up a notch. Miller is gonna be here somewhere around midnight, from what he told Robin Osborne. It's six-thirty p.m. now. Let's get all the video surveillance equipment set up and ready to go no later than nine p.m. That'll give us plenty of time to catch and tweak anything we may have over looked. I want Miller's arrest recorded from start to finish, including Agent Vack, here, doing the cuffing of that scumbag. One other thing, there's way too many rental cars here in the parking lot. I want room eight, nine, and ten's spaces to be empty, giving us a clear shot at to either take down Miller or get a clear shot at shooting him. That decision will be his to make. If he flinches, he's a dead man. Like six-feet-under dead."

"Martinez, I want you and Vack to drive two of the cars over to that Piggly Wiggly lot and park them, I'll have an agent here follow you over and drive you back. So make it quick. We don't have a lot of time left."

"No problem boss, we're on it."

As Vack started heading for his car, I added one more thing. "Oh, yeah, Vack, I have some pizza's being delivered here to the Lazy Day, it'll be here in about fifteen minutes." Smiling, I went on—to rub it in, "I didn't use my FBI cell to call the order in, either."

None of the other FBI agents had a clue what I was referring to, but Vack seemed to find humor and irony in what I'd just said. "No problem, boss, we'll be back here before those pizzas arrive."

"Okay, get out'a here. See ya shortly."

Next I called motel owners, Mr. & Mrs. James, who I hadn't seen since last talking to them when we first arrived. You'd think they were hiding out in a deep, reinforced underground bunker of some type. When I gave them the news about Miller being on the way, I noticed a slight tenseness in Mr. James's voice. I guessed it was because now he realized it was getting close to crunch time.

∾჻∾

Soon we'd be in near-total darkness, except for the blue neon glow of the *No Vacancy* sign flickering on and off out front. Other than that street light attached to a telephone pole, the only other lighting outside was the porch lights mounted next to each room's front door. They radiated out about as much light as you could expect to get from a thirty-watt bulb, not putting out much more light than you'd get from a nightlight plugged into hallway socket, guiding you along the way to the only bathroom in a 1960s house. The only function those porch lights seemed to serve was to attract fluttering moths and fireflies in a continuous circular buzz around each one of the old dated lights.

When Vack got back, we chowed down. Even Carla liked the vegetarian pizza I had included in the order just for her. I knew she disliked fast-food in general, including diner burgers, but I also knew she liked that type of pizza. Once she'd invited me over to her place for dinner to try some of her homemade pizza, and it was vegetarian. Man, that was one good tasting pizza! And I must say the dessert afterward wasn't bad, either, if you know what I mean.

ଈ୬ଈ୬

It was around eight-forty-five p.m. Martinez came up to me with a satisfied look on his face. "We're done, boss. Surveillance is ready to go. All the wireless mini video cams have been tested and are ready to start filming soon as Miller drives up. I've also checked the sound on the ear pieces and the mics we'll be using to communicate with. They all work. The sound is crystal clear, something we'll need when you give us the order to take Miller down to the ground." Martinez then turned and pointed toward the street. "I also had two cams mounted high up on that old telephone pole out there. One will give us a bird's-eye view of the entire motel and the parking lot, and the other one, a northern view of the two-lane road Miller will be coming down."

"You did a good job, Martinez, but I have one more thing I'd like you to do for me."

"Sure, boss, no problem."

That was what I liked about my team. They'd never bitched when I assigned anyone of them a task, no matter how difficult that task seemed to be at the time. "Call the Salt Lake FBI office and let them know we're all set out here and relay my message to have that office be on guard, in case more help is needed out here. Also remind them that I want a chopper in the air and to have it available, just in case something goes sideways."

"I'm on it, boss."

I hadn't informed my team yet about what I planned on doing after all this was over with, and we had Miller behind bars. I was going to recommend to Becker that all three—Carla, Vack, and Martinez—get healthy raises. Maybe Vack's raise would keep him around for a while. I'd hate to see him leave the Bureau.

∾∾∾

I didn't know what else we could do to be more ready for Miller. So as to not assume anything, I'd hold a brief meeting with the agents, making sure we're on the same page as to what each of our jobs were when this went down.

We'd set up laptops in each of the two rooms, seven and nine, on the left and right of room eight. They'd record all wireless transmissions from all the video cams mounted in and around the Lazy Day. Just for my own piece of mind, I personally checked them out by having an agent do a mock drive up test. The cams and laptops worked flawlessly. They recorded every move from the street, up to and when, I told the agent to park right in front of room eight. After the agent stepped out of the car, I had the other agents do a practice take down, with Vack cuffing him as if he were Miller. Then I had a couple of other agents practice wrapping a stun belt around the agent's waist and, just for good measure, I had them shackle his ankles and chain them to the stun belt. It was classic textbook. Just like we were taught during training at the FBI Academy in Quantico, Virginia. I knew then we were good to go.

All of us planned to be on the lookout for Miller rolling in here, driving Old Man Watkins's truck, a 1992 Ford F-150 with a camper shell. I did have an all-points bulletin out to all law enforcement agencies after Mr. Watkins informed me last week that he had sold his truck to Miller, but just to be on the safe side, I put out another all-points bulletin after I found out Miller was headed back this way. So far we hadn't heard a thing. No reports yet of anyone being pulled over, driving a 1992 Ford F-150 with a camper shell. I found that strange. Miller couldn't be that lucky.

Now, all there was to do was just sit and wait it out, other than me calling Becker and giving him an update on what was happening out here. I was sure the director was on pins and needles, knowing, if something did go wrong, President Anderson would be all over his ass. If that happened, I could forget about Becker ever recommending to President Anderson that I become the next director of the FBI when he retired later this year.

Yeah, it looked like it was going to be a long night. If everything went according to plan, the team would be transporting Miller out to the airport later on tonight then taking off in the Gulfstream and transporting him back to San Francisco, landing at approximately three a.m. Frisco time.

Earlier, I had notified both pilots to be on stand-by and to have the Gulfstream fueled and ready to go.

From the moment, I'd arrived here today, I'd thought about this over and over again, hoping nothing went wrong.

CHAPTER 30

Rude Awakening

As Gaf neared the Lazy Day, late that night, he could barely control his emotions, thinking that he and Robin Osborne were shortly going to be giving that motel bed a workout.

Wahoo! I'm within five minutes of the Lazy Day and my hookup with the best-looking piece of ass I've ever had the pleasure of pounding. I can hardly wait!

He was sure Robin was probably feeling the same way he did. Man, how did he ever get lucky enough to meet such a chick? It must have been good old fate. Yeah, that was what it was. Like some jerk-off philosopher once said, "We were destined to meet sometime, somewhere."

He'd made up that last part, the somewhere part. He just never knew it'd be in some redneck bar in Mormon Town. *Go figure.*

Okay, now he was only a few blocks away, and he could see the Lazy Day's blue neon *No Vacancy* sign flickering on and off. He guessed that meant they had a full house tonight. He could have cared less. Robin and he wouldn't be venturing out of bed for two days, any-way, except to take showers and eat. He'd find a diner where they could both chow down, and he could get his favorite food indulgence fix—a patty melt and iced tea with a lemon wedge. It was almost better than sex, but not quite. He wasn't giving up pussy for a patty melt din-er special.

He should give Robin a quick call, just to let her know he was only minutes away. *Naw, I'll just park and head on into room eight.*

℘℘℘

As Martinez monitored both laptops' real-time video feed through the cams set up out front, he spotted a set of headlights coming his way, heading south down the dark-ened two-lane asphalt road out front.

"Boss, do you see what I see?" he asked, talking via our ear pieces and mics.

I was in room nine. "Yeah, Martinez, it's a little past midnight, and I'd bet a month's pay that it's Miller head-ed our way,"

Taking no chance of a glitch in communications, I called out, "Can everyone hear me out there?" I waited for answers to my stress-filled request.

In unison, Vack, Simmons, Martinez, and the other agents came back with, "Yes, we do, loud and clear. We're ready for Miller."

Yeah, I've been waiting for this moment since I came on board to head-up this track down. The moment of truth is near. Jeffrey Miller is in for one rude awakening.

Martinez got my attention again. "Okay, boss. Here we go. There's a blue Ford truck pulling in."

I raised my eyebrows and stared closely at the monitor in room nine. "Yeah, Martinez, I see the truck on my monitor. Miller's supposedly driving the truck Watkins sold him, and that's not it. Let's see what happens here. It could be just a lookie-loo who's maybe gonna try the office anyway, even though the *No Vacancy* sign is lit up."

"Okay, boss—but look, who's ever driving that blue F-250 is pulling right into space eight."

Sensing that Carla could be in danger, I talked to her via her earphone. "Simmons, did you hear that? This could be Miller. We won't know if it is him until that person steps out of the truck. Be ready, just in case it is Miller and he decides to make a run for room eight's door."

Carla was now in her Weaver-stance position, standing inside room eight, ten feet back from the front door Miller would enter if he was that foolish. "No problem, boss, I have my lasered Glock-19s round chambered, and I'm ready to blast that fucker if he steps one foot inside this room."

"Let's hope that doesn't happen, Simmons, but, if it does, like I mentioned before, drop him like a bad habit. No one's gonna shed a tear if a serial killer buys the farm."

"Will do, boss. I kind of hope he does try it. I'd love to have the pleasure of wasting that piece of garbage."

With tension high now, I whispered into my mic. "From what I can see through the windshield, it looks like a male. If it is, he's now shut the trucks engine off. If this is Miller, get ready to pounce when I give the word."

⋞⋟⋞⋟

Gaf was sitting in the truck, fumbling with a couple of duffle bags he had his belongings in. He paused briefly before opening the door and stepping out.

"Okey dokey," he said. "Now I'm ready to see Robin again and get some."

He didn't mention this to Robin on the phone, but after he left the truck stop in Fernley, Nevada, he'd made a quick pit-stop at an all-night 7/11 and picked up a bouquet of some week old roses they had discounted, costing him only three dollars. He felt like he was stealing them! Robin won't know what he paid for those roses and, even if she did, he was sure she'd realize, as he did, it was the thought that counted. After all, he'd always considered himself a friendly people person. *I can be your best friend, if you just let me be.*

With the bouquet of roses in one hand and a duffle bag swung over his right shoulder, he opened the F-250's door and stepped out.

⌒⌒⌒

As soon as Miller's feet touched the pavement, I gave the order. "It's Miller! Take him down!"

Eight FBI agents attacked Jeffrey Miller, slamming him to the ground in a flash. He never knew what hit him. Now he lay there on the ground, face-first, kissing the pavement with pale, red-looking rose petals, from the cheap-ass bouquet he'd brought, loosely covering him and the pavement.

Vack approached. Carla was now standing outside room eight and had drawn down on Miller. "Make a move, *dickhead*, and you're a dead man. Go ahead, give me a reason," she shouted to Miller as he was being cuffed and shackled by Vack, with the help of a couple of other agents.

After Vack got Miller cuffed and shackled, Vack rolled him over. "Remember me, you bastard?" he snarled.

Miller, now looking up at Vack all wide-eyed and not speaking a word through this entire one-minute ordeal, just lay there, squinting his eyes as he tried to focus through the bright flashlight beam Vack was shining right in his face. He apparently couldn't see that it was Vack, who was now leaning directly over him and looking into his eyes.

"Take a good look," Vack continued. "Now, do you remember me? Well, I remember you. You ever heard that phrase, 'What goes Around, comes a Around'?" Well, now it's come full circle, my friend."

"Where's Robin?" was Miller's only response.

Then Vack, who still had some pent up anger still in him at being chained to Miller's basement wall, slapped Miller across the face with the back of his hand. Vack then got up and backed off from Miller, who appeared to just now realize he'd been had by Robin and the FBI.

As he stood there, Vack glared at Miller. "Don't say a word, you fucking scumbag. 'Anything you say, can be, and will, be used against you in a court of law. There, you've been Mirandized you low-life cocksucker. There's your rights!"

"You can't get away with hitting me, I have rights."

"I told you to shut the fuck up," Vack answered.

A couple other agents and I tried to console Vack.

"Sorry, boss," he said. "I couldn't help myself."

"No problem, Vack, I understand. I probably would have done a lot worse than just giving Miller a backhand if I'd been in your place."

As Miller lay on the ground cuffed, shackled, and looking as if he had been hogtied, I looked around at all the other FBI agents, including Carla and Martinez. "Nobody saw that, right? Am I clear?"

"Saw what, Agent Drake?" they all answered in unison.

Next, I told the other FBI agents to check the truck, go over it with a fine-toothed comb. It was a good thing they did. The agents found over twenty thousand in cash, and a revolver that looked like a 44 magnum, hidden behind the rear fold-down seat, along with two Glock-19 revolvers.

Before long, the crime scene technicians arrived on site and took over, searching the truck, bagging everything they found, and taking possession of all evidence, including the cash the agents found.

We'll need to find out how Miller accumulated that much cash. I had a feeling he'd committed other crimes the FBI knew nothing about, while flying around the country as a flight attendant for Docket Air.

I had the pink slip bagged and bill of sale, knowing the owner, Delbert Mitchum, was going to be pissed when the FBI came knocking on his door and confiscated not only the twenty-one grand Miller had paid him, but also Old Man Watkins's truck—which we found out later was part of the deal on the blue F-250 with the ghost flames.

I turned to Martinez. "Call Salt Lake. Let them know we have Jeffrey Miller in custody, and we're now heading for the Gulfstream to launch for Frisco. While you're doing that, I'll get a hold of the pilots and let them know we're headed their way with Miller."

After I called the pilots, I gave a quick call to Director Becker to inform him on the good news. Even though it was past three a.m. his time, Becker was ecstatic. "That's the best news I heard since I brought you on to head up the team. Now I can get President Anderson off my ass!"

With that, we both hung up. I knew as soon as the director got off the phone with me, he'd be speed dialing, as fast as his finger could punch his direct line button, to President Anderson to relay the good news.

Before leaving the Lazy Day, I talked to Robin, who

was really relieved. I sincerely thanked her for everything she'd done in helping with the arrest of Miller. "Robin, I'll have an agent give you a ride over to the Piggly Wiggly so you can pick up your car. And, by the way, I'll be in touch concerning the reward money and also as to whether or not you'll have to testify if Miller pleads not guilty, and there's a trial."

"No problem, Agent Drake, I'll testify if there is one."

Then we hugged. I also called the motel owners, Mr. and Mrs. James, and gave them the all clear. I thanked them for their help, letting both know that I'd be in touch. From the sound of their voices, they were extremely relieved. I also let them know that I'd have the remaining agents dismantle the video surveillance equipment and take out the deck screws, holding the motel's office door shut, so that my team could start transporting Miller back to San Francisco now.

Soon after, we loaded Miller into one of the rental cars, with Vack driving and Carla riding shotgun. Miller was in the rear seat, hogtied and sandwiched between Martinez and myself. Then we caravanned out of the parking lot with SWAT following close behind, again breaking every speed limit law in Utah, as we headed for Hill Air Force Base where the Gulfstream was powered up and ready to launch back to San Francisco.

After getting airborne, I contacted the federal prosecutor's office to get a clearer understanding of what Miller would be charged with during the indictment proceedings tomorrow afternoon. Chief Federal Prosecutor, Laurence McDavis told me that at the news conference he planned on announcing his office would be charging Miller with multiple accounts of first degree murder, first degree kidnapping, burglary, torture, fraud by deception, purchase of stolen property—various vehicles—destruction of personal property, identity theft, plus the State of California would be taking possession of the row house on Green Street that Miller had been living in until just before going on the run, for failure to pay property taxes for the last twenty years.

"Like I said, those are just some of the felony's we'll be charging Miller with as of right now," McDavis went on to tell me. "I'm sure more are coming as our investigators dig deeper into his past. Such as his relationship with his father, who we now believe was the Zodiac, a serial killer who terrorized San Francisco back in the late '60s and early '70s. We'll also be checking to see if Miller's responsible for any robberies while working as a flight attendant. We suspect that he's been committing bank robberies while he worked at Docket Air, otherwise, how would he have accumulated that much cash? As I speak, my office is doing a deep background check on him and, take my word for it, we'll be leaving no stone unturned. If Miller even so much as had an unpaid fine on an overdue library book, we're going to know about it.

"No matter whether Miller decides to plead guilty or not guilty, he'll still be facing the death penalty. There's no question about it. There'll be no plea bargain deals coming from this prosecutor's office. All plea bargains will be completely off the table. Our office will be pushing the court for the death penalty under both scenarios and, Agent Drake, you have my word on that."

I hung up the phone and fastened my seat belt as the pilots began landing the Gulfstream at NAS Alameda. Looking over at Jeffrey Miller, who was now sitting upright in a cabin seat directly in front of me—hand cuffed and shackled, along with a spit guard covering his face, I thought, *Even if Miller does somehow escapes the gallows and is sentenced to life, he'll still end up living the rest of his life in total isolation from the other prisoners. But no matter what, even if he is lucky enough to avoid the death penalty, Miller will still run the risk of eventually being on the receiving end of some street justice from the other inmates, just like Dahmer got after that whack job somehow avoided the death penalty.*

CHAPTER 31

Announcement to the Media

After landing, a team of US Marshals, along with several heavily armed FBI agents, boarded the Gulfstream and escorted Miller to a black FBI armored SUV. They'd be taking him to a holding cell located in the federal court house in downtown San Francisco on Golden Gate Avenue, where he'd remain until Chief Federal Prosecutor, Laurence McDavis, could finalize arrangements to have charges brought against Miller, hopefully, no later than two p.m. today. Prosecutor McDavis, along with the help of other US Government attorneys would be officially charging Jeffrey Miller with numerous first degree felonies they believed he had committed.

Since the track down for Miller had come to an end and before deplaning and walking down the ramp to the tarmac, the team first walked up to the cockpit of the Gulfstream to thank both air force pilots for their help in ferrying us around the country. I wanted to tell both pilots that I knew that, during this hunt for Miller, my calls to them were usually done without notice, giving them only moments to fuel up and ready the Gulfstream. I also let them know I understood how important they were, in that they could be relied on to swiftly get me and my team to the next hot spot without delay, and they had done so without complaining. I then turned, pointing to my team standing behind me, and let both pilots know that not only I, but also Carla, Vack, Martinez, and Director Becker truly appreciated how they'd hung in there during this entire ordeal. All four of us shook the hands of both air force pilots, thanking them again and wishing both the best of luck on their next assignments.

With that, we made it down the ramp to find two FBI squad cars, Crown Victoria's of course, waiting for us, given to us to use for the next couple of days complements of Director Becker.

Before driving away from NAS Alameda, we all agreed we were starved, since we hadn't eaten anything, other than the pizzas I had Vack pickup yesterday while at the Lazy Day. I suggested the four of us grab some breakfast at the base chow hall. Personally, just from my experience, I'd take navy chow hall food over a civilian restaurant any day. Some of my fellow agents found that surprising, and odd, but Carla agreed with me that navy chow hall food was outstanding and, if she didn't think so, there was no way I would have ever made that suggestion. I knew that sounded as if it was coming from a pussy-whipped man, but that was just the way it was in a man's world. *You go along to get along.*

೧൭೧

The news conference, scheduled by the director, began at around eleven a.m. West Coast time. My team, along with the director, and a group of other law enforcement officials, whom I'd call posers, had assembled on the raised platform. We were now fending off questions about Miller, while nearly being blinded by the constant flash of hand-held cameras.

The law-enforcement posers were strictly here for publicity and exposure and, in my opinion, to whore themselves out, seeking the unjustified attention they constantly craved. Those officials had nothing to do with the hard work involved in bringing in Miller to justice. Yeah, the outer fringes of the San Francisco law en-forcement community were all here. I stood behind the director and looked around to see who was up here with us. There were some law enforcement officials who showed up here to somehow get their fifteen minutes of fame by just having their faces shown at this important, nationally broadcasted news conference, as they stood alongside Director or, otherwise, they wouldn't be here. But that was the way it was in all forms of government in general. That was probably the way it'd always be, even in law enforcement.

Just before the director was about to step up to the mic and start the news conference, he pulled me aside for a minute, cupped his right hand, and leaned over to speak into my ear. "David, after I make my announcement here at the podium," he said in a hushed tone, "I'll start field-ing questions from the media. After I answer a few of them, I'll then be asking you, Simmons, Vack, and Mar-tinez to step up here and give the media a brief run down on what it took for the FBI to find, capture, and arrest Miller.

"Explain to the media how your team worked closely with the director of the FBI in overcoming many obsta-cles in making this track down for Miller as successful as it was," Becker continued, with his hand still cuffed next to my ear.

That sounded odd, having Director Becker talking about himself in the third person, but what the hell? He was my ticket to being the next director of the FBI. If nothing else, I could at least give him an atta boy. On the other hand, the director did commandeer that Gulfstream for the team to use and, for me, that was huge. That alone was enough for me to give Becker all the praise he desired.

CHAPTER 32

Guilty or Not Guilty

The news conference was over before noon. All in all, I had to admit it went well. There were over thirty different news organizations there broadcasting a live feed around the country and throughout the world, with a mix of local, independent TV stations recording video to be shown later today on their evening news broadcasts. Even for me, it was a little overwhelming.

The team, especially Vack, did an outstanding job answering all questions the media reporters threw their way. Vack had the room going with his answer to a question from a reporter, when asked how he thought Jeffrey Miller would do if he was convicted and got life and not the death penalty, and had to adjust to prison life.

Vack gave them a condescending smile. "You know Miller's gonna be really pissed when he realizes that jailhouse prison food menus don't include patty melt combo plates and tall glasses of freshly brewed iced tea, along with those big fat lemon wedges that he so dearly craves.

And, by the way, those lemon wedges are oh, so necessary to the taste of iced tea. As they say in the Southern States that I've visited, it just ain't considered iced tea without that lemon wedge."

That comment broke up the seriousness of this whole ordeal and got a spattering of laughter from some reporters who were obviously from the South. That was Agent Vack's sarcastic way of getting a little more revenge on a person he considered a low-life predatory scumbag.

Good for you Vack, I thought.

After answering a few questions, I stepped away from the podium. *When this is all said and done, I hope this deranged psychopathic killer does get put to death for the heinous crimes he's committed. If Miller doesn't plead guilty this afternoon at the hearing, and there is a trial, I'm glad life-without-parole is off the table and won't be considered as an option, according to Prosecutor Laurence McDavis.*

Before the team left FBI headquarters, Director Becker had the four of us gather around him for a minute, just outside the news conference room. He pointed toward the second door, down the hall on the right, of this massively wide corridor that we were standing in. "I'd like to briefly see the four of you in that conference room over there for a few minutes please."

Wondering what this was about, we all entered through the door now being held open by the director.

Becker grabbed one of the black, high-back office chairs—the type the highest-ranking CEO's of a company liked sitting in—rolled it up to the table, and took a seat. Then he leaned back in the chair with his hands cupped up behind his head and, before speaking, just sat there for a while with a wide smile on his face.

I, along with my other three agents, still had no clue as to why we were there.

"Go ahead, have a seat," the director said.

We rolled over four standard office chairs to the massive oval-shaped dark-mahogany table then, more or less, sat at attention, with Becker sitting right across from the four of us. While still not saying a word, the four of us just sat there. We turned and glanced at each other then, in that moment of awkward silence, we looked back over at Director Becker and tried to read his body language—something I'd never been that good at. But it was something Carla was an expert at but, at the time, I couldn't just lean over and ask her what she thought Becker was up to. So we all sat there, quietly twiddling our thumbs, wondering.

"Okay," the director finally said. "Well, I guess you're all wondering what this meeting is all about. Don't worry, you're not getting fired, ha, ha, ha." That apparently was Becker's attempt at being a comedian. He should keep his day job and forget about trying his hand at stand-up. "Relax, that was a joke, of course." Becker said when he looked at us and noticed we weren't laughing. "Okey, dokey, then let's get right to it." He then reached his right hand into his inside suit coat pocket and pulled out four white business-sized envelopes that had each of our names neatly typed on them in big bold fonts. Becker then tossed an envelope to each one of us, as if he were dealing a deck of cards at a Vegas casino, and pointed to the envelopes now laying flat on the conference table, one envelope directly in front of each of us.

"Go ahead, open them."

All four of us ripped open our envelope and then looked at one another with an expression of sheer surprise.

"Those cashier checks are just a little something to show our gratitude to the four of you for a job well done—from the president and myself. By the way, those

$10,000 cashier checks are considered a type of a bonus that you won't have to declare as income when you do your taxes. They came from a special government fund that I can't talk about, so we'll just leave it at that. What I've just mentioned about the special government fund, well, that stays in this room. All agreed?"

We sat there, nodding yes in unison, looking like four wide-eyed, bobble-headed dolls. Frankly, I could have cared less where the money came from. I was just glad to get it, and I was sure Carla, Vack, and Martinez all felt the same way.

"I've also approved a $30,000-a-year raise for each one of you, retroactive from the time this track-down for Miller started."

Now I was getting excited. My mind was spinning, thinking about the things I could do with this new found fortune.

"And on top of that, I'm giving each one of you an extra ten days off with pay, starting tomorrow morning," the director added, as if that wasn't enough. "Of course, you'll all be on call just in case something critical comes up on the Miller case and I need your help back here for one reason or another. Any problem with that?"

I did the answering for the team on that one. "No, no problem with that at all, Director."

We all sat there completely stunned. We'd had no idea.

"Well what do you think?" the director asked.

I spoke first. "Director Becker, I think I'm speaking, not only for myself, but for these other fine agents sitting here with me. Quite frankly, we all worked together as a team, with no dissention at all between the four of us here at this table. If that hadn't been the case, Miller would most likely still be running around out there on the loose. With that said, we are completely blown away. None of us expected this. We were just doing the job we were trained to do. But, on the other hand, it is truly inspiring when the fruits of your labor are recognized by higher ups, such as President Anderson and yourself."

I never was much of an ass kisser and hoped my last comment wasn't taken as being so.

"Thank you, Special Agent Drake, it was my pleasure. Hard work in the FBI is rewarded. That's the way I've run things under my watch." Becker switched subjects and went on to inquire. "Where do you all plan on going, and/or doing, on your ten days off, if you don't mind me asking."

"Since I can afford it now," Vack said, "I'll be traveling to Milan to visit relatives in Italy that I haven't seen in years. I thank you, Director, from the bottom of my heart."

"No problem, Special Agent Vack, you deserve it. It sounds like it's gonna be a fun trip. I hope you take lots of photos and show them to us all when you get back."

"I will do that, Director Becker."

I couldn't tell Becker the truth about what Carla and I would most likely be doing during our time off. I didn't want to see him blush. Martinez mentioned he'd like to visit the Hawaiian Islands, since he'd always heard how beautiful it was there.

"The FBI will now be depending on this team of special agents, sitting right here at this table in front of me, to help solve other major crimes in the US and, also, possibly crimes in Europe that have been instigated by American criminals hiding out over there, creating the same kind of havoc they did while living in the States," Becker threw out nonchalantly, adding another caveat to the equation.

Now that was a total surprise to me. I never saw that one coming, but I did like the idea of my team running all over the globe, putting out fires in the name of the FBI.

Director Becker was now standing near the conference room door he had just opened, shaking each of our hands as we began exiting the room and telling us to take care and try to relax during our time off. "If something does come up," he went on to remind us, "and I need you back here for one reason or another, I'll give Agent Drake a call, and he'll contact you. Thank you again for a job well done."

❦❦❦

Standing out near the curb, in front of headquarters, I shook Vack and Martinez's hands, just before they drove off to start their ten days of R and R, thanking them again for their help in bringing down Miller.

"You two agents take care, enjoy your time off, and, if anything important comes up, I'll be in touch. Until then, I'll see you back here in a couple of weeks."

Both were all smiles, and who wouldn't be with a pocket full of money, a huge raise in pay, and an extra ten days off with pay. Man, it wasn't like this back in the old days. Something Agent Vack was well aware of. I was hoping he'd now change his mind about leaving the Bureau and maybe stay till he got his "thirty" in.

After Vack and Martinez drove off, leaving Carla and I standing on the sidewalk making big plans for tonight, including the next ten glorious days we'd have off together, I got a call from the Prosecutor McDavis.

"Miller pled not guilty," McDavis said. "Don't worry. That happens all the time in cases similar to this one. Whenever we bring a murder suspect up before a judge at these hearings, and after they hear me rattling off the charges being brought up against a felon like Miller, they will plead not guilty nearly one hundred percent of the time. But then, as the trial date approaches, they begin to change their tune, after seeing the mountain of evidence we have against them, and then plead guilty. Most murderers will look for a way out, hoping to make a deal and thinking that by pleading guilty, it's going to save them from the death penalty. Those types are really nothing but spineless cowards. That won't happen in this case. Miller's going to get the needle if I have my way, and it won't matter whether he pleads guilty or not guilty. We'll need you to put together a witness list, Agent Drake, then start notifying all the potential federal witnesses in the case if there is a trial."

"No problem. I'll be off for the next ten days, but I'll work on my list while I'm gone."

After ending the call, I thought, *Yeah, that's all I need. Get all tied down to a trial like this one, where I'll be on call for months just in case the prosecutor needs me, either as an expert witness or to explain the various crime scenes to the jury, which my team had analyzed.* But I didn't mind, considering all the suffering Miller was responsible for. I was sure there were more murders Miller had committed that we knew nothing about at this time.

For now, Carla and I had decided not to use the Crown Victoria, since our vacation time would officially start tomorrow morning. Instead, we took separate cabs, so as not to attract attention, and met up at the Omni, where I'd reserved a bitching suite, costing me more for one night than I'd normally pay for a week's stay somewhere else. But what the heck? I'd be with a beautiful woman, who I was now growing even fonder of. We'd have a great dinner, sex, and then tomorrow morning we'd fly down to the Bahamas for one week and stay right on the beach. I could just picture those seven days on the beach with Carla, gawking at her as she lay there on a beach towel nearly completely nude. It was going to be great.

CHAPTER 33

Trouble in Paradise

The next morning, Carla and I made our way out of the Omni to the street below and caught a cab to San Francisco International, jetting out of town, winging it straight for the Caribbean island of Barbados, for a planned five-day stay. After landing and getting through customs with our carry-on bags, it was now late in the day. I rented a car and we headed straight for Club Paradise. After checking in, we were given keys to our private beach-front cottage that also came with a cabana sitting on the snow white sandy beach, just fifty feet from the shoreline.

The club's private cottages all faced the pristine, warm, clear aqua-blue waters of the ocean, something the Caribbean islands were known for. This place was no Lazy Day Motel. For us, we were now living high on the hog—something most people in our pay grades never got a chance to do. But with the extra loot awarded to us by Becker—what the heck? You only lived once.

I paid for the entire trip, including airfares, just like I'd planned on doing over a month ago if the two of us got a chance to spend time together again. I wouldn't ask Carla to chip in. That was just the way it was in a "man's world." If you wanted to play, you had to pay one way or another. Not that it mattered, but I knew I'd get paid back by Carla in other ways. That alone was making my mind run wild just thinking about our five-day stay here, knowing we'd be having sex every which way known to mankind. We're both horn dogs, when it came to sex.

Club Paradise had a bellhop drive Carla and me, by golf cart, to our private cottage on the beach. By the time we unlocked the door and entered, it was already past eight p.m. Both of us were exhausted and starved, as we plopped our bags on the Saltillo-tiled floor, followed immediately by a face plant on this huge California King bed. After laying there for a short time, we rolled over. Now we were face to face and decided to take showers then head for the Club's seafood restaurant. According to their website, seafood was their specialty, caught daily in the local waters just off shore. Well, we're going to give that claim a test and devour as much shrimp, lobster, and oysters as both our guts could take, especially the oysters. I'd always heard oysters were excellent aphrodisiacs. Yeah, it was for sure we were going to give that old aphrodisiac wives' tale a test run when we returned later on. And when we did, it'd be for more doggie style and for as many hours as our bodies could last. It'd be a great workout—much better than doing that lame yoga stuff.

I just knew this five-day stay was going to be the perfect getaway. It already seemed so perfect. What could possibly go wrong?

Little did I know that trouble in paradise was just around the corner.

శిశిశి

After returning from pigging out on seafood and then completely wearing ourselves out on that California King, our eyes slammed shut sometime after two a.m.

The next day, while lounging in our cabana, I called room service to have a pitcher of margaritas delivered. While waiting for the margaritas, we both decided to take a stroll up and down the beach, something I hadn't done in years.

I knew women liked that stuff. As we walked along the beach, something struck me as odd. Were we the only ones here? I didn't see another soul anywhere, either in or near the water.

When the drinks came, I asked the porter, "Where is everyone?"

The porter glanced over at Carla—who was now topless and nearly completely nude, except for her red string bikini bottoms—and lost his focus momentarily.

Looking over at the porter, I had to reel him back in. "Hey, man, are you getting an eye full? Apparently you didn't hear my question."

Then the porter snapped out of his gawking stare, and looked my way.

"Are we the only ones vacationing here? I haven't seen anyone on the beach all morning."

"Well, sir, or should I say, Mr. Drake, are you aware of the forecasted weather conditions."

"What? What conditions?"

"I'm surprised you aren't aware there's a hurricane headed our way. It's due to hit Barbados in a couple of days."

"What the fuck? I wasn't told this at check in."

Now Carla was rushing around, searching for her top and not at all looking like she was in a good mood. I blew off the porter, telling him to return the margaritas and inform the check-in counter I'd be up there to talk about a refund. "We'll be leaving here and, oh yeah, tell 'em we're fucking pissed!"

With that, we gathered up our beach towels and headed back to the cottage. As we walked up the flag-stone walkway, I noticed that the front door was wide open, flopping back and forth. I thought we must not have fully shut the door and maybe the Caribbean breeze blew it open.

Soon, we both discovered that was not the case. Our carry-on bags were missing, along with my billfold and Carla's tote bag. Luckily, both of us had taken our shields, Glocks, and our FBI cell phones with us to the beach, or else they'd be missing also. Man, that would have been hard to explain to Becker. I could just hear the director now. "David, what was Agent Simmons doing down there in Barbados at the same time you were there?"

Now we were temporarily stuck in Barbados with no cash, credit cards, or passports. Both Carla and I dialed up our credit card companies right away and had them put a freeze on our accounts. They were pretty accommodating, telling both of us they'd be sending replacement cards overnight via FedEx, and we'd have them by noon tomorrow.

We were both now standing in front of the check-in counter, wearing the only clothes to our name. I was wearing a pair of baggy-looking surfer trunks and Carla was in her string bikini. The clerks here were getting an eyeful.

I was going back and forth with the management, trying to get credit for some of the over three thousand dollars I'd blown just coming here.

I was hoping to get credit for at least the days we weren't using, since we'd decided to leave as soon as we could get our hands on the passports and credit cards. I was hoping that'd be sometime tomorrow morning.

Carla also gave management an ear full, but somewhat kept her cool, never mentioning the fact that we were both FBI agents, no matter how tempting it was just to throw that out there. I knew that if they did know, they'd kill that copped attitude and help us out.

While I was haggling, my FBI cell went off. Looking down at the caller ID, I noticed that it was Director Becker. *What the fuck, now*? I stepped outside to take the call. Standing under a palm tree to get some shade, I clicked the accept button and, just when I thought the day couldn't get any worse, Director Becker asks me, "David, where are you now?"

"I'm in Barbados, trying to re-charge my batteries. What is it?"

"Well, I'm sorry to give you this bad news, but Miller has escaped and, in the process severely beat the two FBI guards who were transporting him back from a court-ordered psychiatric evaluation. I don't have all the details right now, but somehow he managed to pick the locks on his waist and leg shackles and then escaped. You'll need to get a hold of Simmons, Vack, and Martinez, and have them head back here to San Francisco right away."

I explained to Becker the situation I was in, stating that I'd be leaving the island in the morning, as soon as I could get my hands on a temporary passport and the overnighted credit cards.

"I've had Ms. Hayes, Mr. Watkins, and Robin Osborne temporarily put in the Witness Protection Program for their own safety, at least until we bring in that sumbitch Miller," Director Becker went on to add.

I thanked Becker. Man, I was glad I didn't have to make that call to Robin Osborne. I knew she'd be freaking right now, knowing that Miller was aware she was the one who set him up at the Lazy Day Motel. The director never mentioned Mindy, the manager at the truck stop in Fernley. I felt it was only right that I let her know Miller had escaped, so I called her right after hanging up.

She was totally panicked. "What am I supposed to do now? What if he comes back, looking for me?"

I assured Mindy that Miller had no clue that we had ever spoken to one another, as I tried to reaffirm she had nothing to worry about. Yeah, that was easy for me to say. I was not in that predicament. Before getting off the phone, she said she was going take a temporary leave of absence from the truck stop immediately and move out of town to stay with her sister in Tennessee until Miller was caught. It was then that I cut in, telling Mindy I'd call the director and recommend that she also be put in the FBI's Witness Protection Program, if she were interested.

"I'm not interested in doing that," she told me.

From the tone of her voice, she was really ticked off, and I didn't blame her. This was exactly why some people chose not to get involved.

I stepped back inside the door, motioned to Carla to join me outside, then gave her a rundown on what the director just told me.

"Fuck Me!" Carla snarled. "I didn't think it could get any worse!"

"My sentiments exactly. We do think alike, Carla. We'll be leaving in the morning."

Going back inside, I noticed management had completely changed the tone of their voice. I didn't know what Carla had told them while I was outside, but whatever it was, it worked. I figured she pulled rank, flashed her shield, and made vague remarks about security— probably hinting she was a phone call away from making a call to the local American Embassy, and God knew who else.

Frankly, right now, I didn't care what she'd told them.

"Mr. Drake, Club Paradise is very sorry for the misfortune and inconvenience you've experienced since arriving."

Okay, enough with the sucking up. I wanted to know what they had in mind.

"Club Paradise is prepared to give you a complete refund on your planned five-day stay, plus each of you will receive a five hundred dollar Amex gift card that you and the lovely Agent Simmons can use any way you like."

Yeah, I was right. She did pull rank. That all sounded nice, but still, it wasn't something they'd volunteered to do earlier. I had to throw in one sarcastic remark, seeing that I was still pissed about our little getaway together being totally ruined. "Okay, well, I thank you. Now we'll take our Amex gift cards and shop at your overpriced swanky clothing store to replace the clothes some asshole stole from our cottage. By the way, both of us believe it's one of your employees. I'd start by looking at the porter first. The one who delivered the margaritas. That's just my professional opinion."

That suggestion by me to the three management dudes was greeted with slightly muted, puckered-up grins—the kind you'd see if someone bit into an extremely bitter lemon.

We got back to the cottage and I made the dreaded phone calls to both Vack and Martinez. Agent Vack wasn't too pleased, since he was now over six thousand miles from Frisco, having landed there just that morning, Italian time. But I knew Vack. He'd want to be involved in getting Miller back into custody. I mentioned I'd do what I could to, at least, get his airfare refunded, courtesy of the FBI.

Martinez was in Maui and had no problem coming back. In fact, he told me he'd be on the next flight out this afternoon. I got the feeling Martinez wasn't all that thrilled about being way over there in Hawaii, anyway. "No, problem boss," he told me. "We're gonna put Miller away this time for good."

I thanked him for the positive attitude and said I would meet up with him, Vack, and Simmons tomorrow afternoon at FBI Headquarters in San Francisco.

After I hung up, I turned to Carla. "What was it exactly that you did to make the management cave?"

"You know that twinkled-toed prissy fuck, Antione. While you were outside, I walked around the check-in counter, got in his face, flashed my shield, then let him know that I was only a cunt hair away from calling the Barbados police, not to mention our friends over at the American Embassy and telling them what's going on here at Club Fuck-Up! Telling him, 'Trust me, Antione, after I explain to both agencies how we're getting screwed over here, they'll come out and investigate, and that means talking to you and, by the time they're through with you, Antione, you're gonna know what a hysterectomy feels like. You get my drift?' After that, he couldn't get the register open fast enough to throw money at us."

"Well, even though what you said wasn't politically correct, Carla, I'm good with it, since Antione more or less just stood there with that creepy smirk, while ignoring everything we were trying to explain. I'm sure he thought we were just another couple of dumb American tourists and what we had to say meant nothing to him. Heck, it worked, so who am I to say? Personally, Carla, I don't plan on ever coming back here again. I'll stick with the good old US of A for my next stint of R and R. Like maybe a dude ranch in Wyoming."

"David, are you crazy. You expect me to sleep in some bunk house and then get up at the crack of dawn to ride a smelly horse? First of all, I wouldn't do a dude ranch unless it had a Spa."

I smiled.

Early the next morning, we managed to get a hold of our replacement credit cards and passports, then we were on our way, jetting non-stop back to San Francisco to meet up with the rest of the team, and Director Becker.

CHAPTER 34

Jeffrey Miller, Wanted Dead or Alive

Meanwhile, at Miller's first hearing, the federal court judge directed FBI Prosecutor McDavis to schedule a full psychiatric mental-health exam on Jeffrey Miller, to determine if he was capable of standing trial. The next day, Gaf was transported via an FBI SWAT armored truck to San Francisco General and examined by psychiatrist, Dr. Zerkerman.

Due to patient privacy laws in California, Zerkerman asked the two FBI agents to wait outside in the hallway, while he examined Miller. Before stepping into the hallway, they shackled him to a heavy metal chair situated near the front edge of Zerkerman's desk. The chair was bolted to the floor for the doctor's safety, eliminating any movement around the room by Miller.

While the doctor was psychoanalyzing Gaf, Gaf was on his best behavior. But as he sat there, unbeknownst to Zerkerman, Gaf was contemplating several escape schemes, anything he thought would prevent those two FBI agents from returning him to his jail cell in the feder-

al court building where he'd await his trial. He knew
without a doubt that if he was returned, he'd likely be
found guilty and given the death penalty. His mind was
racing.

Dr. Zerkerman's office had just the type of creepy at-
mosphere you'd expect to find in a psychiatrist's office
where the allegedly criminally insane were brought to be
examined before standing trial. This office was bare
bones—plain and depressing, with pale-green painted
walls, where one outdated framed photo of General Hospital's founder of the psychiatric wing hung directly behind Doctor Zerkerman's desk. It was a faded headshot of
a man who was now long dead—an obese-looking man
with puffy pink cheeks, beady dark bifocaled eyes, and
thin greasy gray hair combed straight back. The founder
had a rather obese name to go along with his large girth.
He went by the name of Dr. Fuller. That was what was
stamped on a brass name plate directly below his framed
photo.

After doing his fake insanity impersonation, Gaf saw
that Doctor Zerkerman had a rather odd look on his face.
He looked pale, pretty much as pale as that Tide-white
lab coat he was wearing, while he sat there at his old oak
desk, stoned-faced, staring into space and gripping Gaf's
medical file with both hands.

Doctor Zerkerman looked at Gaf then hunched over on
his desk, thumbed through the file to the last page, made
a notation, and closed it. Looking back up at Gaf, he said,
"Mr. Miller, it's my conclusion from what I've just
learned from our physiatrist exam, that you are a very
deranged individual. In all my years at this job, I don't
think I've ever examined an inmate patient who has had a
more profound hatred for the human race than you, Mr.
Miller."

Gaf looked up at Doctor Zerkerman, knowing that if

he weren't shackled at the waist and ankles to this chair, he'd reach over the desk, rip out the doctor's throat, and shove it in his mouth. But since he couldn't, Gaf just smiled and held back his anger, informing the doctor that was the way he'd always felt toward his fellow man, when he thought he'd been rubbed the wrong way. "Whether you know it or not, Doctor Zerkerman, I'm actually a very nice person, and, in fact, I wouldn't harm a fly, like the one that's crawling around on the top of your bald head right now."

When Zerkerman turned to his right and looked at the mirror hanging over the wash basin in his office, Gaf leaned over quickly and picked up a couple of paper clips off this desk with his lips and held them under his tongue.

"Oh, you don't say. Okay, Mr. Miller, tell me about that. Exactly how do you feel toward others, and how come some of your acquaintances seem to end up on the short end of the stick, so to speak? Or should I say, come to end up dead?"

"I've only killed those who have disrespected me in some fashion or another, Doctor. Not to say I wouldn't love to see Special Agent Drake and his team of FBI pigs pushing up daisies. Oh, yeah, and that also includes that bitch, Ms. Hayes, the one who fired me from Docket Air. But now, my list has grown to also include Ms. Robin Osborne. She's the bitch who ratted me out to Drake and his FBI goons, after claiming she was looking forward to fucking me again at the Lazy Day Motel, just like she did that night in Old Man Watkins's shack."

"I see, Mr. Miller. That's interesting. But I'm curious about one thing. Tell me about the infatuation you have with patty melts, freshly brewed iced teas, and lemon wedges. I understand that food group has caused you problems in the past. I'm referring to Rachel, the waitress you killed who worked at the Bay Diner in San Francisco. Do you wish to expand on the reasons why you waited outside the diner, followed her home, walked up on her as she sat in her car, and shot her dead before she even had a chance of exiting her car? Which, by the way, was parked directly in front of her apartment. Do you understand why I'm asking these questions, Mr. Miller?"

Gaf looked straight at this buffoon psychiatrist, who was totally clueless as to why he did what he did. Apparently, no one had ever ragged on him.

"Mr. Miller, my examination is over now. I'll let the agents outside know we're done."

Little did Gaf know that Doctor Zerkerman had made notations in his medical file, stating that he believed Jeffrey Miller had a ranking of 21-30 on the Global Assessment of Functioning—GAF—scale, which basically was a gauge that determined how crazy a person was. With the ranking of 21-30, it indicated that Miller was influenced by delusions, or hallucinations, and had a serious impairment when it came to communicating and judgment. He would sometimes act grossly inappropriately but had an inability to function in most areas of common interaction between himself and other individuals with whom he came into contact. Miller was totally unaware of the medical term GAF, and used the tag name Gaf for an entirely different reason.

Zerkerman got up from behind his desk, walked across the room, opened the door, and motioned to the agents to come back in. Miller was unchained from the chair and, while still shackled with waist and ankle restraints, escorted to the freight elevator, and given a ride down to the lower parking garage of General Hospital.

On the way down, Gaf thought about his next move. His escape move. He knew once they got back to the federal courthouse, he'd have only one chance to escape before he'd be thrown back into that cell.

With only one shot at this, it'd have to be after the agents upfront parked in the underground parking lot of the federal building. That's when he'd make his move— *as they swing open those heavy duty hinged doors to let me out.* They'd never know what hit them. Apparently, neither agent was aware of Gaf's background, working as a locksmith, where he became an expert at picking locks. Gaf figured he'd have less than fifteen minutes on the ride back to open the padlocks at his waist and ankles with the paperclips that he'd lifted off Doctor Zerkerman's desk. No problem for him. It'd be a snap. That gave him plenty of time to free himself.

During the ride back, both the agents sitting up front were totally oblivious to what Gaf was doing, much less what he had in store for them once they parked the SWAT truck in the underground parking lot of the federal building. They continued driving, making small talk about getting together with their girlfriends later that night to party and throw some back, since they'd both be off tomorrow. Those agents should have remembered what they learned in their initial FBI training, and that was, never take anything for granted when dealing with felons, especially Jeffrey Miller, who was previously on their Most Wanted list. That oversight would be a big mistake on their part.

Gaf had managed to pick both locks in only five minutes, so he sat and waited near the rear swinging doors, now holding the chains and leg irons, he'd use as weapons the second the rear door swung open. The one thing he didn't like was the idea of killing again. Recently, he'd been thinking that he was getting soft since going straight.

But he would kill, if need be. There was no fucking way he'd go back to jail again and be caged up like some animal. After all, he wouldn't treat a dog like that. Why should they do that to him? He was a friendly people person, once you got to know him.

They were now in the underground parking garage, and Gaf wasn't making a sound as he sat there near the two rear exit doors, patiently waiting for those doors to swing open so he could break free. He heard one of the agents fiddling with the lock, then he heard the slamming of the bar—the one holding the outer locks—being folded back, then the doors opened.

Bam, right across the heads of both agents. The heavy chains he used left indentations across their faces, causing both agents to stumble backward and fall to the concrete floor. Gaf hopped out and, just for good measure, wacked both across their chins as they lay there on the ground, stunned.

With the agents still alive, Gaf smilingly reached over and grabbed both agents FBI-issued Glock-19 revolvers from their shoulder holsters.

Now standing over the agents, he pointed both Glocks directly at each of their heads. Then he put one in his waistband and patted them down, confiscating their billfolds, shields, car keys, and cells phones. Next, even though they were blooded about the face, he ordered both to stand up and strip if they wanted to live. Then he hustled the two underwear'd agents into the rear of the SWAT truck, telling them, "Don't utter a word, or you're both dead."

Next, he swung both doors shut, hooked the padlock back onto the swinging arm, and snapped it shut. There was no chance they'd get out. He felt good about not having to waste those pig agents. He didn't know why. Maybe he *was* getting soft.

Even though it only took a matter of seconds to pull this off, Gaf knew he didn't have a minute to spare. At any time an officer of the court could enter the garage, and Gaf would probably have to kill him, whether he wanted to or not.

Before running toward a rear exit door he had spotted, he opened the SWAT truck's driver's-side door and found a duffle bag full of ammo, along with an FBI shotgun. He quickly snatched up both, knowing he'd need all the fire power he could get if he got into a gun battle with the law. He knew he'd be wanted dead or alive. The FBI wasn't going to be picky about how he died or if his rights were read to him if they decided to blow him away. If he was spotted, he was sure the command would be, "Shoot first and ask questions later," and, if cornered by agents again, like he was at the Lazy Day, it was going to be different this time. The good thing was he now had— thanks to those FBI agents cooped up in the SWAT truck—some clothes, even if they were suits; weapons; and cash. He was good to go.

With his heart pounding, he ran up to the rear wall of the garage, where he spotted an emergency door exit. He flung it open and, with a flash, he was gone, heading down the sidewalk, looking left and right for a place to ditch his jail garb and change into one of the agent's suits. He left the shotgun behind. It was too big to be carrying around on the open street. He'd make do with the Glock revolvers and a duffle bag of ammo.

Less than a block from the federal courthouse, he zeroed in on a fence surrounding a high-rise construction site. And, with no workers around that he could see, he climbed the chain-link fence and changed in one of those construction outhouses. He knew he needed to get out of the Bay Area quickly because, once the FBI agents were found locked up in the SWAT truck, San Francisco would be on total lock down.

While changing, he thought about his escape. Those two FBI agents were going to have a hard time explaining to their higher ups just how they managed to let Gaf escape, plus having the embarrassment of being found locked up in the rear of the SWAT truck, wearing only their tighty-whities. Ha, ha.

CHAPTER 35

The Plan

After returning from Barbados, I met up with my team in the conference room at the Frisco FBI headquarters. Director Becker was there, and he wasn't happy.

Director Becker didn't hide the way he felt about Miller's escape. "How could anyone working for the FBI let this happen? How could they let that sum-bitch, not only pick the locks on his waist and leg restraints, but then turn around and severely beat the two agents and take their clothes, leaving them both half naked and locked in an armored FBI SWAT truck? Need I say, I'm fucking pissed off? When the media gets wind of what went down, the FBI will be the laughing stock of, not only San Francisco, but Washington DC! Now my ass is now on the line, meaning I'm gonna have to explain this fuck-up to President Anderson."

With a grim look, Becker continued on with his rant, as if getting it all out of his system. "Even worse, Miller now has both agents' FBI shields, their two Glock-19 revolvers, and, from what I just found out a few minutes ago, he also made off with a huge supply of Glock-19 nine-millimeter ammo, left over from an FBI raid last month in Oakland, that some nit-wit agent apparently left behind in the cab of the SWAT truck. I can tell you this, some heads are gonna roll."

The director, still fuming, seemed as if he was on the verge of having a stroke or a heart attack. He looked directly at me. His body language gave me and the other team members the impression that he was looking for someone to pin Miller's escape on. Carla, Vack, Martinez, and I continued stoically sitting there. I wondered if the hammer was going to slam down on us, remembering that Becker had already mentioned that heads were going to roll.

"David, who did you inform in the prosecutor's office about Miller being an expert at picking locks, going back to his days prior to Docket Air when he worked as a locksmith? Please enlighten me."

Now the Director was even more worked up, if that was possible.

"That's noted in his arrest record, Director Becker, the one I personally filled out after we took Miller down at the Lazy Day Motel. And, just for the record, Miller's stint as an expert locksmith is clearly stated and highlighted on that arrest record."

Becker was still fuming, so I continued. "I don't like pointing fingers, but it's clear to me that someone in the prosecutor's office dropped the ball. It wasn't me or my team. I'll also add that none of us sitting here at this table are happy with what has transpired. Agents Simmons, Vack, Martinez, and I had pretty much worked around the clock, with none of us getting a whole lot of sleep while we tracked down Jeffrey Miller."

Of course, I didn't mention the little sex romp Carla and I had in Sonoma.

"I stand by my team," I said. "And, personally, I'd be offended by anyone who points the finger in our direction. With all due respect, Director Becker, hindsight is always 20/20. So under the circumstances, I say now is the time for my team to refocus and put all our energies into bringing Miller back in again, instead of dwelling over something we can't change. My team is ready to meet that challenge. Now it's personal for us. We want Miller back in custody as much as anyone does and, as far as the four of us sitting here at this conference table are concerned, the sooner Miller's back in custody, the better."

I glanced over at Carla, Vack, and Martinez. They were all nodding their heads, yes.

Director Becker needed to get back to Washington, DC, and explain this mess to President Anderson, but he had one parting comment before walking out the conference room door, and he had somewhat cooled off after hearing what I said in defense of my team. "I'm leaving now, David. I'll be back in DC tonight. I want your plan for re-arresting Miller waiting for me when I land in DC. I also want Miller back in jail before he gets desperate and kills again. If he does kill again, we'll probably all be looking for jobs, no matter who's to blame. You get my drift?"

"Yes, I do, Director, loud and clear."

I was relieved this tension-filled meeting was over. It wasn't as if Becker hadn't told me or the team anything we weren't already aware of, but that wasn't to say I didn't understand the position Becker was in, considering he had President Anderson on his ass. Director Becker was the so-called "point man" for anything that went sideways with the FBI.

That made me wonder if being appointed FBI director would be worth it. I might have to re-think that move.

๏๛๏

After Director Becker left the conference room, I stood up and addressed my team. I told them to disregard what had just transpired. "Forget what just came out of Becker's mouth. We did our job by bringing Miller in. The director's just looking for someone to blame it on, so now our job is to do a repeat and bring Miller back in again. This city is on total lock-down, all roads and highways coming in and out of San Francisco have check-points set up. Let's put our minds together and think like Miller. Agent Simmons, that's where I'm gonna be depending on you and your expertise as a profiler."

Carla perked up, giving the impression she appreciated the opportunity to point the team's second track down in the right direction—namely, helping discover the whereabouts of Jeffrey Miller, ending with the team arresting and bringing him back to face the consequences, meaning that Miller got the death penalty handed down by a jury as punishment for the gruesome crimes he'd committed.

Carla walked over to the white board, picked up the marker, and started by outlining what moves she believed Miller contemplated after making his way out of the underground parking lot and into the clear. "This is what I believe Miller most likely did after leaving the underground parking lot. First, since his capture, Miller's face, via the FBI's Most Wanted poster, has been plastered all over every media outlet in the area, plus all news links known to exist on the internet. If seen out in the public, Miller will be recognized. We're counting on the public calling in tips, and those phone tips will be critical in helping us find Miller and put him away for good this time. For him, there'll be no escape from the San Francisco area by land, air, or sea, unless he pulls a Houdini and vanishes into thin air. I don't see that happening. He'll obviously be lying low until he gets desperate, after he either runs out of food, water, or cash, causing him to make a stupid move. My money's on the stupid move, like the one he made by heading to the Lazy Day Motel for a piece of ass."

Even though this was serious business, that last comment brought out silent, tight-lipped grins from me, Vack, and Martinez.

Carla makes another point, as she marks up the whiteboard. "I'm positive Miller will use the lifted FBI shields and Glocks to either steal a vehicle or commandeer one through intimidation. He'll claim it's a law-enforcement matter to any motorist dumb enough to hand over their car or truck. So far, that's not happened. At least not that we know of, but there's a strong possibility he's already pulled that stunt, and we just don't know about it yet. If he has, then he'll need to buy gas to get around the city while he looks for a way out of the San Francisco area. We'll need to request that the SFPD do a face-to-face meeting with every gas station and convenience store owner in the Bay Area, impressing upon them that they need to be on the alert for Miller. We'll pretty much demand that these businesses let law enforcement prominently display, in plain sight for all customers who are coming and going, our re-issued Most Wanted poster of Miller. I want his face burned into the memory banks of every citizen in Frisco, including all the outlying areas," she said, now sounding like a seasoned profiler. "That's how we're gonna get the break that'll enable this team to take him down again. There is one other thing. We need to bring a bloodhound over to the underground parking lot of the federal building and see if it can pick up Miller's scent. Even though it's been a couple of days, I'm sure there's still plenty of skin cells left behind, that'll be picked up by the bloodhound and lead us to the spot where he discarded his prison garb, changed into one of the agent's suits, and disappeared. The bloodhound can also be used to pick up on both the agent's scents coming off the suits they gave up. We'll work it both ways, after locating the spot where he changed, then continue using the bloodhound by focusing in on the scent coming off the suit he changed. From that point, we'll branch out and follow the scent to wherever it takes us and mark the spot where it disappears.

"Our goal will be to tighten the noose around Miller's neck," she said. "When it's tightened enough, giving him nowhere to run, I predict he'll do one of two things. He'll either kill himself or just give up and turn himself in. Either way will work for the FBI. Dead or alive, we don't care which way he's brought in."

Carla then turned, looked directly at me, handed me the white board marker, and sat back down at the table.

I stood, making no notations on the whiteboard, but adding a final suggestion to the plan just outlined by Carla. "Thank you, Agent Simmons. I was actually thinking somewhat along those same lines." I looked over at Vack. "I'm thinking, wherever it was that Miller ended up changing his clothes, I believe after that he then probably either caught a cab or jumped on any bus that came along and rode to who knows where. Our job is to find that out. We need to follow up on that assumption. I'm sure the local FBI and SFSP have thought of that angle, but we, as a team, still need to blanket the area in and around the federal building, just in case something was missed. Vack, I want you to check all cab companies, along with city transit bus lines that were moving through the area surrounding the federal courthouse at the time of the escape. Question all the cabbies and bus drivers who worked the area at that time. Maybe they saw something."

"No problem, boss," Vack agreed, just like the loyal FBI he was. "I'm all over it."

I nodded at Vack as he left the conference room with his small spiral notepad in hand, seemingly chomping at the bit to hit the streets and do what he did best. That was, to start his own Columbo-style investigation.

"Martinez, make arrangements to get an FBI bloodhound and handler out to the escape scene and see if we get a hit on a scent, or scents. Even though you'll have the hound and handler with you, I want you to still use your expertise as a special agent and analyze Miller's possible escape routes as if you were in Millers shoes. Stay with the bloodhound until Miller's scent, or the scents of the both agents' clothing disappears."

"No problem, boss. I'll head upstairs right now and request a bloodhound and handler then head on over to the federal building. I'm hoping the hound will lead us in the right direction."

Martinez exited the conference room, leaving me and Carla all alone. With no-one around, I could now talk freely to her. "You know, Carla, if it were under any other circumstances and not here at headquarters, I'd be tempted to unzip that mini skirt you're wearing, pull your thong down to your ankles, bend you over this conference table, and fuck that ass of yours."

"I know, David. You're like me. We're both horn dogs. That's one of the traits I really like about you. If it weren't for the chance of getting caught, I'd unzip those slacks you're wearing, pull out your stiff hard cock, and suck it until you cum in my mouth, or maybe I'd pull off and let you give me a facial."

Thinking about what Carla just told me gave me a

hard-on. I knew we both had to get out of the conference room before we let caution fly to the wind and got caught doing something we'd soon regret. We'd get a room tonight and fuck each other ragged. I knew that would relieve the stress both of us had pent up in us, since the Barbados fiasco, compounded now by Miller escaping.

I left the conference room, wondering, where Jeffrey Miller was. Surely, he had to be somewhere in the San Francisco area.

Later in the afternoon, while on the phone with Vack, I got a call from Martinez and put Vack on hold.

"Boss, its Martinez. The bloodhound tracked Miller to a high-rise construction site, just a half block from the federal building. Apparently, Miller hopped the security fence there and then changed in a port-a-potty on the construction site. That's where we found his jail garb. Since it was Friday, there were no construction workers on site, thus no witnesses because of the new union rules, giving them every other Friday off. From there, the bloodhound followed Miller's scent to the edge of the curb on Mission Street, and that's where his trail went cold. I'm thinking Miller either caught a bus or a cab and just disappeared."

"Thanks for the update, Martinez. I have Vack on hold. Let me see if he's found out anything. In the meantime, bring the hound back, and we'll start a search in earnest after Vack tells me what he's found after checking out the cab and bus companies."

"You've got it, boss. I'll see you shortly. I'm heading back now."

"Thanks Martinez."

Vack had contacted a cab driver who said he thought it was Miller who he'd dropped off at the docks. That was a good start.

After meeting with the team again, I announced, "Split

up and let the hunt begin. Let's do what we do, what we specialize in, and bring Miller back in again. We need to checkout campgrounds and flop houses in both San Francisco and Oakland. I'm pretty sure we'll find him living in a rat hole in one of these two cities. Vack, you and Martinez hit the road and head down to the docks. Talk to everyone who was in the area Friday morning. I'm sure Miller was seen by someone who may have noticed a strange man wearing a nice suit, looking out of place, no matter how much he tried to blend in. One thing that clown'll never be mistaken for is an FBI agent, even though he's wearing one of the agent's suits and packing their two Glock-19 revolvers. No way."

"You got it boss," Vack acknowledged.

I went on to tell him and Martinez, "While you two are checking out the dock area, Agent Simmons and I are gonna head on over to the taskforce hotline division of the FBI and see what kind of leads they're getting, or have received. I'll make sure nothing was overlooked. I want Miller brought in within the next twenty-four hours, or sooner."

Vack nodded in agreement.

"No problem, boss," Martinez agreed. "With the way the SFPD and the Bureau have the area shut down, I'm fairly positive Miller will have no chance of sneaking out of town. Personally, I believe he's nearby."

"Okay, you two inform me the minute you find something." I glanced back at Carla and then back at both Vack and Martinez. "One other thing before the two of you go. As you well know, I have the director all over me, even more now than before. So if you wanna make me happy, find out where Miller is. That's all I have now, so let's get on with the second track down."

Carla and I then headed to the large hotline conference room the FBI had setup just one floor up.

"Frankly, I'm surprised Miller's not already in custody," Carla commented while riding the elevator up. "It's almost as if he just vanished in plain sight."

I nodded in silent agreement.

CHAPTER 36

Vanished in Plain Sight

After ditching his jail clothes and changing in one of those construction site outhouses, Miller was transformed from a jailbird to a respectable-looking suit-wearing civilian, in his mind. Then he made it to the curb, flagged down the next cab, and had the driver drop him off at Market and Embarcadero, where he caught a ferry over to Oakland. Miller felt like a free man now.

After docking at the Oakland pier, he walked a short distance and found a used car rental yard in a rundown part of Oakland. Frankly, he had always thought most of Oakland was rundown. The cars in the lot looked like rejects from a junkyard. Anyway, he figured this would be his best chance of getting his hands on some kind of transportation without doing a carjacking and attracting any attention to himself.

He walked up to this old, weather-beaten-looking car rental office, peeked through the picture window, and saw some old gray-haired lady sitting behind the counter, smoking like a chimney. He opened the rickety squeaky door and walked into a nicotine cloud that seemed to fill the entire room. That old chain-smoking hag wanted $40 dollars a day, plus a $100 deposit to rent one of those junk cars that littered her lot out front. Lying, he told her he only needed the car for one day, knowing all the while he had no intention of returning whatever piece of junk he ended up with.

Lucky for him, when she asked for ID, he showed her one of the FBI agent's California's driver's licenses. She never compared the photo on the license to his face. He figured she was mainly interested in the money. Between the two agents' wallets, there was over $400 cash, so he paid her, grabbed the keys, and left. He was happy. He still had over two hundred dollars left, and now he had a way to get around, maybe a way out of the area.

That night he slept in the car in the parking lot of a combination strip bar and casino. A place you wouldn't find him, if it wasn't for the fact that he was on the run again. The lot was packed with cars, so he blended in nicely, since most of them were older models. People coming here to blow their money on gambling probably all thought, "Today is gonna be my lucky day! I'm gonna win enough to buy a new car!" But that never happened.

After waking up early the next morning, and while it was still dark out, he climbed over from the back seat to the front driver's seat, stretched his legs, and turned on the local AM twenty-four-hour news station. He was curious to see if his escape made the news and, sure enough, he was the main topic of conversation. Actually, the thing that bothered him the most was that the full story wasn't told. The prosecutor and FBI had a part in giving the media a watered down version of his escape. Gaf figured the FBI was trying to save face, not to mention all the embarrassment and grief they were both getting from the public, because they let a serial killer slip through their fingers. That was not to mention how he rearranged the two agents' faces with the leg and waist chain restraints he'd managed to get out of while en route back to the federal building's holding cell. No problem. He was sure a little plastic surgery would clear that right up.

The on-air news broadcaster sounded like one of those old-time cookie cutter news guys from the 1960s.

"...This just in. Jeffrey Miller, better known as the Gaf Killer, has escaped after returning from a court-ordered psychiatric exam at General Hospital. That's all we have for now, other than that Miller is extremely dangerous and, if spotted, he should not be approached. Jeffrey Miller is a serial killer who's on the FBI's Most Wanted list for the second time around. And, like I just mentioned, do not approach him. If you spot him, please call the FBI hotline at 888-187-1185, and the FBI will take it from there."

"Thank you, Jan. The station will continue with updates as soon as they come in. By the way, we've also posted a copy of the FBI's Most Wanted poster on the station's website."

Still sitting behind the wheel of this piece-of-shit car, Gaf reached over and turned off the AM station. Frankly, he was annoyed after hearing that half-assed news broadcast. Why wasn't he given credit for that slick escape maneuver he pulled off? After all, no one else had ever escaped from a heavily armored FBI SWAT vehicle before he came along.

He was beginning to feel disrespected again, and that was not good for anyone who pissed him off. He might have to make a fresh kill to get back the respect he felt he deserved. What he was hoping was that he'd run into that FBI weasel, Agent, Vack, again and, when he did, this time he wouldn't treat him as nice as before when he had him chained to the basement wall of his row house. Yeah, Vack was going to be a dead man, for sure, if they ran into each other again.

There's some payback coming his way for slapping me around like he did after I was already on the ground and handcuffed that night in the Lazy Day's parking lot. To gain back the self-respect he wasn't given that night, Gaf would handcuff Agent Vack then, as Vack looked death in the face, Gaf would shoot him execution style. He was going to love watching the fear on Vack's pig face, with him knowing this was going to be his last day on Planet Earth.

I'm a friendly people person. I wonder why people don't see that in me. Oh, well, he couldn't dwell on other people's inadequacies. He had more pressing problems to worry about at the moment. Like finding a '50s diner so he could chow down on a patty melt with cheese and wash it down with a tall glass of freshly brewed iced tea, accompanied by a big lemon wedge. It wasn't iced tea without the lemon wedge. He wasn't a hard man to please. He was a simple man with simple needs, like killing his enemies and eating at diners.

Before he pulled out of the parking lot full of losers, he'd pretty much decided he was going to have to rob another bank. Something he hadn't done since his flight attendant days at Docket Air. Those were the days. He always had money then. Plenty of cash. Enough cash to spend carousing bars in the Castro District when he was gay. That was all changed now, thanks to that fine piece of ass he got from Robin Osborne. From what he'd heard, most women really liked to do basically three things— gold dig, fuck off and not work, and shop till they dropped, along with giving blow jobs and fucking. That was pretty much how it worked. So now, while he was on the run, that meant if he wanted to score some more fine-looking female tail, he'd need cash, and lots of it. But first he had to cruise out of this parking lot and find a bank that was in an isolated area of Oakland. Those isolated banks were a piece of cake to knock over, especially credit unions. They seemed to always have the most cash on hand.

Right after he did the bank score, he'd dump this junk car in the bay. He was sure the old hag back at the rental yard would report it stolen after a couple of days, when it dawned on her that he was never bringing that car back. He didn't think they'd ever find it and, even if they did, he'd be long gone from the Bay Area by then.

CHAPTER 37

Hotline Tip

The next morning I got a call from Agent Vack, giving me an update.

"Boss, Martinez and I have split up, hitting diners and flop houses, but, so far, we've had no luck."

"Okay, Vack, keep pounding the streets. By the way, I want you both to also hit up car rental agencies. It might be a longshot, but you never know what a psycho like Miller will try. Especially now that he's desperate. I'm sure he knows by now the FBI is mounting an all-out search for him. Miller's liable to try anything to stay free. If you do run into Miller and positively ID him, shoot first and ask questions later. Right now, I want him, dead or alive. I'll be talking to Director Becker later on to give him an update, so I need something positive to give him, hopefully letting him know Miller's arrest is imminent, or that he's dead."

"No problem, boss. I like that idea. Martinez and I will team up now and start hitting all the car rental agencies in

Oakland and, if I do run into Miller, he's a dead man. You can take that to the bank."

"Okay, Vack. Call me if you run across something."

"You got it, boss!"

ↇↈↇ

At midday Carla and I headed over to FBI headquarters to pay the hotline a visit for the second day in a row. After exiting the elevator and, while we were both standing outside in the hallway, before we entered the room, I said to Carla, "You know, I think it's time I put your talents to some serious use and have you try to think exactly like Miller. We're early in the second day of Miller's escape, and no creditable tips have flowed into the hotline as of yet, other than the cabbie who Agent Vack interviewed. That's the cabbie who claimed it was Miller he picked up at the construction site near the federal courthouse, drove him over to the docks, and dropped him off there."

Still standing in the hallway, somewhat just down from the entrance to the hotline command center, Simmons apparently got the hint. While discreetly huddled together, we begin talking in whispered tones. "That location makes sense," Carla said, taking the lead. "It places Miller at the docks where he could have easily caught a ferry over to Oakland. Next, it's obvious he's gonna need a way to get around, and I don't see him taking another cab or riding a bus. Doing that would be way too risky, now that he's the topic of all the local news broadcasts. I'd bet Miller has either stolen a vehicle or has tried to rent one. If he does manage to get his hands on a set of wheels, Miller could be long gone by the time we find out."

"You know, Carla, I like that. Actually, I was thinking

along those same lines. Maybe I should moonlight as an FBI profiler. I'll bet I'd be a good one!"

As soon as those words came out of my mouth, I knew I had said the wrong thing to Carla, an agent who had spent years perfecting her craft. In return, she gave me a nasty look, the type of look a woman gives a man when she was fixing to cut him off. I had to regroup. I couldn't have that happening.

I knew I had to save face. I needed to comeback with something having the air and sound of the seasoned FBI professional that I was and not to just look at Carla simply as a sex toy. Truthfully, I had a hard time not thinking of her that way since there had been an intense sexual history between the two of us whenever we'd had a chance to work together.

Managing to come up with an on the spot comment, I rattled off an adlib, something sounding like we were meeting for the first time. "Agent Simmons, give me your professional opinion. As an FBI profiler, tell me what you think is going through Jeffrey Miller's mind right now. Where do you think law enforcement should be concentrating their resources?"

Carla perked up, giving me the impression I'd just missed the bullet and wouldn't be penalized sexually, like I'd feared.

"We need every available law enforcement officer, and that includes our team, to scour the entire Oakland area for Jeffrey Miller," she said. "I feel he's close by. That's where we'll most likely find him if we act quick, no matter what rat hole he's crawled into."

Before entering the hotline room, I gave Vack and Martinez a call and told both to keep working the streets and, in particular, car rental agencies in Oakland, because Carla believed Miller had most likely rented a car there somewhere. Carla smiled. Of course, I didn't tell her I had already mentioned to Vack earlier to check the car rentals agencies. I wasn't that stupid. I liked having sex with her.

With that, we both walked into the FBI control center and were immediately motioned over by the agent in charge, Ms. Annette Longstine. She'd been with the FBI since graduating from Brown with a master's degree in criminal science. And, now, twenty years later, she had a PhD in criminal science. Agent Longstine had an A-type personality—a no-nonsense, by the book, take charge personality. The type neither Carla nor I cared for. But, hey, if she could help move this second track-down in the right direction, resulting in the arrest of Miller, I was all for it.

Apparently Carla and I weren't walking fast enough for Agent Longstine. That was when we heard, "Hey, Agents Simmons and Drake, get the lead out. We just got what I feel is a break in this case."

Now we were both standing next to this loud, rather short, intimidating female agent, as she began to clue us in.

"One of the hotline operators has a woman in Oakland on the line who owns and runs a used car rental business. She just mentioned she happened to be watching the news in her rental office and believes it was Miller who she rented a car to yesterday morning."

It was at that time that I took over the call. The rental car owner rambled on, telling me that she now believed it was Miller who she rented a car to, going on to say he hadn't bothered returning the older model Ford Taurus. From there, I got her to give me the name on the ID he used. As it turned out, it was the name of one of the agents who drove the SWAT truck back from General Hospital. I also got the plate number from her and passed it on to Agent Longstine so she could alert all law enforcement agencies. Now I suggested we form a dragnet around the perimeter of Oakland, using all available FBI agents and civilian police agencies. There was no doubt, that customer was our man.

"Thank you, Agent Longstine. I'm contacting the director right now and asking him to make all FBI agents in Oakland available, in an effort to close off all exits, coming and going, giving Miller no way out. If Miller's there, we'll find him."

"I agree with that, Agents Drake and Simmons," Agent Longstine said, sounding like a military boot camp instructor. "I will proceed to help out anyway I can on my end." Now she was getting all worked up, with her eyes bulging, and her forehead veins swelling up. "Let's work together and bring this sum-bitch in!"

If I hadn't known better, I'd have thought Becker and Longstine were related because of the way they both use the adjective "sum-bitch."

Right after Longstine made that comment to Carla and me, I got a call from Agent Vack.

"Boss, I'm at a used car rental yard owned by a little old lady, telling me she thinks she rented an old Ford Taurus to Miller yesterday morning. It's overdue, and he hasn't brought it back."

"I'm way ahead of you, Vack. Apparently that same lady just called the hotline a short time ago. You and Martinez stay where you are. We're headed over there shortly."

"You got it, boss. I have a good feeling about this. I think his ass is ours now."

Agent Longstine alerted all media to be on the lookout for an older model Ford Taurus with California license number 8E6741. By putting that hotline information out there, she knew that the noose would now begin to tighten around Jeffrey Miller's neck, but they needed to work fast. Longstine also knew Miller would dump the Taurus as soon as he heard that info broadcasted by the local media.

Carla and I rolled up to the car rental yard and parked next to the office, located near the back of the lot. We got out and met up with Vack and Martinez, who were waiting for us just outside the rental office. The structure looked like some type of homemade gray weather-beaten wood shed that someone had slapped together, using scrap lumber, and then just simply nailed a hand painted *Office* sign over the entrance, proclaiming "This is where rental transactions take place."

We're definitely not in the high rent district, I thought.

Agent Vack warned me before I walked up and knocked on the rental office door. "Boss, she's a little old black lady who's a tad on the grouchy side. I think it has something to do with her deceased husband."

"What do you mean by that, Vack?"

"Well, boss, just go ahead and knock on the door. You'll see."

"Okay, Vack."

Now standing behind me, Agents Vack and Martinez were both gritting their teeth, trying hard not to grin.

I knocked lightly on the door then opened it to go in and the stench of nicotine hit me right in the face. I backed away, then cracked the door slightly open, just enough to get my head in, and let the lady sitting behind the counter, know who I was. Sticking my head and hand through the cracked-open door, I flipped open my wallet and flashed my shield. "Ma'am, I'm Special Agent Drake with the FBI and, if you wouldn't mind, can you please step outside so we can ask you a few more questions about the tip you called in a short time ago. Sorry, but I can't come in. I'm allergic to nicotine."

That was a lie of course. It's just that I couldn't stomach the smell of nicotine. With a frown on her face, she put her cigarette out in a large round glass ashtray that was already over flowing with a giant mound of cigarette butts.

Standing outside, I planned on briefly questioning her. "I'm sorry, ma'am, I didn't catch your name."

In a rather unfriendly tone, she glared at me. "It's Ms. Bertha Barsdale."

Then Bertha Barsdale started rambling on about stuff that had nothing to do with this case. I tried to remain calm.

"I let my idiot husband, Junebug Barsdale, may he rest in peace, talk me into moving from Arkansas to California twenty years ago," Ms. Barsdale ranted, getting worked up. "And we eventually ended up in this God forsaken place called Oakland. He claimed we'd get rich renting cars! What a crock of shit that was! What the hell was he thinking? Rich my ass. I can't even afford to buy name-brand cigarettes. You know, I have to go over to the local Puff N' Smoke and buy generic cigarettes!" she shouted with a crunched up face. "Do you have any idea how embarrassing that is, Mr. Blake?"

"Ms. Barsdale, my name is Agent Drake."

I knew I had to take control of this one-way conversation, or else I and the team would be here for hours, trying to pick Ms. Barsdale's brain.

"Just for the record, Ms. Barsdale, I wanted to let you know there's a possibility that some reward money may be coming your way if your tip leads us to the capture of Jeffrey Miller."

Her ears perked up, just like the rest of the tipsters ears had done whenever I'd brought up the reward money. She was probably already counting the money, knowing it would be her ticket out of Oakland and back to Arkansas.

"Okay, Ms. Barsdale, let's get started. We need to act fast. Are you aware of the crimes Miller's been accused of committing?"

"No, I'm not. I only called because I saw his face on TV while watching the news on my twenty-year-old black-and-white. Mr. Blake, the main reason I called is because that fucker has my car and I want it back!"

Feeling that this is conversation was still going nowhere, I again tried hard to calm her down and get back on track. "Ms. Barsdale, I can appreciate how you feel. Do you have theft insurance?"

Apparently that wasn't the right thing to bring up.

"Are you kidding, Mr. Blake? Do you have any idea what the blue book value on a 1989 Ford Taurus is?"

"No, I don't, Ms. Barsdale, and, by the way, my name is Agent David Drake." Now I was getting frustrated, thinking maybe the team should just hat up and start working the streets of Oakland. "Okay, Ms. Barsdale, I'll wrap this up with just one more question, then we have to get going. After Miller drove off the lot, did you see which way he went?"

"Yes I did." Then Bertha Barsdale started walking rather quickly toward the drive-in entrance at the front of the car lot, with me and the rest of the team following in tow behind her. We were all were surprised she was able to move that quickly, being she was a chain smoker and all.

Now standing at the curb, this short stocky woman, with an unlit cigarette hanging out of her mouth, struck a pose, like George Washington did when he crossed the Delaware, and pointed north.

"That sum-bitch headed north, up Market Street and, I might add, at a rather fast pace. The bastard probably has a lead foot, and I'll bet he's blown the engine on that Taurus. That's why he hasn't brought it back!"

"No, Ms. Barsdale. Jeffrey Miller is on the FBI's Most Wanted list. He's a wanted serial killer. That's why he didn't come back. Anyway, I appreciate your help. At least now we know what direction Miller was headed when he left here."

I reached inside my suit coat pocket and pulled out one of my cards. "Here's my card. Just in case Miller does return. If you hear from him, please give me a call. We're heading out now. Again, I appreciate your time and co-operation, Ms. Barsdale."

"Are you crazy, Agent Blake? You think I'm gonna hang around here all by myself with no protection, not knowing if that maniac might come back and kill me! Hell no! I'm closing up, and heading home where I can hide out. I'll stay there until you catch him Agent Blake. I can't believe you think I'm stupid enough to just hang out here and wait to get killed!"

"Thank you, Ms. Barsdale, and I agree with you. That would probably be the best thing to do at this moment, even though the chances of Miller coming back here are pretty slim. Oh, by the way, on my name, I'm Special Agent Drake, not Blake, but no problem."

"Okay, Agent Drake. See there? I didn't fuckup your name this time."

Vack and Martinez couldn't hold back any longer. They both exploded in muffled laughter, while holding their hands over their mouths in a vain attempt to not bring attention to themselves, knowing that I was already frustrated.

Vack and Martinez stated at a later date, "This entire attempt to question Ms. Barsdale seemed like a scripted routine right out of a TV comedy sitcom."

Carla also found it rather amusing and would joke about it to me for months to come.

Vack and Martinez jumped into their FBI standard-issue blue Ford Crown Victorias, followed by Carla and I, and drove north up Market Street. As we drove, I turned to Carla and said, "He's here somewhere here in Oakland. We just have to find him."

She nodded in agreement.

CHAPTER 38

Nowhere to Run, Nowhere to Hide

Gaf was now on his third day of freedom. That freedom was quickly coming to an end, seeing how the FBI, the US Marshals, SFPD, and OPD Departments were all roaming around San Francisco and Oakland, shaking down informants for info, in the hopes of locating him. And on top of that, the governor had imposed dusk-to-dawn curfews on cities as far north as Vallejo, California, and south as far as San Jose—a stretch of over seventy miles, running straight through Oakland. The FBI and US Marshals were also conducting an intense nationwide search for him, just in case he'd somehow slipped through the massive dragnet going on throughout the counties surrounding Alameda. Gaf now had nowhere to run and nowhere to hide.

Since leaving the parking lot of the casino strip joint, he'd contemplated his next move while sitting in the rented Ford Taurus that he'd parked inside the garage of an abandoned and boarded up house on Boston Avenue. Strangely, it was located only about a mile from where he'd rented the car. He had decided to restrict his movements to late night, just to avoid being recognized while driving. Now he'd come to the realization that even that was going to be impossible, because of the dust-to-dawn curfew.

With the garage door shut, Gaf scanned the interior of this gloomy, trashy, dark, and dingy garage. Before hiding out, he had stopped at a 7/11 and bought enough of their nasty-tasting junk food to last him two or three days.

"Why me?" he wondered out loud. "How did it come down to this? I'm a nice guy. If only the people I killed hadn't disrespected me, then we could have probably developed a friendship. I just don't get why people think I'm not normal. Yeah, when I think about being disrespected, the first people who come to mind are Ms. Hayes, who got me fired from Docket Air; Racheal, that waitress at the Bay Diner, who viciously mocked me; and, especially, Robin Osborne. She's the bitch who's responsible for putting me in this latest fucked-up situation that I find myself in now. My relationship with her could have developed into something, but no, she had to rat me out to the FBI. Oh, if I ever run into her again, she's as dead as a doornail. Robin Osborne is the real reason I'm cowering here in the dark with this piece of a crap car."

Knowing his cash flow was shrinking, he reached in his rear pants pocket, pulled out his thin billfold, and opened it up. "Fuck! Now I'm down to fifty dollars." He now knew he had to do something desperate, or else he'd soon be out of cash. "I'm gonna have to do something I haven't done for a while. Rob a bank. Yeah, but, this time, I can't be choosy about the type of bank, like I was when I was robbing banks across the nation, while working at Docket Air. Back then I would only rob credit unions, and I robbed a bunch of them."

Gaf got out of the car and paced back and forth. He continued rambling on, as if he were telling his story to someone in this empty darkened garage. "Actually, I lost count after the twelfth bank robbery. I couldn't believe how easy those credit unions were to knock over, and they always had tons of cash on hand, especially on Fridays. After I robbed a couple of credit unions, it became addicting. And, besides that, it gave me a big rush just getting my hands on that much money, knowing I wouldn't be paying income tax on any of it. Frankly, I was surprised that the employees I knew and worked with never put two and two together, seeing how I always paid in cash and never used credit cards for anything I bought. I think it's probably because I was cool and didn't flaunt it."

Still pacing, he went over a plan in his head that he thought might work. Even though it was now daylight outside, about nine a.m. Monday morning, he decided he was going to take his chances and cautiously walk the neighborhood in board daylight, leaving the car here in the garage, and scope out banks that were close by.

He sort of had a plan. When he strolled into the bank, he'd walk in with both Glock 19s out, one in each hand, to show he meant business. Once inside the bank, he'd keep as cool as a cucumber, look around a little, and, just for good measure, fire off a couple rounds right into the ceiling, just to get everyone's attention.

Then he'd announce, "This is a stick-up! Kiss the ground, motherfuckers, if you wanna live!"

That should make all the big-assed old ladies, wearing those balloon granny panties, have them wad up in their butt cracks.

The men would be no problem. Men were pussies. They never resisted. They were always extremely happy that he hadn't chosen to put a round in them, as they lay there whimpering and whining to their mommies, just hoping to get out of this alive.

When he left the bank, he'd zigzag his way back to this abandoned house and stay in the garage until he felt the heat had died down, with the pigs thinking he'd somehow managed to slip out of Oakland. Only thing was, he wasn't sure how long he'd have to hole up here. He knew he could monitor the news on the car's radio then, when he thought it was safe, he'd make his move and leave the Taurus where it was, while he headed for parts unknown.

He didn't know what he'd use for wheels right now, but he'd figure it out once he decided to leave this boarded-up house for good. He would probably have to steal a car this time since traveling by bus, train, cab, or plane was not an option. He'd always been good at hot wiring cars and trucks, so that wouldn't be a problem, as long as he didn't get caught.

Yeah, that was his plan. He liked it. He just hoped it worked but, if it didn't, he had a feeling he was going back to jail, probably for good this time.

Standing next to the Taurus in the darkened garage, he decided that, since the law most likely figured he was wearing one of the FBI agent's suits he took when he escaped, he needed to change clothes and get out of this suit that he'd been wearing for the last couple of days.

Looking through some piled up trash in one corner of the garage, he found a discarded Raiders baseball cap; an old wrinkled-up, oversized, flowery Hawaiian shirt; and a pair of rolled-up, tattered Levis.

How convenient. And even though they weren't clean, he put them on. He didn't care—anything to get him out of this FBI monkey suit. There, now he felt normal again. He didn't know how FBI agents could stand wearing suits for their entire pig career. He had never been a suit guy. He could never shoot and kill anyone while wearing a suit. It would be way too formal.

Next, he quietly opened the garage side door, leading to the backyard, and sneaked out, as if he were breaking out of San Quentin State Prison. He looked around the yard, to make sure the coast was clear, then hustled over to the rear wooden gate, unlatched it, looked up and down the alley, and began walking toward Lincoln. He subconsciously worked at being as nondescript as possible. If anyone walked by him, he definitely didn't look them in the face, while he strolled down the sidewalk, scoping out Lincoln Street for a credit union. Any credit union would do. If he didn't spot one, he'd just have to make do and hit a standard bank.

He'd walked not more than a half block north up Lincoln when he spotted a credit union, the Peoples Credit Union slash bank. He couldn't believe his luck. Before going in, he ducked behind some tall shrubs near the bank and placed one of the Glock-19s in his backside waistband. Then he pulled the oversized Hawaiian shirt down over it. He tucked the other Glock-19 in his front waistband, and now both Glocks were hidden under his shirt. With a confident strut, he emerged from the bushes and entered the credit union. He knew, from past experience, this should be a routine heist, going down just like all the other cakewalk bank robberies he'd committed.

Little did he know, it was about to hit the fan.

He walked in through the swinging glass doors and noticed it wasn't that busy. So, while still in stride, he changed his game plan and decided that whipping out the Glock revolvers, like he planned on doing, and firing off a few rounds into the ceiling would attract way too much attention. Instead, he walked casually over to a counter displaying deposit slips, pulled one out of the slot, and wrote a demand note. *Quickly, put all the money in your drawers in a bank bag and give it to me if you want to live. No dye packs, or I'll come back here and blow you away. Understood?*

At the window, everything was going as planned, and he was thinking he'd soon be out of there with thousands of dollars. It was then that he heard words he didn't want to hear.

"I'm a cop, drop the weapon, slowly turn around, and get on your knees. Do it now, or you're a dead man!"

At that moment, the teller he'd given the note to fainted and dropped to the floor like someone with a serious narcolepsy problem. Gaf knew this was it. It was between him and this cop as to who lived or died. He let the Glock fall out of his hand to the floor then turned around slowly, knowing he still had the other Glock-19 in his rear waistband.

Now that he'd turned around, he saw what was apparently a cop in plain clothes. He was standing there, aiming his 9 mm straight at Gaf and, at the same time, holding out his OPD shield in his other outstretched hand.

"Get on the floor, now!"

Gaf knew there was no way he was going to do that and have this pig cop find the other Glock on him. The seething frustration radiated from the cop's red face. Gaf just stood there, facing him down with his hands in the air, showing no hint of fear. He ignored the command to drop to the floor. He did have one thing in his favor. He knew the cop wouldn't shoot what he thought was an unarmed man because there was way too many witnesses here in the bank, watching this whole thing go down.

Now Gaf knew they were getting closer to the moment of truth.

"Get on the fucking deck!" the cop yelled again.

Gaf just stood there, waiting for his chance to so slightly distract this cop, reach behind, grab the Glock from his rear waistband, and send this wanna-be hero to a dreamland far, far away, from which he'd never return.

Still standing with both of his hands in the air, Gaf found himself getting more pissed-off by the moment with the way the cop was disrespecting him in the middle of this bank lobby. If Gaf got his chance, he was going to enjoy wasting this cop before he made it out the front door with the cash score.

Just then, one of the glass entry doors swung open, and this cop fool—now only five feet away, still standing with his gun drawn down on Gaf—just for a an instant turned his head to the left to see who was walking into the bank. That's when Gaf made his move. He reached around behind his back, grabbed his other Glock-19, and bam, bam, bam!

That cop fell to the floor like a limp rag, then Gaf grabbed the bag of money and rushed out the front door, brushing by the customer who had just entered the bank. He couldn't help noticing the old man was shaking like the leaf on a tree on a windy March day in the country. Gaf was pretty sure the old man would now forever have a phobia of entering banks.

Gaf headed south down Lincoln, making it back to the boarded-up house in only a few minutes, entered the garage, and just sat in the Taurus, waiting for something to happen. He had a strong feeling his luck was running out. He had a feeling of doom, being trapped with nowhere to run, especially if he'd just killed a cop. He knew he'd be tracked down like he was some kind of mad dog if Agent Drake had any say so about it. Gaf was sure his team wouldn't be showing any mercy when they found him, and he was also positive Drake certainly wouldn't be as dumb as that cop in the bank, the one who tried to play hero, who was now, most likely, dead.

Gaf climbed inside the Taurus, turned on the radio,

and monitored the AM news station. While listening, he couldn't help but hear the loud screaming sirens coming from outside the garage, sounding as if they were nearby, and coming from all different directions.

He knew he had to get out of this house. When he decided to make a break for it, he was going to need other wheels, because the law would be looking for the Taurus. Maybe he'd put the suit back on then walk up on some unsuspecting soul stopped at a red-light, flash one of the FBI shields, and demand their car, telling them, "I'm an FBI agent, and it's an emergency. There's been a bank robbery. I need your car."

It was a weak idea, but it might work.

CHAPTER 39

We've Got Him Now!

After leaving the car rental yard, I drove for a while up Market Street, then I slowed down, and motioned out the window to Vack and Martinez, following behind, that I was pulling over.

I decided to call Director Becker and update him for the umpteenth time. Something I'd been required to do from the start, something the director expected. I got out of the Crown Victoria, and walked to the curb. Carla, Vack, and Martinez remained in their cars.

"Director, its Drake. So far, we've had no other eye witness accounts of Miller, other than Bertha Barsdale, owner of the rental yard, who I just spoke to. I don't think he's made it out of Oakland, and neither does Agent Simmons. But I'll say this, if Miller's given enough time, he's gonna find a way out of Oakland. Both Simmons and I are sure he's close by, but where? That's the sixty four thousand dollar question."

That update, or excuse I'd just given the director, seemed to fall on deaf ears.

"I don't care what you have to do, David, I just want Miller found!"

"We're doing all we can, and I think you know that,"

"Well, Agent Drake, apparently you're not doing enough. Miller's still running around free, making the FBI and me, personally, look like the Keystone Cops."

It was at this point that I felt like telling Becker he could take my planned-on appointment to the director's position and stick it up his ass, and to also get another agent to take over the second track down for Miller.

Just when I was about to unload on Becker, Carla jumped out of the car, in a panic, and came running toward me, waving both arms and shouting. "I just got a report from dispatch about an armed robbery that just went down over at the People's Credit Union on Lincoln. An off-duty Oakland cop has been shot and killed. Eye witnesses say the shooter's identity matches Miller's. David, let's go!"

I blew off the director, then Carla and I jumped in the Crown Vic, yelled back at Vack and Martinez to follow us, flipped on the lights and siren, made a U-turn in the middle of the street, and laid rubber as we all headed west to Lincoln Street.

"It means he's nearby!" Carla told me in an animated and excited voice. "There's a half-mile perimeter being set-up out from the bank as I speak. Witnesses said he was on foot, but they lost track of him after he took off running south, down Lincoln. We got him now!"

We all pulled up to the crime scene at the bank to find it crawling with OPD and FBI agents from the San Francisco headquarters. Vack, Martinez, Carla, and I all showed our shields and were allowed to step under the yellow crime-scene tape and enter the People's Credit Union. It was gruesome. The cop hadn't been wearing his Kevlar bullet-proof vest, because he was off duty. Lying there, his body was surrounded by a big pool of blood and, from looking at the body, I could tell he took three shots to the upper torso at close range. If this indeed was the work of Miller, he most likely used one of the FBI-issued Glock-19s that he took during his escape over the weekend. How ironic that a weapon issued by law enforcement was used to kill a member of law enforcement.

Now the FBI wanted Miller even more than before. Killing a cop shed a whole new light on the urgency and importance of locating him. I was sure Miller knew that if he was found and tried, he'd surely get the death penalty for killing a cop. That made him even more desperate than before, and now I was confident he'd kill again, without hesitation, if he thought it would prevent him from being caught and sent back.

I looked over at Martinez. "Call San Francisco and have them get a couple of handlers and bloodhounds over here ASAP. We'll have the hounds track his scent, starting here at the bank entrance then south down Lincoln, which will hopefully lead us directly to him. Also call the OPD and have them send us over a couple of canines and handlers. They're also good at sniffing out a bad guy. Miller's gotta be nearby, because the eye witnesses who saw the robbery go down didn't see him driving away. When the canines and handlers get here, we'll split up into teams, Simmons and I, and you and Vack, and we'll start knocking on doors within a two block radius of the bank. I have a hunch he's either holding someone hostage in their house, or he's hiding out in a vacant house or building close by."

I looked over at Martinez again. He was now standing off to the side, holding one hand over his ear, as he tried to block out the sound of sirens while talking to OPD on his cell phone. "Any word on how soon the OPD can send over a couple of canines and handlers?" I asked him when he hung up.

"Yes, boss, they're en route now. They'll be here in five minutes."

⌇⌇⌇⌇

Carla, Vack, Martinez, and I all started walking south on Lincoln, then we broke off. Simmons and I went left on Boston, and Vack and Martinez went right on Calla Avenue, with both teams being followed closely by an OPD canine and handler. All four of us were now wearing our bullet proof vests, and each of us had our Glock-19s chambered with a round and ready to fire if we spotted Miller.

I had a good feeling about this, thinking that Miller's crime wave was nearing its end—a feeling agents, and law enforcement in general, had when we thought our gut-check was correct.

I knocked on the front door of the first house on Boston Avenue, then stepped away from this rather dated front stoop that was attached to what looked like a house built in the 1950s. A house right out of *Leave It to Beaver*'s neighborhood. Standing there, alongside Carla, with the handler and canine standing directly behind us for back up, I was trying hard to project a friendly persona but, at this moment, was feeling the stress of extreme tension and anxiety. Neither Carla nor I, nor the handler and canine, had any idea what was going to happen when, or if, that front door opened. All three of us had our hands on our weapons, just in case something ugly went down.

The old, brown-stained, cracked and faded door slowly opened, and out stepped an elderly gray-haired couple, probably in their middle eighties. The husband was wearing a pair of pajamas, that looked like something he most likely wore around the clock, and his wife was in a house coat, mu-mu-looking thing. For lack of a better word, those were probably the uniforms they wore every day, all day long, while lounging around, watching TV— unless, of course, they dared to venture out to the local Walmart one mile away and, even then, if they didn't change into their regular clothes, no problem. They'd fit right in at Walmart.

Carla and I flashed our shields at the couple then tried to engage them in conversation, in hopes they might have seen something or somebody they didn't recognize come through their neighborhood this morning.

"Hello, sir, I'm Special Agent Drake." I then pointed to Carla. "And this is Special Agent Simmons. We're with the FBI. If you wouldn't mind, I'd like to ask you a couple of questions. It will only take a few minutes."

The old man, who had cupped his hand up to his ear as I was talking—as if he was straining to hear—nodded. "Yes, sonny, but first can I ask ya if you could please call the Oakland Sanitation Department for me and have them come over here and pick up our trash. Look out there by the curb!"

Trying to be nice, I begrudgingly turned and looks toward their front curb.

"Trash day was yesterday, and our recycling and regular issued trash cans haven't been touched, and now they're overflowing with garbage. The misses and I think that's awful. Can you help us out?"

I was now having visions of déjà vu all over again, thinking this conversation was sounding like a retake of the Bertha Barsdale interview I tried to have with her at the rental yard. "Yes, sir, I'll do that, but first I'd like to ask you just a few questions please."

The old man with his hand cupped back up to his ear again and his little gray-haired elderly wife, who was now squinting as if she were taking an eye exam at the DMV, because she was legally blind, stared up at me. "You say you're taking up donations for the FBI? I've never heard of them doing that before."

"No, ma'am, it has to do with a bank robbery this morning. Did you notice anyone coming through the neighborhood that maybe you haven't seen around here before? Please, this is very important."

"Why would we notice anyone? We never leave the house except to drive over to Walmart once a month."

I could see this was going nowhere and decided to move on to the next house. "Okay, I thank you. Now we'll be moving over to the next house. Have a nice day." Carla, the handler, and I turned around and started walking down their walkway, back to the sidewalk, when the old man yelled out, "What did you say your name was Mr. FBI man?"

I looked over my shoulder. "It's Agent Blake, sir." I smiled at Carla and we continued on to the next house, hoping we'd have better luck.

At the next house there was no answer, so we continued on to the next one and, just before I started to go up the walkway to knock on the door, an FBI Cruiser with its lights flashing, pulled up next to the curb out front. It was Special Agent in Charge Steward Harden, of the San Francisco FBI office, who while sitting in the cruiser, motioned with his left arm for us to come over to the car. As we began quickly walking over to Harden, I heard a sound and looked to my right to see a bloodhound trotting down Boston Street in our direction. He was making a low-pitched howling sound and practically dragging his handler along behind him.

Now out of the Crown Vic, Harden pointed toward the hound headed our way. "Drake, the bloodhound immediately picked up on Miller's scent at the bank's entry door, and when bloodhounds make the sound he's making now, it means Jeffrey Miller is nearby and has gotta be holding up in one of the houses here on this street. I've already called for backup for an FBI SWAT team and just got the word that they're headed this way now. Miller's here within this square block. I'm sure of it."

"Okay then, I'll call Vack and Martinez back from Calla Ave, and get 'em over here."

"Good, we need all the fire power we can get. We both know you can never have enough backup. I'd like to take that cop killer in alive, but if he even so much as flinches when we spot him, he's a dead man," Agent Harden continued, making a statement you wouldn't find in writing but was clearly understood by FBI agents and cops connected with this case.

We held the canines and handlers back while waiting for SWAT to show up. In the meantime, I got a call from the chopper flying overhead, saying that, less than a block away from where we were standing right now, stood an old abandoned, boarded-up house. After hearing that news, all of us agents and both canine handlers sensed that, if Miller was holed up anywhere near here, that had to be the house he was most likely going to be found in. Now I realized that was probably why the bloodhound was making all that commotion.

CHAPTER 40

Trapped

Gaf looked through a crack between the single garage door and its jamb to see what was going on. It was now starting to sink in that his plan of leaving this boarded-up house and stealing a car nearby wasn't going to work. He heard the loud sound of rotating chopper blades directly overhead and, off in the distance, the howl of a bloodhound and the barking of another canine, both sounding like they were headed his way.

He was now feeling trapped, with no way out. He paced around in the cramped garage, talking to himself—as if anyone cared about what he had to say. "What the fuck am I gonna do now? Maybe I should just jump in the Taurus and make a run for it. Naw, that won't work."

Gaf realized that his short taste of freedom was about to come to a swift end. Even though he was a serial killer, he didn't want to die going out in a blaze of glory. He was like all serial killers—chicken-shit losers whose only fear was their own mortality or demise

❧❧❧

The old boarded-up house was now completely surrounded by SWAT, my team and I, the US Marshals, plus
countless cops and sheriffs from Oakland and other nearby law-enforcement communities, not to mention several
other canines with handlers, who would have loved nothing more than to be given the order to strike and watch
their canines sink their teeth into Miller. I grabbed the
bullhorn and blasted a warning directed at the boarded-up
old house.

"This is FBI Special Agent Drake. Miller, we know
you're in there. You have one minute to come out with
your hands in the air. If you don't, we're gonna gas the
house. You have one minute, starting right now." I
looked at my watch, letting thirty seconds go by. "Miller,
you have thirty seconds. Come out with your hands in the
air. If you comply, no harm will come to you."

With only ten seconds left to go, Miller slowly swung
up the old rickety wooden garage door and stepped out
with his hands high in the air.

I yelled through the bullhorn. "Get down on your
knees then lay flat on the ground, spread eagle. Do it
now!"

Now lying face first on the ground, Miller was rushed
by a half dozen of the burliest FBI agents sent over from
the San Francisco office. They searched him for the
Glock-19s he'd taken from the two agents during his escape and later used in the bank robbery. Then he was
cuffed. No weapons were found on Miller, but later on
the Glocks were found when they searched the Taurus.

Miller was dragged over to a waiting squad car and
placed in the back seat between two FBI agents.

Agent Vack couldn't resist. He walked over, peered
inside the squad car, and really let Miller have it. "Re-

member me fuck-head." Miller glanced over at Agent Vack. "Listen, you cock-sucking punk," Vack continued. "We got you this time for good. This time your ass is going down. I personally would like to see you die an agonizingly slow death but, fortunately for your sake, you low-life scumbag, the law is on your side. Murderers like you get the needle in California. Oh, and by the way, here's your fucking Miranda rights. Anything you say can, and will, be used against you in a court of law, motherfucker. Is that understood?"

"You can't talk to me like that. I have my rights," Miller answered.

Vack turned and looks at the team. "Did anyone of you hear a discouraging or disrespectful word come out of my mouth?"

All of us stood there shaking our heads no.

"I thought so." Then Vack turned back to Miller. "You're so delusional, you're starting to hear things."

The agents in the front and rear seats smiled and gave Vack a thumbs up. Vack then backed away from the car and told the agents inside the Crown Vic, "Go ahead and get this piece of shit out of here."

With that, the squad car tore down Boston with lights flashing and its siren blasting, heading for the federal courthouse where Miller would be locked up and guarded around the clock, until he could be arraigned for the second time with additional charges: escape, bank robbery, and—the most serious charge—killing a cop during the commission of a bank robbery. In addition, if that wasn't enough, Miller would have these additional lesser felony charges filed against him: use of stolen identification, forgery, and auto theft.

Before my team and I left the scene, I got a call from Chief Federal Prosecutor, Laurence McDavis requesting that we be at the arraignment tomorrow morning at eleven a.m., just in case the judge had any questions.

I agreed, telling McDavis, "No problem, my team and I will be glad to do whatever's needed to put that bastard away, for good this time."

CHAPTER 41

Arraignment

The next morning, Carla, Vack, Martinez, and I met with Federal Prosecutor McDavis in his office. McDavis went over a few questions he thought might come up, telling me and the team, "Most likely this will be a quick and simple arraignment, just in and out. I don't expect any questions out of the ordinary coming from this judge."

Then, as a group, we all headed for the courtroom, took a seat, and waited for Federal Judge Bernard Michaels to enter through the side door. Miller was already in court, shackled at the waist and ankles, and, for good measure, strapped securely to his chair. Nevertheless, the tension was high.

At exactly eleven a.m., the judge entered the courtroom and the bailiff blared out, "All stand. Court is now in session, the Honorable Bernard Michaels proceeding."

The judge took his seat, and the second Jeffrey Miller arraignment was underway.

The judge got right to the point. "Prosecutor McDavis,

let's hear the additional new charges you've now filed against defendant Miller."

"Yes, Your Honor, and as I've stated on the arrest warrant, these new charges are all felonies: escape, bank robbery, and—the most serious—killing an OPD off duty detective during the commission of a bank robbery. In addition to those charges, Mr. Miller is being charged with these additional lesser felonies: using stolen identification, forgery, and auto theft."

"Thank you, Prosecutor McDavis."

Judge Michaels looked over at Miller's public defender. "Mr. Blankenship, is the defendant ready to plea?"

"Yes your Honor, Mr. Miller pleads not guilty."

The judge looked at Miller. "Mr. Miller is that your plea, not guilty?"

"Yes, it is, Your Honor."

Judge Michaels then looked at both the prosecutor and the public defender. "Very well, this court will set a trial date sixty days from today's date. Are there any matters we need to clear up from the prosecutor's or PD's offices while we're here?"

"Yes, there is, Your Honor," McDavis said. "Just for the record, the federal government will be seeking the death penalty if the defendant is found guilty. His horrendous disregard for life in, not only killing a member of law enforcement during a bank robbery, but also for several other unsolved murders we believe the defendant Miller is responsible for—ones that we are now investigating. In addition to the unsolved murders, we believe the defendant is also responsible for numerous other bank robberies committed during his employment with Docket Air. There's a possibility the prosecutor's office will bring those additional charges against the defendant at a later date, when our investigations are complete," McDavis continued. "And, just for the record, there will be no plea bargaining on the part of the prosecutor."

Miller seemed to turn a whiter shade of pale after hearing what McDavis had just said.

The judge glanced over at Public Defender Blankenship. "Does the PD have anything to add?"

"No, Your Honor," Blankenship replied. "Mr. Miller stands by his plea of not guilty."

Judge Michaels then ordered the defendant held without bail, grabbed his gavel, and slammed it down on his desk. "Very well, this proceeding is adjourned. I'll see both parties back here sixty days from today."

In unison, the Prosecutor and PD stood and said, "Thank you, Your Honor."

The judge exited back through the side door leading to his chambers, and both parties then left the courtroom. The bailiffs escorted Miller back to his holding cell where he'd stay until he was later transported to the Atwater Federal Prison where he'd remain until the trial started. This phase, of what could be a long drawn out struggle to bring justice to Miller's victims, had begun.

As we rode the elevator down, Simmons, Vack, Martinez, and I all decided we should do lunch together. It'd been some time since we'd had a chance to get together as a group and enjoy a good meal.

It was Agent Vack's idea to have lunch at a place called Fish Island. He told us he had eaten at Fish Island several times since joining the team. "Their steaks and seafood are cooked on an oak-fired, open-flame grill," Vack went on, as we all walked out of the court house together, "giving them a unique taste—something that you don't get at any other sea food restaurant on Embarcadero. It's also a good place to just sit, relax, shoot the breeze, and maybe throw back some vino and just enjoy the ocean view."

We were sold. Besides, we all liked the idea that the restaurant had an ocean view, something we could enjoy while we chowed down and gossiped during lunch. After all, we didn't have any other pending bad guys to track down, at least not just yet, anyway.

With all of us looking forward to having some down time, we got into our Crown Vics, and followed Vack over to the Fish Island Steak & Oyster Company.

About half way through our leisurely glorious lunch, I got a call. Looking down at the caller ID, I noticed it was from Federal Prosecutor McDavis.

"Hello, Agent Drake, are you busy?" he asked when I answered.

"No, but the team and I are having lunch together—something we haven't done for some time."

"I have some good news, Drake."

"Okay, what's the good news?"

"Well, apparently, after Miller went back to his holding cell, he had a change of heart. He's decided to change his plea to guilty after hearing all the present and future possible charges we're filing against him, that not only link him to first-degree murder, but also the long laundry list of other felonies we believe he's committed. So therefore, we're going before Judge Michaels again at ten a.m. in the morning, to put his plea on the record, but I'd like to see you and your team back in court again tomorrow, just in case Judge Michaels has any questions for you."

"Oh, man, that's great! That's the best news I've heard since starting this track down. Director Becker is gonna be very pleased with this turn of events. Of course, we'll be there. No problem. I'll let Simmons, Vack, and Martinez know as soon as I hang up, although as I look around at their smiling faces I think they've heard. Thanks for calling, McDavis. See you in court."

I knew right off that Agent Vack had heard everything. The smile on his face was as wide as the Grand Canyon, and he had already began tipping his wine glass in the air, motioning and suggesting for the rest of us to join in and make a toast.

Indeed, we all were very happy to hear that news. It made the steak and seafood, on those combo platters we shared, taste even better, if that was possible.

CHAPTER 42

No Mercy

The next morning, my team and I, along with Federal Prosecutor McDavis, assembled in the small courtroom at nine-forty-five a.m. and waited for the Honorable Bernard Michaels to enter. Miller, like yesterday, was strapped securely to his chair, with Public Defender Blankenship seated beside him. Miller and Blankenship were leaning toward each other and talking in hushed tones, to prevent McDavis from overhearing.

At ten a.m. the bailiff bellowed loudly, as the judge entered the courtroom. "All rise. This court is now in session, the Honorable Bernard Michaels presiding."

The judge, looking out at both the prosecutor's and the public defender's tables, notated on his docket. "I notice all parties are present and accounted for. I understand Defendant Miller wishes to change his plea." Looking at PD Blankenship, the judge asked, "Is defendant Miller ready to change his plea?"

"Yes, Your Honor. Mr. Miller wishes to plead guilty and throw himself on the mercy of the court."

Judge Michael looked over at Miller. "Mr. Miller, is that correct? Are you now changing your plea from not guilty to guilty, and are you doing so without any encouragement or influence from any outside source, whatsoever? And is your change of plea to guilty solely your choice, and your choice only?"

"Yes, it is, Your Honor."

"Okay then, duly noted, Mr. Miller. I understand you wish to address the court."

"Yes, Your Honor, I do."

"Okay, Mr. Miller, the court will now hear your statement."

ℰ∽ℰ∽

Gaf thought he had a chance of getting some sympathy from Judge Michaels, since he'd plead guilty. In his scheming delusional mind, Gaf thought if he made a strong enough case, Judge Michaels wouldn't send him to death row to face death like the victims he'd slaughtered in the past. Like all serial killers, the only person they didn't want to see die was themselves. Jeffrey Miller was truly sociopathic.

"Your Honor, I am truly sorry for all the misery and sorrow I've forced the victims' family members to go through. I would personally like to apologize to each and every one who I've hurt by taking their love ones from them. Judge Michaels, Your Honor, I throw myself on the mercy of the court, and ask that I be given a life sentence. If I'm given mercy by Your Honor, I promise I will reach out and try to do what I can in seeking forgiveness for the terrible crimes I've committed. Thank you, Your Honor."

Judge Michaels looked over at Prosecutor McDavis. "Does the Prosecutor have anything to say in response to the defendant's statement?"

"Yes, Your Honor, I do. Jeffrey Miller is a sociopathic serial killer who's never had any qualms about snuffing out the lives of once-living, breathing human beings whom he sought out and murdered. These were random, no conscious, vicious killings. Defendant Miller killed for the sadistic pleasure he got from seeing the fear on their faces just before he murdered them. Now he stands before this court, insulting our intelligence with a weak and flimsy excuse, for lack of a better word, Your Honor, just to save his own ass."

"Thank you Prosecutor McDavis. We'll break for a two hour lunch, and I'll meet both parties back here at twelve-forty-five p.m., then I'll render my verdict."

෩෩

The bailiff gave the order to stand, and the judge departed back to his chambers. Prosecutor McDavis, Carla, Vack, Martinez, and I all decided to walk down the street for some lunch. We were all keeping our fingers crossed, in the hopes Judge Michaels didn't cave to Miller's plea for leniency, and that he would give Miller what he deserved, a cell on San Quentin's Death Row, where he'd sit and wait to meet his maker.

While at lunch, I called Director Becker to fill him in, letting Becker know there was a decision coming down on Miller's fate as soon as we returned to court.

"David, if Miller gets what's coming to him, I'll be doing cartwheels around my office and, for me, that's saying something. Heck I can't even do one push-up."

I heard the director chuckling into the phone. I always knew Becker had a bizarre sense of humor and wondered why he couldn't understand why the agents working under him at the DC headquarters didn't roll around on the floor with laughter when he told what he thought was a good joke. Personally, I thought it was his timing. He had none.

But to appease Director Becker, I mustered up a phony, forced half laugh over the phone. "Now that's funny. Do you write your own stuff?"

"Yeah, David, it's totally all adlib, spur-of-the-moment stuff. I've always had a great sense of humor and style. You know? Like those great-looking suits I buy off the rack at Walmart and those dollar-saver stores."

My eyes began to roll as I realized I had to cut Director Becker off. I didn't want to spend my entire two-hour lunch listening to him boast and rant on about how well-dressed he thought he looked and what a great story teller he also thought he had become, ever since he purchased and completed a college-level correspondence course titled *How to Win Friends and Influence People*.

The director did give me some good news just before hanging up, though. "Here's what I'm gonna do for you and your team, David. It's something to make-up for having called you all back from that last hiatus I granted the four of you. I'm gonna grant you and the agents the same deal again, ten days off with pay, starting tomorrow, and it won't be charged against your vacation time. It's all good now, David, even if the Judge doesn't give Miller the death penalty."

Right away, I started thinking about that dude ranch I had told Carla about—the one we'd go to when we got some time off. I got aroused just thinking about it. I knew that meant Carla and I would get into some good dude ranch sex in the bunk house, because she told me she wasn't interested in riding smelly horses or mules. It was fine with me if we stayed in the bunkhouse cottage bed during our entire five-day stay there. "Thank you Director Becker. Simmons, Vack, and Martinez are here with me now. They'll be ecstatic when I tell them the news," I said, thinking to myself, *But not half as much as I am.*

After I hung up, I informed my three agents about what Becker had just told me on the phone, then I finished off my fried artichoke hearts, garlicky sourdough bread, and the side dish of marinara dipping sauce. Finished with lunch, we headed back to court. With both parties back in court, the Judge entered the courtroom.

"All stand. Court is back in session, the Honorable Bernard Michaels presiding."

Judge Michaels looked out over the small courtroom and, again, made a notation in his file. "Okay, I see both the defendant, Miller, and prosecutor, McDavis, are here and accounted for, so now I'll read my decision, unless either party has something to say before I render my verdict."

Both the prosecutor and public defender told the Judge they were ready to move forward with the verdict.

"Mr. Miller, for me this was an easy decision. How dare you stand before my court and ask for forgiveness and mercy? It's clear to me, with all the misery and carnage you've managed inflict on innocent human beings, you'll get no mercy from this court. Therefore, I sentence you to death by lethal injection, to be performed at San Quentin State Prison, where you'll remain incarcerated until the sentence is carried out."

Now it was beginning to sink in. Miller obviously knew this was it and wished to speak. "Your Honor, in that case, I would like to have my sentence carried out as soon as possible."

Judge Michaels stared at Miller in utter disgust. "If it were up me, Mr. Miller, you'd be executed tomorrow but, unfortunately, in California there is an automatic appeal process. Your PD, Mr. Blankenship, will explain. Bailiffs, get this garbage out of my court."

"All stand. This proceeding is over," the bailiff announced. "Court is now adjourned."

Miller was then hauled out of court by four US Marshals and escorted to San Quentin's Death Row.

CHAPTER 43

Case Closed

After walking out of Judge Michaels's courtroom, I had the team huddle up in a spare courthouse office to set a schedule, seeing how they'd been granted ten days off by Director Becker. I also wanted to give Special Agents, Vack, Martinez, and Carla a well-deserved pep talk, seeing that this case was now really, officially, closed. I closed the door to the small office that looked like it was used as a place for employees to take breaks, with its wall-hung cabinets and coffee maker sitting atop of its beige Formica counter.

Carla, Vack, and Martinez were seated at the break table, but I stood. "Okay, well, without saying it, I think you all know how thankful that I am to have had FBI agents of your caliber and talent working on this team. You haven't bitched or complained during this entire manhunt. That's something I can't say about some agents I've either worked for or had the displeasure of having them work under my direction."

Of course, Columbo, aka Agent Vack spoke up.

"Boss, I have to say it's been a pleasure. We're all a team here. We're kinda like a family now. That's just something I wanted to say."

"Thank you, Vack, I think we all feel the same way," I summed up. "Anyway, I'm not gonna keep you all for some long drawn-out boring speech. I just wanted to mention the good news again. Number one, Miller's on death row now, and number two, we've been granted another ten days of paid time off, and it won't be counted as vacation time."

That got a polite round of applause.

"Before we take off for ten days of what, I'm hoping will be uninterrupted time off, I have a couple of suggestions. Just in case, for some reason the director calls me, and says, 'Sorry to do this to you, but I need you and the team back here ASAP, something important has come up.' You all know how Becker is, so we can't assume that he won't. I would suggest that none of you travel outside the Continental US. Reason being, like I just mentioned, that Becker, knowing him like I do, there's always an outside chance of us all being called back early if an emergency comes up. If that happens this time, I want all of you back here the same day I call, or at least by early the next morning."

Vack waved a hand in the air to get my attention. "Hey, boss, don't worry about me. This time, I'm staying somewhere here in the great US of A. You know, boss, I've never been to one of those dude ranches I've read about in all those western magazines, so I'm thinking I'll give that a try. Even though I'm a New Yorker from Manhattan, I've always wanted to be a cowboy."

I knew I had to talk Vack out of that idea. There was an outside chance he could book a stay at the same dude ranch I had in mind for myself and Carla. "Agent Vack, I don't picture you as the cowboy type. By the way, do you

know that on those dude ranches they make the visitors
staying there clean out horse and mule stalls and have
them haul off all that manure to the local landfill so it can
be recycled as fertilizer?"

Vack had a bewildered look on his face and came back
with a couple of F bombs, a word he rarely used. "Well,
boss, fuck that. I'm not cleaning up horse shit for anybody, especially when I'm on a vacation. Scratch that
idea. My second choice was to go on one of those one
week cruises down to Cabo San Lucas and hang out at
Sammy Hagar's Cabo-Wabo Club. Yeah, I think I'll do
that. It sounds better than having to clean up after a bunch
of smelly horses and mules."

With that comment from Vack, I looked over at Carla
and noticed she had a smile on her face, knowing that that
was pretty much what she had told me in reference to
horses and mules. There'd be no smelly horse or mule
riding for her. Personally, I'd liked being around horses
and mules when I lived in Texas as a kid.

Martinez raised his hand and mentioned he'd be going
to Florida this time, saying it with a big wide smile on his
face. "You know what, boss? Florida's beaches and
weather are just as good as Hawaii's, if not better. Besides, I'd frankly rather spend my money here on the
mainland."

"Okay, here's some more good news," I said. "Today
is Thursday, take the rest of today, and all of Friday, off,
and enjoy your weekend, then your ten paid days off will
officially start on Monday. I'll expect all of you to meet
with me back at the San Francisco FBI office on Thursday of the following week, but give me a call the day before, and confirm it. That's all I have, except to say, enjoy your time off and, by all means, do not turn off your
FBI cell phones, just in case."

After another round of muted applause, we all got up

from the table and headed out the front door of the federal courthouse.

My plans for today were to meet up with Carla later on at that Sonoma bed and breakfast we had stayed at before, for another couple of days of good wine, good food, and a whole lot of riding that crest, before we headed out for our one week stay at the Cowpoke Dude Ranch in Wyoming. But before leaving, I planned on requesting a one-on-one interview with Jeffrey Miller at San Quentin's Death Row on Monday. I was hoping he'd grant my interview. There was something about him I'd been curious about from the time I was asked by Director Becker to head up this special FBI taskforce.

CHAPTER 44

The Interview

F riday, the day after sentencing and before heading to Sonoma with Carla, I got through to Warden Daniel Rivers at California's San Quentin State Prison and requested an interview at ten a.m. Monday morning with Jeffrey Miller. The warden informed Miller of my request, and Miller told Warden Rivers he'd do the interview only if certain conditions were met, asking the warden to relay them to me.

"These are the parameters that must be met for Drake's interview," Miller had said. "I can't be questioned about any crimes I may or may not have committed. Any and everything I say is strictly off the record. No video, sound equipment, or prison guards are allowed in the room while the interview is going on."

I agreed to all conditions, and the warden informed Miller. Driving up on Monday then parking and walking through the gates of San Quentin, a place I'd never been to before, and ending up sitting in a secluded room on death row all alone with a convicted serial killer, literally made the hairs on the back of my neck stand up.

Before entering the interview room, I could feel the pure evil permeating from the death row cells as I was being escorted by Warden Rivers to the designated room where the interview would take place.

Those cells held the worst of the worst. At present they were occupied by over seven hundred criminals, who were mostly men who had committed unspeakable crimes against humanity. Walking by those cells, the size of a walk-in closet, I thought these inmates had only themselves to blame. So now here they sat, day after day, until their time was up and they met their fate. That was a chilling thought. It made me wonder why anyone would commit murder.

I walked into what looked like a cell used to temporarily hold death row inmates until just before being wheeled into the death chamber for their date with death.

There he was, Jeffrey Miller, sitting behind a small, older-looking, simple wooden table and secured to a chair with thick leather straps and chains, allowing him to only move his head from side to side. Miller looked cool, calm, and collected, giving off the vibe of a celebrity who was about to be interviewed by *Rolling Stone Magazine*.

"Hello, Mr. Miller," I said. "I want to thank you for granting me this interview."

"You're lucky, Agent Drake, because I've already been contacted by various news agencies, and I've turned them all down. You wanna know why?" Before I could answer, Miller told me. "None of them would interview me off the record like you've agreed to do, that's why."

"Thank you. I appreciate that, Mr. Miller."

"Just call me Jeffrey. There's no need to be formal. After all, look where we're at."

"Thank you. Actually, I only have two questions, and they're simple ones. Both are something I've wondered about from the time I was asked by Director Becker to take on the case."

"Okay, go ahead, shoot."

"Here's the first one. Was the Zodiac your father?"

"Yes he was. He taught me everything about the killing process, but as I got older, I got sloppy and careless, so now here I sit."

Watching Miller's expressionless face and listening to his monotone voice gave me the feeling I was listening to someone who was totally devoid of guilt. He came across as cold as ice, a true sociopathic killer, who I knew would put a bullet through my head if he were given that chance.

"Here's my second and final question. Why did you call yourself Gaf or the Gaf, in the beginning?"

Miller didn't know I had done some research on Wikipedia and learned that GAF was a numeric scale used by mental-health physicians to rate a person who they suspected was mentally ill to determine, in laymen's terms, how crazy they were. It was called the Global Assessment of Functioning.

"That's an easy one to answer," Miller said. "When I began killing for enjoyment, I was gay and sometimes went bi. Later on, while I was on the run from you and your team, I hid out in the outskirts of Mormon Town, and that's where I met Robin Osborne one night at a redneck bar. And she turned out to be the finest piece of ass I'd ever had. Robin Osborne is the reason I decided to go straight. Now I hate that bitch. She snitched on me, and she's the main reason I'm sitting here now."

"Okay, but I'm still wondering why you called yourself Gaf?"

"All right Drake, I'll tell you what. You gotta scratch pad and pen on you? I know you do, that's standard. All you agents carry a pad and pen around."

"Now that you mention it, you're right." I reached inside my suit coat pocket, pulled out a spiral note pad like the one Vack carried around, and moved both across the table in front of Miller. "Okay, here you go."

"No, man, what are you thinking? I can't write all shackled up like this with my arms strapped to this chair. Fuck, I can barely move my head from side to side, much less my hands. That is unless you wanna have the prison guards at least remove the leather straps holding my arms down."

I knew that wasn't going to happen. I wasn't that stupid. "Well, Jeffrey, I'm afraid I can't do that, under the circumstances."

Miller frowned and, from the look on his face, I could sense he was contemplating ending the interview then, but had second thoughts. "All right, Drake, just jot this down, then it'll all make sense."

I moved the pad back across the table, clicked the ballpoint, and was ready to write. "What now? What do you want me to write?"

"Write the word Gaf, then write it backward."

I did what Miller said, then it all started to dawn on me. "Is this correct, Jeffrey?"

"Yes, it is. It spells fag. That's what I was before I went straight. I was a fag, so I did a play on words. That's why I called myself the Gaf Killer."

He stared back at me and gave a wide, grinning, muffled chuckle. I had to admit that in all my years as an FBI agent, investigating crimes, this was a first for me. It was stranger than fiction. You couldn't make this stuff up. Personally, I thought it might have had something to do with the psychiatric GAF gauge I found on Wikipedia. What Jeffrey just said proved to me than he was truly a crazed psycho.

Now that the interview was over, I thanked him, departed San Quentin's Death Row, made my way out the front gates, and headed to someone I really cared for in Sonoma, Carla Simmons. And, for me, it wasn't a minute to soon.

That was one creepy experience that I was hoping I'd never have to repeat. But, anyway, I was glad I did it. Now I knew what sitting on death row felt like. Still, even after doing my short interview with Jeffrey, I wondered why some people turned out the way they did.

When I got back to the bed and breakfast in Sonoma, the first thing I did was take a long hot shower to wash off the bad karma that I believed was clinging to me from my visit to San Quentin's Death Row.

CHAPTER 45

Best Laid Plans

That Monday afternoon, I returned from San Quentin to the bed and breakfast in Sonoma, where Carla and I planned on spending one more night before we jetted out to Casper, Wyoming, for the five-day stay at the CowPoke Dude Ranch. Although Carla told me she wasn't interested in riding no smelly horses or mules, she was interested in seeing that part of the US, an area she'd never visited.

I placed a call to Director Becker and checked on the status of the reward money for Robin Osborne; Old Man Watkins; Mindy, the truck stop restaurant manager in Fernley, NV; Mr. and Mrs. James, owners of the Lazy Day Motel; and Bertha Barsdale, owner of the used car rental business in Oakland. I wanted to see if his office would go ahead and release the one million dollars in reward money to the main tipsters who helped us locate and arrest Miller. The director gave the okay, but went on to add that the auto-shop owner, Jake Barley on the outskirts of Fernley would also be granted reward money for his tip. Man, I had completely forgotten about Jake Barley. I was glad the director caught that.

Anyway, I was thrilled I'd gotten the okay to call those who were mentioned and give them the good news, telling each one that, since the case was now closed and Miller was sitting on death row, they'd be receiving their share of the one million dollars in reward money in the form of a cashier's check from the director's office next week. The director and I went over the dollar amounts. The main chunk of change would be going to Ms. Robin Osborne, in the amount of six hundred thousand dollars, and the remaining four hundred thousand was to be split up equally among Old Man Watkins, Mindy, Mr. and Mrs. James, Bertha Barsdale, and, of course, Jake Barley.

For me, other than arresting Miller, this had to be one of the best parts of this entire track down, calling these folks and giving them that good news. I had to admit, I really enjoyed talking to Robin Osborne the most.

She was ecstatic, nearly out of her mind, when I told her how much she'd be receiving next week, and she went on to give some good news of her own. "Number one, I divorced that loser husband of mine, and now, with the reward money, I'll be able to quit my crappy day job and be a romance novel writer, something I've always wanted to do since I was a teenager! And number two, I got that AIDS test back, and it was negative. Thank God!"

I congratulated Robin and thanked her again for stepping up to the plate like she had. I went on to wish her good luck with her writing and told her that I hoped to be reading one of her bestselling novels in the near future.

That night at the bed and breakfast, Carla and I ordered wine and prime rib, cooked medium rare, and had it delivered to our room. After that great tasting dinner and the nice bottle of Cabernet Sauvignon, we followed it up with four hours of some intense sex. We fucked every way known to man, so much so that we both literally passed out from exhaustion. I had to say, we both still liked the hard pounding doggie style the best. We always had.

Tuesday morning, Carla and I got up early, headed for the Sonoma County Airport, and caught an Alaska Air flight, and winged our way out to Casper, Wyoming, to the Cow Poke Dude Ranch.

While in flight and, out of sheer boredom, I came up with what I thought was a funny line and passed it on to Carla, who was now practically sitting on my lap in the first-class cabin.

"Carla, I'll be the dude who'll be doing the poking at the Cow Poke Dude Ranch…ha, ha."

Carla thought my line was somewhat amusing. Now she was straddling me like a lap dancer at a strip joint. "As long as I'm not getting poked by one of those smelly horses or mules."

I thought that was funnier than my line.

We landed two and a half hours later in Casper, and a Cow Poke shuttle bus gave us a free ride out to the ranch, where we checked in and were given keys to our private rustic cabin on the range. It looked like a cabin from *Little House on The Prairie*. I was liking this, already.

Even Carla was impressed with its furnishings. "Yeah, it's not bad, seeing how it was probably built by a bunch of tobacco-chewing rednecks, but who cares? It looks nice.

We put our things away, looked at our Cow Poke brochure, and read the flyer insert, listing the upcoming scheduled events during our five-day stay. Both of us looked at each other and frowned when we read the one for tonight. *All guests are requested to gather around the giant fire pit, located adjacent to our Chuck Wagon Steak*

House, for the opportunity to sing some old "home on the range" songs that the early settlers sang way back in the good old cowboy days.

We both looked at each other and just shook our heads. And we both reaffirmed it with an audible, "No way."

"Oh, well, tell you what, Carla. Let's go on over to the steak house and grab some grub, then come back here and take a nap. I'm still tired from last night."

"David, where did you get that term, grub from?"

"Oh, I don't know. I think it was from watching those old black and white cowboy movies when I was a kid."

After getting back from the Chuck Wagon Steak House, we decided to first take showers before hitting the sack for naps. Of course, while showering together, we both got aroused, so what was new? After all we were both horn dogs. Besides, we were thinking, "Who knows when we'll get another chance to do what we like to do best?"

Getting out of the shower, I sat at a side chair with a hard-on that was carried over from fooling around with Carla in the shower. We both knew, when we hopped in the sack, there wouldn't be a whole lot of napping going on. Carla, who was now completely nude and standing right in front of me, pretending she was still drying off, with me sitting there gawking at her with a throbbing erection. She smiled. She knew what she was doing to me. Just as she reached down, as if to stroke me, my FBI cell phone began to ring on the nightstand. We each had a bad feeling in the pit of our stomachs, as we moved over to the nightstand and leaned over to look at the caller ID.

"Ah, fuck!"

That's about all Carla and I said out loud together. It was Director Becker calling and both knew what that meant. Before I answered, I told Carla, "You know, even if Becker is calling us back, we made the best of it and, for me, Carla, I've loved every minute that we've had together these last couple of days."

We quickly kissed, and I answered the call.

EPILOGUE

Director Becker was forced to call Special Agent Drake and his team back early, at the request of President Anderson, to seek out and bring down another member of the FBI's Most Wanted, with the director planning on flying out to give Drake and his team the details Wednesday morning

Jeffrey Miller was executed on Monday, August 19, 2013 at 12:01 a.m. For his last meal, he requested a patty melt, with freshly brewed iced tea and a lemon wedge. He was served a cold patty melt and instant iced tea, with no lemon wedge, by a smiling death row prison guard.

About the Author

Jerry Otis is a SAG Actor who turned to writing about a half dozen years ago. The entire publishing process has taught him one thing, "Never give up." Even after getting over forty rejection letters from other literary agencies or editors, he continued to forge ahead. He's found out that if you have a good story, a literary agency, or editor out there somewhere will recognize your manuscript for what it is and decide to sign you.

Otis lives in a rural section of Eldorado County called Pollock Pines, Calif. Although he's now a newly published author with Black Opal Books, it's something that in his earlier years he would have never dreamed of becoming, considering the crappy grades he received in English classes, from elementary all the way up through high school. It wasn't until he got into college that he found out he liked to write, and it was at that point in time he realized it's not just the grammar that's important, it's the story telling. Remember this, "Without a good story, you have nothing but a bunch of rambling, mumbo jumbo, so no matter what kind of degree you have in Literature/English etc., that degree will get you nowhere unless you're a good story teller. Grammar can be corrected, but story telling can't be faked."